HERO TYPE

HERO TYPE

BY BARRY LYGA

G RAPHIA

Houghton Mifflin Harcourt
Boston New York

www.hmhbooks.com

The text of this book is set in Legacy Serif Book.

Library of Congress Cataloging-in-Publication Data is on file.

LC Number 2008007276

HC ISBN: 978-0-547-07663-8   PA ISBN: 978-0-547-24877-6

Manufactured in the United States of America

DOM 10 9 8 7 6 5 4 3 2 1

DEDICATED TO CAPTAIN PETER G. MADRIÑAN
AND MAJOR GREGORY C. TINE,
UNITED STATES ARMY,
BOTH SERVING IN THE MIDDLE EAST
AS I WRITE THIS.

FINE SOLDIERS, BETTER FRIENDS.

"There I was one night, just a normal guy.
"And then there I was the *next* night . . .
"Goddamnit, I was still just a normal guy."

—Bruce Springsteen, speaking to
the crowd on July 7, 1978,
at The Roxy, Los Angeles, California

Overture

You know those pictures of fat people?

I'm talking about the ones in the ads for diets and weight-loss drugs and stuff like that. You know them. They always show the "Before" picture of the person back when they were a big fat slob. And then they show the "After" picture, which is like this totally buff hottie.

Here's the thing about those pictures, though: For the longest time I couldn't figure out why the pictures were labeled "Before" and "After," because to me it was obvious they were two completely different people.

But I get it now—we're at least supposed to *think* that it's the same person, made over thanks to the miracle of whatever the company is peddling. It doesn't have to be just for weight loss. It can be for any big life change.

I've always been skinny, so I don't need to lose weight, but I think about those pictures a lot. Especially now. After my own big life change.

So why do my "Before" and "After" pictures look exactly the same?

Hero

CHAPTER 1
SURREAL

EVERYWHERE YOU GO, it seems like there's a reminder of what happened, of what I did. You can't escape it. *I* can't escape it. I wouldn't be surprised if someone suggested renaming Brookdale "Kevindale." That's just how things are working out these days. The whole town's gone Kevin Krazy.

Take the Narc, for example. The big sign out front, the one that normally announces specials and sales, now says THANK YOU, KEVIN, FOR SAVING OUR LEAH. That's just plain weird. The same spot that usually proclaims the existence of new flavors of Pop Tarts or two-for-one Cokes is now a thanks to me. It's just surreal, the word my friend Flip uses when he's slightly stoned and can't think of a better word to describe something strange.

But I sort of understand the Narc sign. After all, Leah's dad owns Nat's Market (called "the Narc" by every kid in town *except* Leah), so I get it.

But ...

Then there's the flashing neon sign that points down the highway to Cincinnati Joe's, a great burger-and-wings joint. Usually it just flashes JOE followed by SAYS and then EAT and then something like WINGS! or BURGERS! or FRIES! or whatever the owners feel like putting up that day. Now, though, it says:

Joe
Says
Good
Job
Kevin!

Even the sign at the WrenchIt Auto Parts store wishes me a happy sixteenth birthday. And when you drive past the Good Faith Lutheran Church on Schiffler Street, the sign out front reads: GOD BLESS YOU, KEVIN & LEAH. Which almost makes us sound like a couple or something. And I don't even *go* to Good Faith. I'm what Mom calls "a parentally lapsed Catholic." (Usually followed by "Don't worry about it.")

Continuing the Tour of Weirdness that has become Brookdale in the last week or so, you can see similar signs all over. My favorite—the most *surreal*—is the one near the mall, where someone forgot to finish taking down the old letters first, so now it says, SPECIAL! SAVE KEVIN ROSS IS A HERO!

Gotta love that.

And, God, don't even get me *started* on the reporters.

You probably saw me on TV. First the local channels and then—just this past weekend—the bigtime: national TV, courtesy of *Justice!*. I didn't want to do the show, but *Justice!* was one of the big contributors to the reward money. I don't have the money yet, and it's not like the producers are holding it hostage or anything, but when someone's planning on dumping thirty grand into your bank account . . . I sort of felt like I *had* to go on. Dad said it was my decision, but I could tell he was waffling. It's like, one part of him figured I deserved the money, and another part of him hated the idea of this big media company having that over my head, and *another* part of him probably wanted the whole thing just to go away.

Anyway.

They (you know, the *Justice!* people) filmed in Leah's living room, Leah being the girl whose life I saved.

See, here's the deal, the way I told it on TV and in the papers: I'm walking along near the Brookdale library and I hear this scream from down the alleyway. So I go running and there's this big guy and he's hassling Leah and he's got a needle in his hand.

He was big. I was—and am—small. But I couldn't help myself. I just threw down my, y'know, my backpack and I charged him and somehow I managed to get him in a wrestling hold like they taught us in gym class. He dropped the needle and Leah screamed again and the guy grunted and tried to shake me off, but I was sticky like a parasite, man. I just held on and tightened my grip and he couldn't move.

And Leah called 911 and that would have been that, but it turns out the guy in question was Michael Alan Naylor. The Surgeon. Or . . .

"The man responsible for a series of abductions, rapes, and murders throughout the Mid-Atlantic," said Nancy deCarlo, the host of *Justice!,* just before she introduced me to the nation in all my zitty, sweaty, panicky glory.

They stuck me on Leah's sofa with Leah, who looked poised and calm and radiated perfection. It was like "Beauty and the Beastly" or something. Nancy talked. I listened. I answered her questions, but I can't really remember it at all. I was too caught up in the moment, sitting so close to Leah that I could smell her perfume and the hot TV lights and the *Justice!* people running around and everything. It was crazy.

They showed a reenactment of the whole thing, shot in grainy black-and-white, with some little emo kid playing me, running down the alley, jumping . . .

It was TV. They didn't tell the whole story, of course.

Maybe that's because *I* didn't tell *them* the whole story.

CHAPTER 2
BUS RIDE OF CHAMPIONS

IT'S HARD TO GET USED TO the way the world's treating me. No one ever really paid attention to me before, and now . . .

Well, for example, there's *People*. They wanted to put me on the cover along with other "Teen Heroes!" like the kid who woke up at night to smell smoke just in time to get her family out of a burning house, and the other kid who went to computer camp even though his home had been devastated by Hurricane Katrina. (I don't know how going to computer camp makes you a hero, but *People* says it, so it must be true, right?)

But let me tell you something—bad enough I agreed to have my face plastered all over TV. I wasn't about to give *People* an interview, so they cut me from the cover, thank God.

Oh, and then there were the reporters. *Billions* of them.

OK, not billions, but a lot. It's down to a few local guys now, but for a while there, there were about ten or fifteen of them and they were sort of camped out on the sidewalk and in vans on the street where me and Dad live. Which was embarrassing because we live in this crappy basement apartment in an old house and people took pictures of me coming out of it. They took pictures of Dad, too, when he came home from work, which is also embarrassing because he's usually in his overalls and doesn't look all that impressive. I tell people my dad works for the government, which isn't a total lie. He used to be in the army and now he's a garbage man. That's sort of a government job. Government contracted, at least.

You'd think that it would be against the law to hang around outside my home and wait to take pictures of me, but Dad says it's not.

"You're considered a public person now," he told me in a rare moment of lucidity. "The privacy laws are a little less strict around you. The sidewalk and the street are public property, so they can wait there as long as they want."

He told me to just ignore them, that they'd go away as soon as there was another story to cover.

Easy for *him* to say. Dad doesn't care what anyone else thinks. But I'm *ugly*, OK? And I have face pizza like you wouldn't believe, so I really, really hate having my picture taken. Bad enough everything was splattered all over TV courtesy of *Justice!*, but now I also have to deal with the thought that my picture might show up in the *New York Times* or *US Weekly*?

I was pretty much fed up with walking into a solid wall of bodies and flashbulbs every time I left the house, so it's actually cool that *Justice!* has aired, because now they've mostly gone away and I can just go to the school bus like a normal person.

I hop on the bus and the doors close and it's totally silent. Like someone just cut a nasty fart and won't own up to it.

And then someone clears their throat and says, "Way to kick ass, Kevin."

I don't know who says it. I can't even turn in time to look

for the person before suddenly the whole bus erupts into applause. It's like drums in a tin can.

God, even on the school bus. I can't escape it. I thought this was over last week, but I guess the airing of *Justice!* over the weekend just got people going again.

I expect the bus driver to shout for us all to get quiet and for me to sit down, but when I look over my shoulder, *she's* standing up, clapping her little heart out for me.

This is unreal.

What do I do now? What do I say? Am I supposed to make a speech or something? God, I hope not.

I smile as best I can—when I smile, my face becomes even uglier, so I avoid it whenever possible. See, my lips sort of peel back and my teeth just hang out there like they're dangling in space. So I keep my lips pretty tight together when I'm in situations where I have to smile.

"Thanks," I say, because I don't know what else to say. The bus driver slides back into her seat, which I take as my cue to sit down.

I take the first seat I see, not pressing my luck. It's next to a kid I don't know, a freshman.

"Saw you on TV," he says. "You looked OK."

You'd have to cut through ten miles of bad jungle overgrowth before getting within pissing distance of "looking OK" for me, but he's not pulling my leg. He seems sincere, a sure indicator of some horrible variety of brain damage. Poor kid. So young.

"Way to kick that guy's ass," he goes on. "I read about him online, you know? They called him 'the Surgeon.'"

"Yeah. I know."

"Because he would anatize his victims," the kid announces proudly.

"Anesthetize," I tell him. I have some trouble pronouncing it myself, but at least I *try*.

"Yeah, that's what I said. And then he would cut them up, all surgical-like. With a scalp. Like the Indians."

Wow. He managed to mess up vocabulary *and* history all at once. That's impressive.

"He used a scalpel. That's what doctors use."

The kid snorts as if I'm pulling his leg. He turns to look out the window, muttering something about "big-shot hero." I let it go. I don't need to add shoving a freshman out the bus window to my list of problems.

CHAPTER 3
SCHOOL DAZED

AT SCHOOL, THERE'S OCCASIONAL SMATTERINGS OF APPLAUSE and some cheers, even from people who don't know me. People who just saw me on TV or who maybe heard about things from Leah or one of her legions of friends. I hate the attention. I duck my head down and do the best lips-over-the-teeth grin I can in response. I hate my teeth. Along with the rest of my mouth.

And the rest of my face, for that matter.

I'm only in homeroom for five minutes when the phone rings on Mrs. Sawyer's desk. "Dr. Goethe would like to see you, Kevin." So I trudge off to the principal's office . . .

. . . where Dr. Goethe leans back in his chair, beaming, as he reminds me that this afternoon will be the "very special town assembly" to honor me for my "unwavering heroism," with plenty of "important people and press" in attendance.

"You know, you've always sort of flown under the radar, Kevin," he goes on. "So it's great to see this. I hope you'll take all of this attention as a sign and really step up your game."

Whatever. My grades are OK. I could do better, but why bother?

This will actually be the third such assembly for me; Dad

says I can ditch them if I want, but he also says it would be polite to keep going, since people are going to so much trouble. There was already one at the Elks Club and the VFW, and now the whole town is showing up at school this afternoon.

I assure Dr. Goethe that I haven't forgotten and then I try to have a normal day, but that isn't going to happen. I don't know if it'll ever happen again.

There's a palpable silence when I enter the lunchroom, everyone turning to look at me. Leah is eating lunch with her usual group, and everyone seems to be waiting to see if I'll sit down with her, even though that hasn't happened yet and *won't* happen. Not a chance. I know my place.

Tit waves to me from his table in the corner. He's with Jedi and Speedo. I sit down with them and try to ignore the million eyes boring into me from all angles. Why does everyone have to stare? Why can't they just let me be?

And then it's like the entire cafeteria sucks in its breath all at once. Like we were all watching TV or something and a car blew up out of nowhere. Or something. I don't know. I'm bad at metaphors or similes or whatever they are. Ask any of my English teachers.

Tit clears his throat really loud, trying to get my attention. Jedi makes his *vvvvvvvvvhnn* noise, and I look up from my dry hamburger and Leah is standing there. I try to swallow, but I'm nervous and my throat's dry and I think, *Oh, cool, Kross— you're going to choke to death right here,* but that doesn't happen and instead I sort of cough and I think, *Oh, even better—you're gonna spit up a gross brown wad of partly chewed burger while Leah's standing here and the whole school is watching.*

But somehow that doesn't happen either. I manage to keep my mouth shut and my food somewhere between my teeth and my throat.

There's an endless moment of silence. It's like church. Been a while, tell the truth. But I remember it well—this is what it sounded like in church, just before Mass, when the processional music stops and Father McKane stands at the altar and everyone's perfectly quiet for just those few seconds between the last strains of music fading away and Father McKane saying...

Leah saves the day by speaking, because I'm just sitting there, lost in my Catholic past. First she flashes me this *totally* dazzling smile that nearly blinds me and makes me ponder the awesome power of those tooth-whitening strips. Then she says, "I wanted to invite you to my party."

In a way, I'm glad for the burger plug jammed in my craw; otherwise, I'd probably say something witty and brilliant like, "Huh?" Instead, I just nod wisely.

"My parents are letting me throw a party next Friday, and I wanted..."

She looks around, suddenly aware that everyone in the lunchroom is staring at us, that the usual dull roar of conversation has quieted to a burble of whispers. "Beauty and the Beastly" all over again. Good for her—she doesn't let it bother her.

"I wanted to invite you," she says, smiling perkily and bouncing a little bit. I force my eyes *not* to follow the bounce, which is easier said than done.

She holds out a little cream-colored envelope. After fifteen or twenty years, I realize that it's for me. I take it.

"I really hope you can come," she says again, and spins around and marches back to her table.

I rediscover my ability to swallow just as the lunchroom erupts into applause. Oh, God. Not again.

"Dude, you rock *and* you roll," says Tit.

"Cut it out."

Jedi jumps in. "Man, you know who'll be at that party? All the hotties, man."

"Can I go with?" Speedo asks.

"Shut up, guys." They're talking too loudly and I don't want someone to overhear my buddies acting like the horn-dogs they (OK, OK, *we*) really are. It's embarrassing.

"I wanna go with," Speedo says.

Tit reaches out for the invitation, but I shove it in my pocket before he can grab it. "Stop it, guys. No one's going."

Tit shakes his head. "You saved her life and stuff. You should go."

"Yeah," Jedi says. "Maybe she'll give you a *special* reward." He mimes oral sex with a french fry.

I look around, panicked, making sure no one notices. The guys crack up. They don't know. They don't care.

Later, in science class, I examine the envelope. I'm supposed to be taking notes, but I sit in the back and for once no one is looking at me.

A little cream envelope, very lightweight. My name written across the front in what must be Leah's handwriting: "Kevin." I like the way she makes the *K,* with a sort of flourish, like it's something special.

Green ink. Green is her favorite color.

It isn't sealed. I pry out the card inside. It's a stiff piece of matching cream paper, preprinted—in green, of course—with Leah's name and address and the time of the party. Leah has written at the bottom "Don't forget a bathing suit!" and I think for a second that I might pass out.

And then, off to one side, is another handwritten note. Did she write this on all of them? I don't think so—the handwriting is slightly different here, as if she jotted this last part down quickly, in an uncertain rush.

"Please come."

That's all it says. Two words.

God, how do I get into these things?

CHAPTER 4
THE COUNCIL OF FOOLS

OK, I'VE HAD ENOUGH MIND-NUMBING WEIRDNESS for one day, so after bio I decide to skip math. I head off to the auditorium instead. There's a janitor's office back there, behind the stage and off the wings. It's locked, but Speedo scammed a key last year and made copies for all of us. The office is always empty at this time of day because that's when the custodians all head out to McDonald's for lunch.

I'm not the only one who needed some time away, it looks like. Flip and Fam are here, slobbering all over each other on one of the pitted metal desks.

"Whoa, sorry, guys." I start to back out.

"No, no!" Flip jumps up. Fam looks a little annoyed, but she just runs her fingers through her hair and straightens her clothes. "Hail, Fool! Dude, stick. Stick."

I sort of want to leave because I'm sure they have better things to do than hang with me right now, but Fam doesn't look annoyed anymore, so I guess I'll stay. I wish I were alone, though. I really just want to be alone right now.

"Hail, Fool," I say back, and Fam repeats it.

"So today's the big day, huh?" Flip gets this gleam in his eye, and for a second there, I'm worried. As soon as I knew about it, I begged him—honestly *begged* him—not to pull any pranks at the ceremony this afternoon. Bad enough I'll be on display for everyone in town; I don't need some craziness interrupting it and stretching it out.

No sooner do I think it than the door opens and in comes the rest of the crew: Speedo, Jedi, and Tit. The gang's all here, and the room's a confusion of "Hail, Fool!" as everyone says hi.

And then Tit starts chanting, "Kross! Kross! Kross!" and the rest pick it up, except for Flip, who just looks bored, and I don't blame him.

"Guys, come on." But they're not listening to me.

"Guys, you're making too much noise. Someone will hear."

They don't care. They just keep chanting.

"We're proud of you, Kross," Flip says once the chanting has died down.

"Yeah, man." Jedi chimes in. "*Vvvvvvhhhn.* You put Brookdale on the map!"

"I did?"

"Sure," says Flip. "It's freakin' hilarious. I mean, people are talking about *Brookdale.* When's the last time that happened?"

"Uh, that whole thing with that teacher screwing Crazy J," Speedo says.

"Crazy J" is a senior named Josh Mendel. He gets into a lot of fights and it's generally agreed that he's a class-A nutjob from way back, when he had sex with a teacher back in middle school.

Flip waves it off. "Whatever. There's one of those in, like, *every* town, so who the hell cares?"

"I was just in the right place at the right time, guys." It feels like a lie when I say it, but it's true in its own weird way. I sort of wish I could *be* Josh Mendel, even with all his problems. He's tall and good-looking; he takes no crap from anyone. I take a moderate amount of crap and I wish it was less. He could have any girl in the school. I only want one. I don't see why it has to be such a big deal.

I guess I should explain about the Council of Fools and all of this "Hail, Fool" nonsense.

See, back in middle school a bunch of us decided that school was crap. School was for fools. So we became the Council of Fools, an organization dedicated to proving the absurdity of school and all aspects of social life.

If that last bit sounded rehearsed, it's because it's part of our charter, which every Fool has to memorize. Yes, we have a charter. We're pretty scarily organized, tell the truth. Especially considering that there were five of us at the time (Fam joined later, in high school), and *you* try to get five middle-schoolers to do anything for any length of time. The fact that we're still together speaks well for us, I think. Of course, we're dedicated to generally messing with people's heads, so maybe it's not all in the best cause, but you can't have everything.

We all have Fool names, like Kross. Bill Yingling became Jedi because he's constantly making this *vvvvvvvvhhnnn* noise, this weird little humming thing that sounds just like a light saber, so we all decided he's a Jedi. Speedo and Tit are tied for most embarrassing names—Tit got his because his last name is Titus, so how could he *not* be Tit? Speedo got his name because when we all took swimming classes a few years ago, he wore this nearly gone Speedo while the rest of us wore surf shorts. You can't let a guy forget that kind of shame, not if you're a real friend.

Last but not least, there's Fam and Flip. Fam's our only girl member—and she's only a member because she's Flip's girl-friend. She joined at the beginning of this school year. She was just this little freshman chick who for some reason glommed on to Flip. I don't get their relationship—it's like all sex and Flip driving her places. But I don't try to figure it out. Her real name's Julia, which became Jules, which became Jewels, which became *Family* Jewels, which . . . You get the point.

Joseph Brenner—our fearless, peerless leader (his own words)—is "Flip" because his mom was always telling him to watch his mouth and "stop being so flip!" which seemed really hilarious back in, you know, seventh grade. He's sort of our Head Fool because even though he's in the same grade as the rest of us, he's the oldest. He flunked out of third grade, not because he's a dummy but because he's so smart. He would get bored in class and zone out all the time and his teachers thought he was a retard or something because he never did his work so they "held him back." That's such a stupid phrase, but it's so accurate, too. I mean, on the one hand it's totally teacher-talk for "flunked." On the other hand, in Flip's case they really *were* holding him back. Literally.

Fortunately, Flip didn't let it stop him. He just kept on do-ing his thing, but he was careful to wake up in school long enough to get a C average and keep on plugging ahead.

"No way I'm staying in school one day longer than is strictly necessary," he told me once.

Repeating third grade was pure torture for him. He already knew everything there was to know up to grade six by then, but he couldn't be bothered to do the tests because he thought they were boring and stupid.

Which they were. Most of us don't have the balls to say so, though.

Flip doesn't suffer fools gladly. Which is why we sort of went with an ironic twist and called ourselves the Council of Fools. And the best part of Flip being in charge is that he could drive earlier than any of us, so we've been pretty mobile ever since we started high school.

We started out with stupid little pranks in middle school. Just dumb kid stuff, really. Like exploding lockers and turning off the water to the girls' bathroom. Junk like that. But freshman year, Flip topped himself. He hacked into the school computer and started changing grades. Only instead of screwing people and lowering their grades, he went in and gave a bunch of jocks *better* grades, high enough that they could keep playing lacrosse. Why?

"Because it's a Foolish thing to do," he said. Sometimes when Flip talks, you can hear capital letters in his voice.

I got his point, though. Usually you hack into a computer to do damage, right? But Flip was doing something wrong that was actually helping someone.

"It's a moral, ethical, and philosophical paradox," he told me, puffing away on a cigarette, hunched over his computer. "And besides, why not?"

The whole thing became the Council's greatest triumph/failure (they're sort of the same thing to us, really). Someone found out about the hacked grades and assumed that the lacrosse team was responsible (we never clued them in, of course) and they had to forfeit the entire season.

"Unintended consequences," Flip intoned when the news broke. "Not just a good idea, but the law." I didn't quite get that one. But that's OK. If you understand half of what Flip says, you're on solid ground.

Probably Flip's finest hour, though, was the amazing kidnapping and debut of Officer Sexpot.

CHAPTER 5
THE INCREDIBLE TRUE SECRET ORIGIN OF OFFICER SEXPOT

NO, SERIOUSLY. I'M NOT MAKING THIS UP. You think I could make this stuff up?

See, all kinds of speeding and stuff goes on here in Brookdale, but no one ever wants to pay for more cops. And when folks *do* get pulled over, they just bitch and moan about getting pulled over anyway. So I guess it's a Catch-22 for the mayor and the cops.

A couple of years ago, someone got the bright idea to do like they do in other towns and put a dummy on the road dressed as a cop. No, really. They actually do this. They take one of the town police cars and stick it along the highway like it's just parked there. And they stick a dummy at the wheel and people seeing it think they're busted so they slow down and by the time they drive by and realize they've been had, it's too late—they've already slowed down, mission accomplished, no money spent, no overtime, yadda yadda.

It's not a bad plan because you never *really* know if that cop car up ahead is legit or a fake. So you slow down no matter what.

Or at least, you *used* to.

See, six months ago Flip stole the dummy.

Well, that's not how *he* put it.

"I kidnapped Officer Sexpot," he told us all triumphantly. "But really, she wanted to come with me. She was pretty tired of sitting in that car all the time. She craves excitement. She wants a *life*, boys." (He said "boys" even though Fam was right there.)

And when you see her up close, she sort of *does* look like one of those blow-up dolls. I don't know where the town got her, but she looks like she sort of had a shady past, you know?

So she became our unofficial mascot, and then one day Flip got this brilliant idea: we would start dressing her up in outrageous outfits and pose her places and take pictures and then Flip would hack the pictures into people's e-mail accounts and websites.

It's a *blast!* Honest! The lovely and wooden OSP has done time as a call girl (in front of the First Baptist Church), a French maid (bending over a grave marker at the cemetery), and—my personal favorite—a very naughty Mrs. Claus on Christmas Eve.

On the mayor's roof.

Doing something very jolly with the mayor's Santa statue that put the "X" in "Xmas."

And let me tell you, it was a *bitch* getting that thing up to the roof and back down before the mayor and his wife got home from church, but it was worth every sore muscle on Christmas morning.

These are the things we do, we Council of Fools. We're bored a lot.

CHAPTER 6
A BIG MOMENT (OH, JOY)

BEFORE LEAVING THE JANITORS' OFFICE, I secure another promise from Flip not to mess around today.

He looks at me like I just kicked him in the shin. "Kross. I'm hurt. How could you think I would embarrass a fellow Fool like that?"

His expression is so sad and forlorn that I almost feel bad for bringing it up. But then his face splits into the grin I know so well. "Besides," he says, "it'll be much more fun watching you go through the whole thing. If I pranked it, you'd get a break."

Fam slaps his shoulder. "Be nice."

I go to my last two classes and try to focus, but when the day ends, I feel no relief because there's more to come.

The ceremony takes place on the football field. I can't say "football stadium" because that would imply that South Brook High has, well, a *stadium*. And the truth of the matter is that all we have is a field with a bunch of hard-on-your-ass bleachers and two goalposts and a scoreboard that isn't even digital—it still has those numbers cut in half horizontally that flip over themselves to update.

So, this is how Brookdale treats its hero-types: it tortures them.

They've put up some kind of stage at one end of the field,

and that's where I stand, along with the mayor, Dr. Goethe, and a bunch of other people I don't know. I think they're aldermen or councilors or something. I guess if I cared, I'd ask to be introduced.

All I know is that the entire town of Brookdale is sitting on the field on folding chairs or on the bleachers. Or at least that's how it feels. There's a whole hell of a lot of people out there, and I squirm every time I think about it, which is all the time at the moment because they're right in front of me, so I'm basically one big ball of squirm.

Leah is up here, too, standing near me. She smells nice—like lilacs. I guess. I don't really know what lilacs smell like, so it's tough to say. But in poems and stuff, people are always talking about the smell of lilacs and they say it with this sort of emotion that makes me think lilacs must be just about the best thing in the world, and that's what Leah smells like right now—the best thing in the world.

OK, settle down, Kross.

I don't even want to *think* about what *I* smell like. I think my deodorant gave up a couple of hours ago and it's hot out here and I really hope that some of the funk I'm detecting is just radiating from the crowd.

Flip was right: If he suddenly overloaded the speakers with feedback or had the Council set off firecrackers over by the parking lot, I'd at least get a minute without everyone staring at me.

But there's no break in sight, so I have to stand here the whole time, while Dr. Goethe introduces me and talks about what I did and how I'm Brookdale's new TV star, which gets some laughs—*Ha ha, the ugly kid is a TV star.* Then the mayor takes the mike and babbles for a while about Civic Pride and Lending a Hand and how I am, apparently, the New Face of Today's Youth, which, let me tell you, does not bode well for Today's Youth's chances of ever getting laid.

Thankfully, I'm not asked to speak. Because I would probably puke.

Unbelievably, it turns out there's a key to the town—the key to Brookdale. This makes me think of a big dome over the town, with a little door and a teeny, tiny keyhole. Now *that* would be cool.

Leah is the one who gives me the key. Of course. She's wearing a cream dress with green trim. She wears it at least once a month, usually for something special. She wore it today for me.

She hands the key to me and she's smiling and she's beautiful and she's lilacs and I think—no, no, wait, I'm pretty sure—I'm going to pass out here and now, which would just be *perfect*, wouldn't it? Right there in front of Leah, in front of the entire town of Brookdale and probably half of Canterstown, too.

But I manage not to pass out. Leah gives me a little hug that sends sparks all along my body and makes me rigid with fear that I'm going to pop a boner right here on stage. Oh, man, that would suck.

Fortunately, Little Kross decides to behave. Leah steps away from me, leaving a fog of lilac confusion in her wake. There's applause as I perform the supremely heroic act of standing there with a dumb look on my face, holding the key in one sweaty hand. Looking out at the crowd, I see Dad and

Leah's parents and Tit's mom and the Council, everyone applauding except for Flip, way in the back, his arm around Fam's shoulders. She's clapping and cheering, but Flip just looks sort of bored and isn't applauding at all, which is cool because this is *so* not a big deal.

Now what do I do with the key? I feel like everyone expects me to hold it up over my head like a trophy or something, but it's sort of small, only a little bigger than a *real* key, so no one would even be able to see it. It's sort of a brassy color, but it doesn't feel all that heavy, so that's probably just paint. It has a little red stone set in it, and it's engraved BROOKDALE, MARYLAND with the date.

God, this is stupid.

And, sadly, it's not over yet. Because now there's more speech-making. People saying incredibly stupid things about me, going back to the whole hero thing, making me sound like I tracked the Surgeon from his lair with my trusty bloodhound and a sniper rifle before besting him in hand-to-hand combat on top of a speeding bus filled with orphans and nuns. And ninjas. Ninjas are involved somehow, too.

I zone out long enough to imagine all of that and snap out of it to more applause. I have, apparently, just been offered free manicures for life at a local salon. Why would I want a single manicure, much less a lifetime's supply? (And how many manicures *are* there in a lifetime's supply?)

It gets better: free DVD rentals (I don't have a DVD player!) and free meals at some local restaurants (yeah, because I love eating alone in public) and a bunch of other crap.

By the time it's over, there's sweat soaking through the

back of my shirt. My armpits are a swamp. I imagine my zit cream running down my face like melted makeup.

"We have one last surprise for you, Kevin," the mayor says, and beckons for me to join him at the microphone. Oh, Lord.

"You turned sixteen last week, didn't you, Kevin?"

I lean into the microphone. "Yeah." Oops. I'm supposed to say, "Yes, sir," or something like that, right?

"Don't have a car yet, do you?"

"Nah." Oops. Again.

"Well, stop by the lot. We'll take care of you."

The crowd goes crazy with more applause.

And then it's all done, thank God. The final round of applause dies out and the mayor thanks everyone for coming and that's that, and I breathe a sigh of relief.

Dad starts to make his way toward me while the mayor makes sure to get one last picture with me.

"Are you serious?" I ask the mayor. "About the car?"

"Of course! We'll help you spend a little of that reward money, huh?" He slaps me on the back and laughs like it's a joke, but it's not. "I'll get you a great deal, don't worry. Give you my cost on the whole thing. I've got the perfect car in mind already."

Being mayor of Brookdale is not exactly a high-paying gig. We learned that in an elementary school unit on local government. I think he gets like ten grand a year, which—if you ask me—is probably ten grand too much to run this place. So he has to have a regular job, too, and this particular mayor owns a car dealership.

This is actually a pretty sweet deal, all things considered. Dad wasn't going to be buying me a car any time soon, after all. I wouldn't need Flip to drive me everywhere all the time. I could have some freedom.

Even though I don't really deserve it.

Because . . .

And then Dad's on the stage, shaking the mayor's hand, and he puts his other hand on my shoulder and the mayor says, "You must be so proud of Kevin."

And it kills me when Dad says, "Yes. I am."

SELF-LOATHING #1

MY DAD—NOW *THERE'S* A HERO, I GUESS. He carried a gun. He served his country. He walked the desert sands, never knowing which step might be the last he would take.

And me? Yeah, I saved Leah's life.

But I did something else, too. Something no one knows about.

I don't know which would be worse—the world learning the truth, or the world *never* learning. Because if people find out, my entire world would crumble.

But worse than that is this: if no one *ever* knows, I think this secret is going to eat me alive from the inside out.

CHAPTER 7
SMART PEOPLE

DAD ALWAYS SAID THAT MOM WAS THE SMARTEST PERSON in the family, and I agree with him. She proved it the day she left us.

If Dad thought Mom was the smartest in the family, she always returned the favor: "Your father is too brilliant for his own good," she would say. I never believed it because I never saw it. Dad was just . . . Dad. One day I was feeling particularly snarky, so I asked him why he didn't do something more with his life, something important. I didn't put it that way, but that's what I was getting at.

He leaned back, stared at the ceiling, and thought for a while. Then he said, "I had to opt out of the opt-in society."

Which to this day still makes no sense at all. Not even to Flip.

So maybe he's just the smartest garbage man in the world. Doing all that physical work is good for him, he says. It lets the brain shut down and the body take over and maybe that's kind of like his own personal safety valve.

Isn't that what Mrs. Sawyer called it in history class—the safety valve? When America was young and things would get rough and then everyone would just move west and things would calm down because everyone was spread out and not getting on each other's nerves anymore?

Yeah, that's what they called it—the safety valve. That's what my dad has. That's what everyone needs.

Dad has to get up at like two in the morning for his job, so he goes to sleep at four or five in the afternoon most days, which is why he gets the apartment's only bedroom. I don't have a room of my own—I have the foldout sofa in the living room. See, when Mom left, Dad couldn't afford to keep the townhouse anymore, so we moved into this little apartment on Main Street.

The apartment is basically a basement with "delusions of grandeur." (That's one of Flip's pet phrases and I stole it because I like the way it sounds.) Mrs. Mac is our landlady—she lives in the house above us. She's like ten million years old and even though she's supposed to make sure everything is running right in the apartment, she usually ends up calling Dad when *her* pipes are acting up and stuff. She makes these really lousy blueberry muffins that are as dry as sand and half as tasty, and she's always bringing bunches of them to Dad and me.

So we've got one bedroom and one bathroom and a tiny living room and this little hallway with appliances that counts as a kitchen. There's junk piled just about everywhere because Dad goes off to work and comes home with all kinds of crap. I mean, sometimes I wonder if anything actually ends up *in* the truck. It all seems to make its way to our place instead.

Dad's all like, "We live in a disposable society. It's reprehensible." (He uses that word a lot.) And, "People throw away perfectly good things." And things like that.

He's got all of this old sporting equipment, like dented baseball bats ("I can pound that out") and rusting barbells

("They just need to be cleaned up") and other junk. At last count, there were ten broken VCRs stacked up in a corner. ("I just need to take 'em apart and get them working again," Dad says.)

I used to fold up the sofa every morning and unfold it every night, but eventually it hit me that no one visits us anyway, so now I just leave it open all the time. Fortunately, Dad has gotten used to this because now I hide my video camera and my tapes under there. I should toss all of it now. I really should. Can't bring myself to do it, though.

Not that I would throw it away *here*, anyway. I'd have to go to a Dumpster or something. I *never* toss anything incriminating at home. You never throw away anything that could prove you guilty when you live with a garbage man. Trust me on that one.

I mean, it's bad enough he digs crap out of *other* people's garbage. "Rescuing," he calls it. Which is why we have stacks and piles of "rescued" junk all over the apartment, so that there's barely enough room for us to move around. Bad enough he does *that*. But he totally checks out *our* garbage, too. I threw away a tube of toothpaste once that hadn't been rolled all the way up and he just about freaked on me. "Do you realize how wasteful this is?"

And heaven forbid I toss a piece of paper! As long as it's blank on one side, he'll cut it up into quarters and use it for note paper or shopping lists or whatever.

"We live in a limited world, Kevin," he told me once. "Everything runs out at some point. People need to realize that. I'm not going to have my son contributing to the problem."

I said something smart-alecky at that point about recycling bread crusts . . . and he just launched into a tirade about how bread crusts could be ground up to make bread *crumbs*, which could be used in recipes (because he *totally* cooks all the time), and I realized—then and there—that there's just no point arguing with my dad.

CHAPTER 8
TWO SPARROWS

THE COOL THING ABOUT A DAD WHO SLEEPS in the evening (the *only* cool thing) is that I get to do what I want most nights, as long as I'm in bed by two a.m., when Dad gets up. So tonight, like so many others, I meet the Council at SAMMPark.

SAMMPark is the Susan Ann Marchetti Memorial Park, but no one in their right mind calls it that. Everyone just calls it SAMMPark. The town built it about five years ago, and it's pretty much one of the only places worth going to in Brookdale.

When they first opened the place, it was a big deal. It was like Fourth of July and Memorial Day rolled into one. People took off work to come with their families, to listen to bands play, to barbecue, play Frisbee, all that stuff.

I was ten or eleven. My little brother, Jesse, was five or six. We were still a family back then. Dad and Mom and Jesse and me.

I couldn't believe how big the park was. There had once been an office park here, right on the edge of town, but after the economy went bad, the place just sat abandoned for years. Then the town suddenly had a wad of cash and the next thing you know—ta-da! SAMMPark.

Before Dad would let us run off to play with the other kids, though, he dragged us over to a spot near the entrance to the park. There was a statue there—a lifesize replica of a woman dressed like a nurse.

"See this?" Dad asked.

Jesse was all fidgety. Mom put her hands on his shoulders to keep him still.

"Yeah, Dad," I said.

"All of these people are just here to have a good time, and that's OK, but..." And then he started rambling and I couldn't understand half of it.

"What your father is trying to say..." That was a big phrase for Mom. She said it all the time. When I was younger, I thought she had telepathy or something, seeing as how she could figure out what Dad meant to say. Especially when it seemed like *he* had no idea.

"What he's trying to say, is that people should know why the park is here. That's important."

Dad took a deep breath and nodded. "Right. Right. See, it was built for... It was built by..." He blew out his breath. "Look. Here. See it?"

I read the inscription on the pedestal: *Susan Ann Marchetti Memorial Park*. Under that: *Dedicated and built in her name by the man who gave her life and the man who gave her death*. There were also two dates, just like on a gravestone.

"What does it mean?" I asked Dad.

"She was killed back before you were born," Dad said, "by a drunk driver." Dad had found a rhythm now and was comfortable. "Ran her off the road while she was on her way home from nursing school. The guy who did it wasn't much older than you—he had just turned eighteen. And he killed someone. He got off pretty light, too. His family was from Breed's Grove."

Breed's Grove was on the west side of Brookdale. Rich people lived there. Like *super* rich, you know? I suddenly felt guilty, even though I hadn't done anything.

"A few years ago, he came back to Brookdale. He was a big success, made a lot of money. But he came back here and the next thing you know, he was working with *her* father to build this park in her memory."

Dad stared at the statue for a long time. Jesse started fidgeting again. I kept waiting for Dad to say something else, but he just stared. Finally, Mom cleared her throat and told me and Jesse to go play. We ran off, but I looked over my shoulder. Dad was still just staring at the statue. Mom took one of his hands and stood there with him.

I went over to the playground area. It's like every kid in Brookdale was there—the place was all chaotic fun. Except for Jesse, who sat on a swing, not moving at all, staring down at his feet.

"What's wrong, Jess?" I thought maybe he wanted me to push him. He knew how to swing on his own, but he still liked being pushed.

I crouched down next to him and that's when I realized he was crying. I got angry and confused at the same time. "What happened? Did someone hit you?"

He shook his head ferociously. He never let Mom cut his hair, so it flopped all around his face. "No."

"Then what's wrong?"

"Why did she die?" And he started bawling. Other kids looked over.

"Calm down, Jesse." I knew who he meant—the dead girl. The one they'd named the park after. I should have known this would happen. Jesse cried at cartoons, for God's sake.

I pulled him off the swing and took him over near some bushes where I could calm him down and get him settled. "Remember how Pandazilla created Aquahorse?" I asked. It was this totally silly memory. We'd been playing together in the backyard and this gigantic stuffed panda—we named it Pandazilla because it was the bad guy for our army toys and superheroes—picked up a horse to throw it at something and instead Jesse tripped and the horse went flying into the wading pool. Jesse was four and this was, like, the height of comedy for him. The horse was taking a bath, we decided, and then we decided that the horse loved the water and we named it Aquahorse. I could always count on that stupid memory to make him laugh.

It worked again this time. "The horse took a bath," he said, sniffling a little bit.

"Yeah, that's right." And pretty soon he was doing all right and I helped him wipe up his tears with the edge of his shirt and we went off to play.

Later that night, when we were home and tucked in bed, I asked Mom why Dad had told us the story about the dead girl.

"Dad just likes for you to know these things. It's important to him."

"Why?"

A troubled look flitted over Mom's face for just a second. Looking back, that was probably my first clue that she was going to leave him. *Us.* "It's just important to him," she said, in a tone of voice that added, *Beats the hell out of me, too.*

That story—that day—always pops into my brain whenever I come to SAMMPark, which is actually a lot these days because the park is the Council's official outside-of-school meeting place. It's big enough that we can always find someplace to sneak off to when we need to discuss whatever mayhem we're going to concoct next.

Flip picks me up in his beat-up old orange coupe. We're the last to arrive; everyone else is already at the park. He keeps up a running stream of commentary about the ceremony at the school and all of the great ideas he'd had to disrupt it.

"But out of respect for a fellow Fool, I held back," he admits, then waits for me to fall all over myself thanking him. I'm not in the mood, though, so I just sit there.

"We should do something with the key," he says after a moment, pretending that the silence never happened. "I mean, there's got to be *something* we can do with it, right?"

I think about the key. It's actually on my key chain now, because . . . Well, because it's a *key*, right? Not much else to do with it. And besides . . .

"If we do something with the key, they'll know it was me."

Flip's eyebrows shoot up. "Very true, Fool Kross! Very true. Nicely done. Good show."

Just then, we pass the big sign that reads, KEEP BROOKDALE BEAUTIFUL! I bite my lip because Flip is about to say . . .

"You know the problem with that sign, Kross? It pre—"

"'It presupposes that Brookdale was beautiful to begin with.'"

"Guess I say that a lot, huh?"

Only, like, every freakin' time we drive past it.

"The truth must be spoken." He steers into the parking lot at SAMMPark. "Let us disembark!"

Just inside the entrance is the statue of Susan Ann Marchetti. As he does every time he comes to the park, Flip saunters over to it and slaps it on the ass. "Hey, there, Susie baby!" he calls out. "Lookin' good, sweet thang!"

I hate it when he does that.

"So hot for someone made out of cold stone," he says on his way back to me. "I would have hit that, Kross. I really would have."

I almost tell him that he *wishes* he could have hit that. That Fam only hangs out with him because she's a freshman and she likes having a boyfriend who can drive. But there's no point to it. I mean, Flip once told me that he *knows* Fam is only his girlfriend because it's convenient. He doesn't care. He just likes having someone who hangs on his every word.

But I don't say anything because Flip'll just come back with something I have no answer for. So instead, we head further into the park for the party.

When I say the Council's having a party, you have to realize that a Council party is just the six of us hanging out at SAMMPark until it's too late at night, eating buckets of take-out wings from Cincinnati Joe's and drinking beer in the bushes so that no one busts us and smoking and listening to Flip, who blathers on about whatever wild thoughts have invaded his brain lately—radiation from quasars, prime numbers, college student plagiarism, last night's TV, sex. Whatever.

By the time the sun's gone down and the park has emptied out of the families, we're all pretty smashed, except for Flip, the designated driver. ("Dying in a car wreck isn't Foolish—it's just stupid.") Then again, Flip's permanently high on his own adrenaline and brainwaves, so he doesn't *need* booze or drugs.

Speedo had the foresight to bring a little baggie of pot, so we roll up and light up and sort of blunder around the park, losing more and more touch with reality. It's a great way to access Fooldom. You think and say stuff while drunk or stoned that you'd never think or say otherwise.

I end up lying in the grass near the baseball diamond with Tit, the two of us just staring up at the stars, which suddenly look like giant, winking eyes. I've known Tit the longest of the whole Council. We grew up together in my old neighborhood, back when Mom and Dad were still together. We always end up doing this—splintering off—when the Council gets together. Flip calls us the Subcommittee.

Tonight, it's like the sky is *watching* us from every angle, and even though I'm stoned, this doesn't worry me or make me paranoid. It sort of makes me feel safe and secure. Like someone has my back.

It makes me think of my favorite verse from the Bible. Not that I know much about the Bible, tell the truth. I mean, I'm no scholar or anything. But I paid attention back when I used to go to Mass, and this one verse really hooked me one time when Father McKane was giving his sermon, so I looked it up later.

"Are not two sparrows sold for a penny? Yet not one of them will

fall to the ground apart from the will of your Father. And even the very hairs of your head are all numbered."

That's from Matthew. And what it basically means is that God's watching and he doesn't miss anything, which is a good thing.

And it makes me think like maybe tonight God punched holes in that big black vault overhead so that he could keep tabs on me and keep me from doing anything else really, unbelievably dumb or evil.

It's too late for the dumb, evil things in my past, but maybe there's still time to rescue me from my future idiocy.

Tit starts blabbing about girls.

We Fools, we tell each other everything.

Almost.

We keep no secrets from each other.

Almost.

So Tit's babbling about girls and that makes me think about Leah, and I wonder how the universe can be so screwy that I've ended up in this position—called a hero when I know I'm nothing of the sort.

Flip says that chaos dominates the world. That everything is made up of these things called fractals, which I don't understand, but Flip's brilliant, so I just believe him and he says that with fractals, the *ending* of something is completely dependent on how it *starts*. So what if . . . What if I'd never bought the video camera? What if I'd never worked at the Burger Joint two summers ago? Would I still have ended up in that alley? And would the world still believe the great lie, maybe the *ultimate* Fool prank, that Kevin Ross is a hero?

I don't know. I'm not smart enough to know. But I think

Leah would probably be dead, if that was the case. So do I have to bear the burden of my guilt to save her? Is that the price I pay?

My head starts to hurt from all of the thinking. Fortunately, Tit interrupts me.

"Who would you do?" he asks. He blows out some smoke and passes his cigarette over to me. The pot and beer are gone, and the two of us are down to two cigarettes, which we're sharing to try to make them last longer. Neither of us feels like getting up to look for the others to bum more smokes.

"What do you mean?"

"C'mon. Of the girls at South Brook. Who's in your top ten?"

I don't want to talk about this. I was enjoying just lying on my back in the cool grass, toked out of my mind on some *other* cool grass, watching God's billion eyes above.

Flip comes over. He's stone cold sober, which seems funny to me, so I start giggling and Tit joins in. "I'm driving Jedi and Speedo home," he tells us. "I'll be back for you guys in like twenty minutes."

Tit goes right back to the question as soon as Flip leaves: "Who would you do? C'mon, man."

"I don't know."

He laughs, spilling out smoke. "Sure you do."

"Doesn't matter what I think," I tell him. "I'm so damn ugly no chick is gonna look at me twice. Much less do me."

He turns to look at me. "You *are* an ugly son of a bitch. I'll give you that. You gotta do something about the zits. You wouldn't be so bad then."

"Whatever." Like it matters. My buzz is slipping away now. Damn.

"But let's pretend that some girl has lost her mind and wants to straddle the Kross-Town Express. Who do you want it to be?"

I shrug, which really doesn't communicate much when you're flat on your back.

"Come on, Kross. Tell me."

"Get off my back. You tell me."

"OK," he says, as if he doesn't care. "Number one is Michelle Jurgens."

"Oh, please! You can't say Michelle Jurgens."

"Why not?"

"Because *everyone* says Michelle Jurgens." It's true. Michelle Jurgens is sort of the Official Wank-Bait of South Brook High, a promotion from her previous role as Official Wank-Bait of South Brook Middle.

"So?"

"So, the whole point of making a list like this is to make it, like, individual, you know?"

"OK. *Dina* Jurgens." He grins.

"She graduated last year, you moron. She doesn't count."

"Fine. Kayla Meyer."

"Not bad."

"Now you."

"No. Keep going."

"I'll give you my top three. Kayla and then, uh, Lisa Carter."

"Lisa Carter? Really? I don't see it."

"Awesome ass."

"If you say so."

"And then, uh, Kyra Sellers."

"Who?"

"Kyra Sellers. You know. Sellers. Kyra."

"I don't know who the hell you're talking about."

"Junior. Wears all black . . . Little piercing right here." He points to the corner of his mouth.

"Her?" Because now I know who he's talking about, and let me tell you—there is no less doable girl on the planet.

He sits up and shrugs, then flicks the butt of the cigarette off into the bushes. "Something about her . . . So, what about you?"

Back to me.

"I don't want to do this."

"You have to."

"Says who?"

"I told you. Come on. I told you I want to nail Kyra Sellers. Come on."

"No." But he *did* tell me.

"Dude, is it a *guy?* Are you gay or something?"

"No!"

"Because I'm cool with that. With you being a fag and all. I don't care. But you gotta tell me the guy you want to do, then."

"Shut up, Tit."

"Because I can forgive being gay, but I can't forgive you holding out on me."

"It's just one," I say to him, slowly. I don't want to say it, but it's late and I'm tired and stoned and buzzed and at peace. And it's *Tit.* He's not just a Fool—he's my buddy.

Besides, God's watching me through the sky, and he wouldn't let me do anything too stupid, right?

"Leah Muldoon," I tell him. "And that's it. That's my whole list."

"That's your whole list?" he asks.

"Yeah." And maybe it's the pot, but I feel relieved to tell it, finally. I've kept it a secret for a long, *long* time.

"Leah? That's . . ." He shakes his head. "Just one? That's serious, then. That's not just wanting to nail someone."

I don't say anything. What is there to say?

"I mean . . ." He stops for a second. "It's just weird, man. I don't get it. You never even mentioned her before all this hero crap. At all. Do you even *know* her?"

"I have a bunch of classes with her." It comes out more defensive than I intended, but I don't care. It's true—before I saved her life, I had had maybe three encounters with Leah that you could call conversations. But it doesn't matter. I know all about her. "I know her," I tell him.

"OK . . ." He doesn't sound convinced.

"She wants to go to Syracuse," I say. "She takes ballet and she's in Drama Club and she thinks she might want to try it professionally, for a little while at least." I can't stop myself. It's like I'm suddenly reeling off this bizarre testimonial to Leah Muldoon. "Her parents have more money than God, but they make her pay for her own car insurance. Every Christmas, she volunteers at the Good Faith soup kitchen with her dad."

Tit stares at me. Oh, crap. What the hell did I do? Now he's going to ask: *How do you know all that about her, Kross?* That's what he's going to say. And then I'll have to tell him. I'll have to tell. God.

I lie there, perfectly still, waiting for him to ask. I wait and I wait and it doesn't come, thank God. Instead, he just says:

"Wow. You've got it bad, huh?"

I don't say anything. It's weird now, having someone else know. Having someone else know a *part* of it, at least.

"I guess it makes sense," he says. "You saved her life. So I guess that makes sense." He sounds like he's trying to justify it to himself. Like it doesn't *really* make sense, but if he keeps saying that it does, maybe it will.

But here's the thing: It didn't start with the rescue. No. It started long before that . . .

CHAPTER 9
WHERE IT BEGAN

THE VIDEO CAMERA IS—*WAS*—MY PRIDE AND JOY. It's the only thing I've ever really worked for in my life.

When Mom left, she told me to e-mail her all the time. She also said, "Be sure you take pictures of yourself and send them to me so that I can see you growing up."

This was right around the time that my face started losing the Battle of the Zits, so I wasn't too keen on taking lots of pictures of myself. But one day I got this idea: I thought to myself, *What if I shot video of the things going on around me and sent that to Mom?* I could make these mini videos and sometimes I would be in them, but otherwise it would be friends and stuff.

As soon as the idea landed in my skull, I became obsessed with it. I scrounged around in the apartment for something I could use. I figured there had to be at least *one* usable camera in all that mess, right? But no—of all the things Dad had scavenged and brought home, a video camera was not one of them.

I had just turned fourteen, and in this state you can work at that age as long as you have a work permit. So I bugged and badgered Dad until he let me get a job that summer. I think he figured I wouldn't get into trouble if I was working eight hours a day.

So I got a job bussing tables and doing scut work at this

burger joint called—I swear to God I'm not making this up—
the Burger Joint. It was within walking distance of the apartment . . . if you don't mind walking *a lot*. And I didn't.

If Dad thought I'd stay out of trouble, he totally didn't
consider the Council. Once they knew I had a job, they all
started showing up for free food. I would smuggle them free-
bies and get the cooks to screw up orders so that I could give
the goofs to the Council. The owner—this big fat slob of a guy
named Carl—never figured it out. He thought the Council was
buying all of that food and was happy to see them around, so
he didn't spaz out when I would take a few minutes and shoot
the breeze with them.

Anyway, by July, I'd saved up enough money for a camera.
I went to the library and got on a computer and found a cheap
auction on eBay and sat on that sucker until I was the top bid,
and next thing you know, I had a camera. I filmed *everything*.
First thing I filmed was the apartment because I wanted to
show Mom where I lived now, but Dad caught me and freaked
out and made me erase it.

I carried the camera everywhere. I took it to work with me
because I was spending so much time there. (I was only supposed to work eight hours a day, but Carl gave me extra hours
if I wanted them and paid me under the table.) The Council
would come in and goof off and I would film them and Carl
called me the next Tarantino and that was all cool.

Everything *was* cool. For a while.

There's a time stamp on the tape, so I know exactly
when it happened. When it started. It started at 2:36 p.m. on
August third, two years ago. That's when my . . . my interest in
Leah began. I just didn't know it yet.

* * * *

I found out the next day. I was zipping through the tape I'd recorded the previous day, going on fast forward, looking for anything I thought Mom would be interested in. I would save that part and kill everything else.

All of a sudden, the camera swung around, making me dizzy, then stopped dead. I hit "pause." The camera wasn't pointing at the Council or at anything interesting at all. What had I done?

I fast-forwarded a little bit more. It was just the same table in focus. What was I—?

Duh. I'm an idiot. I must have put it down. Yeah, I remembered now—I was tired of holding it, so I put it down on the seat next to me while I ate lunch with Flip and Speedo. I thought I'd turned it off.

Man, I probably wasted half the tape!

I fast-forwarded some more, just to see where it picked up again, or if at some point I stumbled over a clue and, y'know, turned it off. A few seconds later, someone came into the frame with a tray of food and sat down.

It was Leah Muldoon.

I hit Play and the tape went back to normal speed.

I don't know *why* I hit Play. She was just sitting there. It's not like she was doing anything interesting.

With the tape on Play, I could hear Speedo jabbering about his new PS3 controller and an occasional grunt from me and the background noise of the restaurant. I muted the TV.

Leah just sat there for what seemed a very long time. She picked at her fries.

I crept closer to the TV. For some reason, I looked over my shoulder to see if Dad had come out of the bedroom. I don't know why, but I suddenly felt like I was doing something wrong.

But I wasn't doing anything wrong, right? It's not like she was—I don't know—naked. Or alone somewhere. She was just sitting there, eating. I hadn't done it on purpose—I thought the stupid camera was turned off.

Still, I kept my finger on the Stop button so that I could kill the tape *fast* if Dad showed up.

I watched her. She was in this weird kind of zone that I guess people get into when they're out in public but all alone. They forget that people can see them. She was just totally . . . I don't know the word for it. What's the opposite of self-conscious? Un-self-conscious? That can't be it; that sounds stupid.

But whatever it is, that's what Leah was. It was wild, watching someone, being able to just . . . *watch*. Just to *stare*. Without worrying about being caught or being polite. At one point, she reached up with one hand and adjusted her boob. I'm serious. I swear she did that. She just did it really fast and she didn't even look down and she was grabbing a fry with the other hand at the same time! But right there in public, she just—wham!— grabbed her boob real quick and *shoooped* it into place.

Unreal. I bet people do all kinds of crazy stuff all around, all the time. And people just don't notice because it's too fast and there's too much other stuff going on. Except maybe sometimes you just happen to look up at the right second and you catch something.

And maybe sometimes you just happen to catch it on tape.

So that's where it started. Yeah. I kept rewinding and watching Leah over and over that night. It's not that she was doing anything exciting or crazy or sexy. It wasn't even the boob adjustment. It was . . .

I can't explain it.

I wish I could.

I want to.

It was like I missed Mom and Jesse so much, it was almost a physical thing. And when I watched that tape, the *missing* went away. Just a little bit. But it went away.

So I had to keep watching.

CHAPTER 10
CONFESSION-OR NOT

OF COURSE, I DON'T TELL TIT ANY OF *THAT*. He rambles on about Leah for a little bit, comparing various portions of her anatomy to the girls on his list. The word "nice" is used a lot, usually stretched out to *niiiiiiiice*, so that it doesn't sound, well, nice anymore.

I just lie there next to him and find myself caught in a moment of memory, that moment when I threw down my backpack and charged at the Surgeon. Maybe it's the pot. Maybe it's confessing to Tit. I don't know *what* it is, but for some reason the memory is really intense and I'm lost in it, in that endless moment of decision . . . And then . . . Throwing down the backpack . . .

I throw it down over and over and over.

I remember one of the cops coming up to me, afterward. He held my backpack by one strap and held it out to me and something made a noise inside and he said, "This yours?" and I nodded and he said, "Sounds like something broke in there."

"What?" says Tit, and I realize that I mumbled that last bit out loud.

"Nothing," I tell him.

That's when Flip gets back. Fam's with him. He leads us through the park, back to the entrance and the statue that stands there. He jumps up on the pedestal, wraps his arms around the statue, and dry-humps it for a little bit.

"You're *soooo* mature," Fam says.

"Don't be jealous, baby," Flip says. "I just gotta give her what she needs, you know?" He pulls back, slaps the statue on its ass, and says, "That ought to hold you for a while, huh, sweet cheeks?" before jumping down.

CHAPTER 11
HOW I GOT SCREWED OVER

IT'S JUST ABOUT MIDNIGHT BY THE TIME I GET HOME. I creep into the apartment as quietly as I can. Dad's a pretty sound sleeper, but he'll be up in a couple of hours and I don't want to wake him.

As usual, Flip provided all kinds of sprays and lozenges and stuff to take the smell of beer and smoke and pot out of my clothes and my breath. He's always prepared like that. Just to be safe, though, I take off all of my clothes and stuff them deep into the laundry hamper. I'll do laundry tomorrow and Dad will never know.

I lie there on the sofa bed for a while, thinking of the broken camera under me, thinking of the tapes, thinking back to Flip's whole deal with fractals and how the end of a situation totally depends on its beginning. And I wonder: Is it all Mom's fault? Does it go back that far? I mean, if Mom had been here, I never would have bought the camera. I never would have accidentally filmed Leah. I never would have . . .

Been there.

Leah dies. But am I innocent? Am I guilt-free? Does it all come down to Mom?

When she left for California, I was thirteen, almost fourteen. So they let me decide where I would live and which parent

I would be with. And you know what? That's total bull. Because it's so not cool to sit down a kid and say, basically, "Who do you love more?"

Especially when you do it the way my parents did it. They sat me down and Mom did all the talking. I already knew they were getting divorced and that Mom was moving to California. I guess I thought Dad would move there, too. I don't know—maybe that's stupid. Maybe it's wishful thinking. I look back on it now and I think I was just in shock from everything. I wasn't thinking straight. I was thinking really, really crooked back then.

So Mom said to me, "Kevin, your father and I think you're old enough to make this decision. You know I'm going to California. We want to let you decide if you want to go with me to California or stay here in Brookdale with Dad."

I was thirteen, remember. The idea of picking up and moving across the country was scary. I would have a new school. I would have to make new friends, and—tell the truth—I wasn't very good at that. And who knew what it would be like in California?

Plus, I liked the townhouse we lived in. It was in a nice part of Brookdale. I could ride my bike all over the place.

"We might have to move," Dad said, popping that particular balloon. "I don't know yet. But we would stay in Brookdale and you would still go to South Brook."

That sounded good.

Mom chewed her bottom lip. "Honey, you don't have to decide right now if you don't want to."

I suddenly realized that my little brother was nowhere to be found. "Where's Jesse?"

"He's at Gramma's house for the day."

That was another reason to stay, I guess. Gramma Ross lived in Baltimore.

"What did he decide?"

A look passed between my parents just then. To this day, I don't know what the hell it meant. It looked like guilt and accusation and anger and resignation all mixed up and mashed into one big dripping wad of emotion.

"Jesse's too young to make this decision. He's only seven. He's . . ." Mom hesitated for a second. "We've decided . . . your father and I, that is. We've decided he's going to come to California with me."

That pretty much decided it for me right there. My little brother could be a big pain in the butt a lot of times, but he was still my brother. We were a set. A pair. We were like peanut butter and chocolate, like Batman and Robin, like spaghetti and garlic bread. I took care of him. And he . . . ?

He made me feel good that I was taking care of him.

I would just have to get used to California.

I could see Dad over Mom's shoulder, standing there, his shoulders slumped. He nodded, his face sad. It was like I'd said something already. It was like he could read my decision off of my face.

"If you go with me, you'll be with me and with Jesse," Mom said, her voice even. And then—because Mom was always fair above all else—she went on: "If you stay here, you'll be in the same school, have the same friends. And your dad will be there to help you when you're becoming a man."

I barely heard her. I mean, the words went into my ears and into my brain and I understood it all, but it's like it didn't matter. I couldn't stop looking at Dad. I felt so sorry for him. All I could think was *If I go to California, he'll be all alone.*

"I'll stay here with Dad," I heard myself say, and when Dad smiled, I knew I'd done the right thing.

After Mom and Jesse left, we moved into Mrs. Mac's basement apartment and things just . . . sucked.

I started hanging out with the Council more and more, and our pranks really took off. It helped a little bit. It kept me distracted. Sometimes.

Always only sometimes.

I realized pretty quickly that I'd made a mistake. Without Mom around to keep him even and read his mind, Dad started having more and more problems communicating. With the hours his job demanded, we saw each other less and less.

For the first time, I noticed how many pills my dad took each day. I had gotten used to him popping a few before he went to bed, but now that we were sharing the same tiny bathroom, I couldn't avoid the fact that our medicine cabinet had a lot of medicine in it! He's on antidepressants and antianxiety drugs, which . . . You'd think they would just cancel each other out, but I guess not, because the doctors at the VA keep prescribing them and he keeps taking them.

One time Mom called when Dad was out and I got to talk to her without him lurking around and overhearing. I came right out and asked her: "What's wrong with Dad?"

"The divorce has been tough on him, too," she said diplomatically.

"Mom, come on." I wanted to say, *Is it about the army?* but I knew better. Dad's time in the army was *taboo*. Or, better yet, proscribed. (That's not like getting your medicine at the pharmacy. It's a different word. It's this cool word that Father McKane uses. It means things you can't do. Forbidden. Like how adultery is *proscribed* by the Ten Commandments and all that.)

But Mom wouldn't spill. Some old, lingering loyalty to her ex-husband? Guilt? I don't know. But in the end, no matter how much I begged, all she would say was "There are a lot of things wrong with your father. The world didn't turn out the way he thought it should. He didn't turn out the way he . . . Look, Kevin. Just don't bother him when he's like this, OK?"

He has good days and bad days, she told me. He's *always* been like that, she told me. You know that.

I thought a bunch of times about telling him I'd changed my mind. But Mom's place in California was small. How could I force her to make room for me? I had made the decision, right? She'd left it up to me, and that was that. I couldn't go back on it now.

I also had this weird inkling, this feeling that I couldn't get rid of. It was the idea that maybe this was what Mom and Dad had wanted, what they'd agreed to. I knew other kids whose parents had huge custody battles when they got divorced. I think Mom and Dad figured they'd just split up the kids. Make it easy. No fighting that way. And I knew something that my parents didn't *know* I knew—I knew that they had had Jesse to try to save their marriage. I overheard them one night. (It wasn't tough—they were yelling.) I mean, he's six years younger than I am. They were desperate.

I couldn't decide if that made Jesse more important than me or less important. I mean, on the one hand, he was this Golden Child, born to save the marriage.

On the other hand, it didn't work.

I still felt like he was some kind of prize, though. Mom pretty much talked me into staying with Dad, didn't she? It was never *really* my decision. But she made damn sure she took Jesse, no matter what.

Maybe it didn't matter, though. As miserable as I was, Dad was even worse. If I left, Dad would be all alone. I couldn't do that to him.

Even though I really, really wanted to.

The only thing that helped the misery . . . was Leah. When I stumbled over those stolen moments of her, it's like my life changed. For a little while. I didn't feel as lonely. And that was good.

Right?

I don't know. I roll over and feel for my keys on the coffee table I use as a nightstand. The key to Brookdale is on the ring. I hold it in a tight fist.

I wish it opened something.

In my dream, I know it's the Surgeon. It's not just some creepy guy in an alleyway threatening Leah—it's Michael Alan Naylor and I know that from the get-go.

I throw down my backpack, just like in real life.

But in my dream, I do more than just tackle him, do more than just hold him while Leah calls the cops on her cell. In my dream, I knock him to the ground, land on top of him, thrashing him over and over, beating his face into a mass of red pulp.

He tries to beg, to plead, but he can't even talk for the shattered teeth and the mucus and blood and crap clogging up his throat and my fists pounding his face over and over. Because in the dream I knew it was him, see? And I threw myself at him anyway, with reckless abandon, not caring about my own safety, not worried that he's raped and murdered four girls already, that he's bigger and stronger than I am. All I know is that I've followed him here, stalked the stalker, and now I'm beating him, maybe to death.

In my dream.

In my dream, I'm a hero.

I wake up, and my fingers are moving on their own. I'm crossing myself, like I used to do back when I prayed. When we stopped going to Mass, I sort of lost the habit of praying—it seemed weird without Mass to back it up.

So now here I am, like I'm back at Mass, my hands folded together, the key pressed between them, eyes aimed at the ceiling, ready to talk to God.

But I don't know what to say.

SELF-LOATHING #2

DAD'S GONE IN THE MORNING, OF COURSE. Off heaving other people's garbage, probably solving world hunger in the back of his mind while he's at it. Mom used to say that Dad had two compartments in his brain and that they didn't connect. There was the part that kept him showered and fed and shaved—that was the smaller part. Then there was the part that wanted to save the world. That's the bigger part. Problem is, without the one regulating the other, the big part just sort of runs amok sometimes. He can't stop it; he can't direct it.

What happens is that sometimes his mouth can't keep up with his brain. So he starts talking, like, ten words ahead and then he realizes he's out of sync and he tries to catch up, but his brain's still running a mile a minute, so he just gets even *more* jumbled up. And in *his* brain it all makes sense, so then he gets frustrated that you don't understand what he's thinking and that just makes him even worse. He's like a kid who needs Ritalin, which my dad might need, actually, now that I think of it, so we can just add that to the list of drugs he's already taking.

Anyway, since I'm alone, I do what I do on most mornings—I rummage around for a videotape and watch it for a little while. It's that first tape I made at the Burger Joint, way back when. It's cued up to the part with Leah. I watch it a little bit.

Then I switch it out for another tape. The picture is jerky and moves too much—even with the motion stabilizer turned on.

I swallow with a dry throat. On eBay, I've seen people sell cameras that can see through clothing. Or special lens attachments that shoot at ninety-degree angles, so that you can aim at one thing but record something in a different direction, without anyone knowing.

God, I hate myself.

I hate myself, but I can't stop myself. If the camera wasn't broken, I could bring it to the party at Leah's. To the *pool* party.

An X-ray lens. Filming right through a wet bathing suit . . .

God. Stop it, Kross! Stop it!

I watch the tape and I hate myself over and over again.

At times like this, I wish I *could* pray. For strength. Strength to stop. But I can't do either.

CHAPTER 12
VILLAIN-TYPE

I DON'T KNOW MUCH ABOUT CARS. The one the mayor has picked out for me is brown.

After school, Dad takes me to the lot and literally kicks the tires—don't ask me why. He pokes around under the hood, grunts and clucks his tongue a couple of times, and then, as if he can't believe he's doing it, nods and gives me the OK to buy the thing.

There are reporters here for the Big Event—two local guys with their photographers and a kid from the school paper with his little digital camera. It cracks me up that there needs to be five people here to record me getting a car.

Poor mayor, though. He's getting his free publicity, but he's a little depressed to find that I don't actually *have* the reward money yet. The producers of *Justice!* have to fill out all kinds of legal paperwork and stuff. But there are press people right here, and I guess he doesn't want word to get out that he denied the Hero of Brookdale his pre-owned wheels.

"You come back in a couple of hours and I'll have some paperwork figured out."

So that's how it goes, only Dad has to get to bed early for work, so I call Flip later that day to take me there.

It's like nothing's changed—the press people are still here, and I amuse myself for maybe half a second by imagining that they've been waiting this whole time for me. But they all look sort of cranky and pissed off, so I imagine the truth instead: The mayor got all up in their faces and made them come back to see the actual Hand-off of the Car.

Flip checks out the car and pronounces it worthy (like I care) and then goes off while the mayor puts the papers together for me. I sign everything and we're good to go. He hands me the keys and puts an arm around my shoulders, with a look on his face that says, *I'm so glad there's a camera here to catch this!*

"Enjoy the car, Kevin. God knows you earned it and more." He probably wishes there were a TV crew, too. He can probably envision the headlines: MAYOR ADVISES LOCAL HERO.

And then, just as I'm about to hop into the car, the mayor suddenly snaps his fingers. "Wait a minute, Kevin!" He rushes into the office and comes back with two magnetic ribbons that he slaps on the back of the car—the one on the left is yellow and says SUPPORT OUR TROOPS. The one on the right is red, white, and blue and says UNITED WE STAND.

"Can't let you drive out of here without those, can I?" He winks at me.

The two newspaper reporters and their camera slaves leave, but the school reporter hangs around. "Mind if I follow you for a bit?" he asks.

"Uh, why?"

He shrugs. "My editor thought it might be a cool idea to show you with the car in your driveway or something like that."

It's official. This whole town has gone Kevin Krazy. "Fine. Whatever."

And then I'm driving home. Wow!

It's weird, driving by myself. It's like I'm super-aware of all the other cars. When you're a passenger, you don't have to pay attention to them, but now that I'm behind the wheel it's like they're all up in my face. And I guess the mayor was right that you can't drive without those ribbons, because every single car I see on the way home has at least one and usually two of them. There are so many people from here serving in the military—Brookdale's always been a patriotic place.

I park the car right up against the house on the side that faces the main road. There's a parking pad there with room for two cars—Mrs. Mac always parks in the back, so there's always been this empty space, and now it's mine. God, it's so cool! I stand there for a few minutes, looking at *my* car, in *my* driveway. The school reporter takes a couple of pictures of me standing there with my hand on the car and I'm so happy that I can't help it—I smile for the camera.

Inside, I get a surprise—Dad's still up, yawning and grumbling, but still awake. This happens sometimes, when he just can't sleep. I try not to annoy him as I start to throw together something for dinner. Man, this reward money has totally changed my life . . . and I don't even have it yet!

And then suddenly Dad's yelling, "Kevin! Kevin!"

It takes me a second to realize that he's walked over to the apartment's only window, looking right out into the driveway.

"What's that?" His voice has gone sharp, like that time I tried to set a frog on fire back in sixth grade. (Long story.)

"That's my car, Dad." I've got a can of ravioli half opened and I almost cut my thumb off when he yelled.

"Don't be smart. That ribbon."

"Oh. The ribbons."

"Plural?" he says, as if someone just dipped his big toe in battery acid. "There's more than one?" He cranes his neck, looking for the other one.

"Yeah. The mayor put 'em there before I—"

"Get rid of them."

"Why?"

And he starts to do that whole brain-moving-too-fast, flustered thing: "Because . . . Because . . . Don't you *get* it? It's just a—"

"OK, OK." I cut him off before he can go into total spaz mode. "I'll get 'em after I eat."

"Do it *now*." He says it with such venom that it takes me a second to figure out that he's still just talking about the freaking ribbons.

"OK," I tell him, and go back to opening the can.

"I'm serious!"

You've *got* to be kidding me. But he's not. So I slam down the can, go peel off the magnets, and toss them in the trash can.

"Happy now?" I say once I'm back inside.

But Dad's nowhere near happy. If happy was the earth, Dad would be out there orbiting Pluto.

"How could you drive around with those things on?"

"Chill out, Dad. Everyone has them."

"That's exactly my point," he says. "People think . . . Do you know what people *think*?" And here he goes again: "People, they, you know . . ."

"Yeah, Dad."

"Let me tell you something: When I was in the army, those things didn't mean anything at all. You think they helped me over there? You think they helped any of us?"

It's the most he's talked about the army in, like, *forever*. I just stand there, stunned. He glares at me and then he shakes his head. He looks like he's about to say something else, but he just goes off to his bedroom and closes the door and I'm able to eat my dinner in peace.

In the morning, I drive to school for the first time, which is great. Tell the truth, I'm starting to get used to this "hero" thing. People treating me well in school, Leah inviting me to parties, the mayor bending over backwards to get me some wheels . . . There are worse ways to live a life.

And at school, I experience one of them.

I don't get it. All of a sudden, no one's talking to me. Or high-fiving me. As I walk through the halls to my locker, I just get stares and glares. What the hell?

Oh, God, wait. Did someone find out? Did someone find out the truth, about what *really* happened at the library that day?

No. No, that's impossible . . .

And then I get to my locker.

Someone has taped a sheet of paper to the front of it. It's a printout from the school newspaper's Web page. There's a picture of me taking one of the ribbons off the car and then another picture right next to it of me tossing both ribbons in the trash can.

And a headline:

LOCAL "HERO" TO TROOPS: DROP DEAD!

Oh, boy.

Zero

CHAPTER 13
UNINTENDED CONSEQUENCES

THE REPORTER. That pain-in-the-butt school reporter. He hadn't left yet. From the angle and the size of the shots, he must have been just across the street, getting back into *his* car when he saw me and . . .

Crap.

I keep my head down in homeroom, moving only to rise and then sit for the Pledge of Allegience. I try to imagine there's a bubble around me and no one can see through it, but I don't have that great an imagination.

Like a junkie looking for a needle, I look for Leah in the halls between homeroom and first period. Which is stupid because I know her schedule by heart and she's never in my path this time of day.

I do catch Fam, though. Actually, she catches me, grabbing my backpack and pulling me off against the wall before I even realize it's her.

"Hail, Fool," I tell her.

"Kross, please be careful," she says, skipping the "Hail, Fool" nonsense. "People are pissed."

"Yeah, I know."

She pats my hand sympathetically and gives me a look like

I'm a dog going to the vet for the last time. I get this weird vibe that, if we weren't both carrying armloads of books, she would give me a hug. Which, like, I totally don't want.

All day, I get the stink-eye from everyone around me. It's like I chopped up a baby and deep-fried it for lunch.

That whole hero thing was annoying, but it was better than the villain thing, let me tell you.

I finally spot Leah in the hall between classes—she's on her way to trig and I'm headed to bio, just like every Wednesday. She's not giving me the Death Glare for Unpatriots like everyone else, but she's not giving me the hero-worship look, either.

I guess at this point most guys would just go ahead and tell everyone "My dad made me do it!" and that would be that, but come on! Is there anything in the world more pathetic than blaming your parents for your problems? That's so whiny. And it would just make me look like even more of a wuss. So, no.

I decide I can't handle a lunchtime of everyone watching, so I ditch lunch and head to the janitor's office. My hand actually shakes as I try to unlock the door with my copied key. I guess I'm more worked up than I thought.

Fam opens the door from the inside. I want to kiss her for it and then I'm grossed out by the idea.

"Hey, make up your mind, Kross." It's Flip, lounging at the desk. God, when did *he* learn to read my mind?

"What do you mean?" I ask, all fake innocent.

He holds up a copy of the Web printout. "Hero or villain? Which is it?"

Fam goes ahead and hugs me quickly, then moves to Flip's

side. "Leave him alone, Joey. He's having a bad day. Can't you tell?"

Flip grimaces at the use of his real name. "He should have thought of that before he decided to piss all over the troops." But then he shrugs. "Not that I care. There might be something to this . . ." And he leans back on the desk and goes off into Flip-space, where he can think about such things.

I shake my head. Fam gives me that dog-to-the-vet pity look again, and I can't handle it. But I guess it's better to be here and getting the pity look from her than to be in the lunchroom and getting pelted by flying utensils, right?

Tit shows up and that's it—Speedo and Jedi must not have been able to slip away. "You're having an interesting day," Tit says, because Tit has a black belt in understatement.

"Tell me about it. What the *hell*, man? Why are people so pissed? It's not like I *did* anything."

"Beats me. What are you gonna do about it?"

I throw my hands up in the air. "How can I do something about it when I don't know what the big deal is in the first place?" My voice goes all high and cracky, which I hate, but I can't help it. "I can't believe people actually care about this!"

Fam pipes up. "Maybe you could—"

"Hey!" Flip sits up. "Some quiet, please! Genius at work. Heavy thinking going on here!"

"Sorry."

I enjoy my respite from the halls of South Brook as long as I can, but eventually I have to leave.

The rest of the day is just hellish. No one confronts me directly, but I hear mumblings and mutterings everywhere I go.

And no one is giving me the worshipful hero look anymore. I don't get it. I can't believe people are so worked up!

The burnouts and the band geeks and the goth kids are the only ones not ganging up on me, which doesn't help at all because I don't fit in with any of those people.

This doesn't make sense. None of it makes any sense. They're *magnets,* for God's sake!

"Not everyone hates you, Kross," Speedo tells me at one point during the day. "It's just that the people who *do* hate you are really loud and the people who *don't* hate you just don't give a crap at all, so they're not gonna rush to defend you."

"Thanks for the good news."

Speedo doesn't catch the sarcasm. "No problem, buddy." He punches my shoulder. "See ya."

I try reading the story from the school paper, but it's just a mishmash of stupid. Stuff about how everyone thought I was a hero, but can one good deed wipe out what is clearly a deep character flaw and stuff like that and let me tell you: I *know* I've got deep character flaws. I mean, I've got character flaws like the Grand Canyon, but what's the big deal about tossing those magnets?

It's funny, because if they knew the *truth* about me . . . I guess if they knew the truth, they'd hate me for the right reason, not the wrong one.

At the end of the day, when I get to the parking lot, there are about a million freakin' magnetic ribbons on my car. Poetic justice or general cluelessness? Who knows?

When I get home, voice mail is jam-packed with reporters. Real reporters, not idiots from school. There's a guy from the

Lowe County Times—the same guy who interviewed me after the thing with the Surgeon—and he's all freaky on the message. And then there's the *Baltimore Sun,* and I start to think, *What the hell? Did nothing else happen in the world today?*

Everyone wants a piece of me again. They want to "discuss your political beliefs" and "get inside your head" and find out "why you've chosen now to expound on your leftist ideology" and stuff like that.

I didn't know I *had* a leftist ideology. All of this over some strips of magnetic . . . stuff. Whatever those ribbons are made of.

"Is this some kind of joke?" Dad asks. He's looking out the window at my car, which is still brown, but not that you can tell with that swarm of yellow, red, white, and blue all over it. "Didn't I tell you to get rid of those things?"

"Dad, do you even *listen* to voice mail?"

"Don't change the topic."

"I'm not! Everyone in the whole world thinks I hate America!"

"Don't be ridiculous."

"Dad, they want to interview me about it."

Dad blinks at me, like it's a totally alien concept. "You're in high school, Kevin. Trust me—nothing terrible is going to happen."

"Dad!"

"Did you do anything wrong?"

"No."

"Is anyone shooting at you? Trying to blow you up?"

Jeez! When you put it *that* way . . . "No, Dad, but—"

"Then don't worry. It'll pass. Just deal with it."

I can't believe it! I can't believe he's that clueless! I mean, yeah, I understand that when he was a little bit older than me, he had people shooting at *him* and trying to blow *him* up, but still.

"Compared to that," he goes on, "you're just—"

The phone interrupts him and Dad picks it up. "Hello? What? No. He has no comment. I don't care. Uh-huh. Lose this number." And hangs up.

"Who was *that*?"

He shrugs. "The *Washington Post*."

"*Washington Post*!" Holy crap, this has gone national!

"Or *Washington Times*. One or the other. There are bigger things to worry about than this, Kevin. The war. The economy. The environment. College."

I get the feeling he could go on all day listing things for me to stress about, but then he actually *yawns,* as if his son being assaulted by the media happens every single day and he's bored with it all.

"I have to go to bed. Now get rid of those things. I want you to think for yourself, not like the rest of the sheep."

"You don't want me to support the troops?"

He pauses halfway to the bedroom door. I can almost see the conflict in the set of his shoulders. He turns back to me. "You think putting a stupid *magnet* on your car supports the troops? Do you? Because I thought you were smarter than that. Putting a magnet on your car does *nothing* for the troops. They're still over there, still dying."

"Well, what am *I* supposed to do about it?"

Which, hey, shuts him up for a second. Now, if it was anyone else's dad, I would think that maybe I'd scored a point or two, but it's my dad, so he's probably shut up just long enough to actually figure out what I'm supposed to do about it.

He looks like he's going to say something, but then he shakes his head. "Just . . . Just get rid of those magnets, Kevin."

Which is a total cop-out as far as I'm concerned, but I'm not an adult, so I don't get a vote.

CHAPTER 14
MEET THE PRESS

MY CAR SITS THERE IN THE DRIVEWAY, covered with those magnets.

So, like, I wonder who gets all the money for those things? And do they do anything good with it, like give it to a veterans' charity, or do they just pocket it? And I never really thought about it before Dad brought it up, but . . .

How stupid is it to pin all your patriotic fervor on a *magnet?* On something temporary that can be removed and replaced at will. Even an actual bumper sticker is kinda cheesy, when you think about it. Want to brag about going to a theme park or that your kid's a stud athlete? Sure, a bumper sticker's the way to go. Kind of weak for matters of life and death, though.

It seems like someone got the magnet idea and they just went to town and everyone else followed along like sheep, like sheep following *more* sheep, everyone putting those things on because everyone *else* is putting them on and that's supposed to, I don't know, supposed to ease their consciences or something.

Man, I hate it when Dad's right. It messes with my world.

So I start to pull the magnets off. First I look around to make sure there aren't any school reporters lurking in the bushes or ready to pop up from the sewer or anything. Not that it matters anymore. The damage has been done, and it's not like I'm not used to being in the paper at this point. People can't hate me any more than they already do.

Man, I'm really riding the fame roller coaster, huh?

I've got a nice little pile of about twenty-five magnets when someone walks up to me. I sorta kinda recognize him; he's the reporter for the *Lowe County Times*. Bill Something-or-Other. He interviewed me after the whole thing with the Surgeon. He was pretty cool, so I kinda give him a little half smile, but his expression is greedy and hungry.

"Here we are again," he says, his voice tight. "Want to talk?"

Crap. He wants to talk about the ribbons. Just like all the idiots on voice mail. Hell, he *was* one of the idiots on voice mail.

"No comment, dude."

"Come on, kid. What are you scared of?" He thrusts a tape recorder into my face.

"Hey, watch it," I tell him, pushing the recorder away.

"What are you afraid of? The truth? Afraid to show the world your true face, Mr. Hero?"

He comes down on the "hero" part really sarcastically. I don't get it. Right after I stopped the Surgeon, this guy was so far up my butt he could have given me a dental exam. And now it's like I'm an enemy of the state or something.

I shrug and keep peeling ribbons off my car.

"Why do you hate this country?" he asks.

"Man, what is *with* you?"

"Come on, Ross. Talk to me. Give me an exclusive."

I stare at him. "You're kidding, right? Have you heard how you're talking to me? Why should I help you?"

He shrugs. "It's win-win. I get the interview. You get a platform for your beliefs."

"Oh, yeah, because the *Loco* is such a great platform." The *Loco* is what we call the *Lowe County Times*.

"Are you kidding me? With this story, with an exclusive? I could go to the *Sun*. Maybe higher. Maybe get it put out on the AP or something."

Oh. Now I get it. I'm his ticket to the bigtime. I see.

"So come on, kid." Greedy eyes. "Why did you throw away those ribbons?"

The easy answer would be "My dad made me do it," but I'm not ducking like that. Tell the truth, I don't want to see a new headline that reads: LOCAL "HERO" ACTUALLY BIG WUSS.

When I don't say anything, he shoves the recorder at me again. "I know how you 'heroes' work. I've been covering people like you for years. I know all about your father's past. You want to see *that* in the paper?"

What? What about my father's past? I want to ask him, but even *I* have the brain power to know that that's a bad idea. So instead I just keep my mouth shut.

"Apple doesn't fall far from the tree, does it?" he goes on.

"Dude, totally shut up about my father, OK?" I can't help myself.

"Why? Did I push a button?"

"Man, you really think what I do with some cheap magnets is more important than stopping someone from getting raped and killed?"

"See, that's the problem, Ross. You don't get it. You don't

get why the rest of us hate people like you. It's because of a little something called patriotism. You don't see it. People like you. People like your dad. People who want to outlaw the Pledge. People who think it's OK to burn the flag. You can say they're just magnets, but you know damn well they're more than that. They symbolize something."

I look down at the stack of symbols in my hands. "I guess I don't get it."

"You need to support the troops."

"How do magnets support the troops? Seriously. Look." I slap one of the ribbons back on the car. "There. Did some kind of magic energy wave just fly off overseas and wrap a soldier in a force field or something?" I slap on another one. "There. Did a bomb just *not* go off somewhere?"

"You're a little smart aleck. Aren't you proud to be an American?"

"Well . . . yeah. Sure. I guess I just don't feel the need to tell everybody."

He sniffs and nods at the pile in my hands. "What are you going to do with them?"

"Give them a deserving home." And I hand them right to him, shoving them at his chest. His hands come up by reflex and he takes them from me without even thinking, which is awesome.

"Make sure you read the paper in the morning," he snarls.

Oh, great. But I'm not going to let him know he got to me. I grin, throw him a salute, and head back inside.

CHAPTER 15
LOVE IT, LEAVE IT

UGH. WHEN WILL I LEARN TO KEEP MY MOUTH SHUT?

Next day, I wake up and look at the newspaper and there's Reporter Guy's byline in the *Loco,* right over a story about me and right under a headline that says, LOCAL "HERO" UNMASKED. I can't even bring myself to read it.

If I thought that this ribbon thing would just go away, not only am I a moron, but I'm also a moron brought right back down to earth *very* fast. Mrs. Mac is watering the azaleas next to the porch as I head to the car in the morning, and she gives me a brief snort. Great—now even old ladies are pissed at me.

"They said you're a hero on the TV," she says. "Now I'm not so sure."

Lady, I agree with you, I want to say, but don't.

On the way to school, I try not to think about the *Loco* and the school paper and all of that, but Reporter Guy's words from last night keep echoing in the empty chamber I call my head. He was talking about going national with this, maybe. That's the last thing I need. Could *Justice!* take back my reward? Man, that would suck. I've gotten used to having this car, and I've only had it a couple of days!

But worse than that is what could happen if someone

learned the truth about that day at the library. About me catching the Surgeon. I think of my tape of Leah, how I captured her on video at the Burger Joint and she didn't even know. How I watch it over and over, looking for something new every time.

What if someone else has done the same thing to me? What if someone out there taped my appearance on *Justice!* and is watching it over and over and over again, until the truth about that comes out? I don't know *how* that could happen, but that's what I worry about. Someone mean and smart, like Reporter Guy, watching me fidget and *lie* on TV until he figures it all out.

I'm sweating all of a sudden. The air conditioning is blasting cold air all over me, but I'm still sweating.

School sucks as much today as it did yesterday. I'm an outcast. I bump into a senior in the hall and mumble, "Excuse me," and he just shoves me against the lockers. Hard.

His friends laugh. Two weeks ago, I might have said something, but now? Now I know that there's absolutely no one in this hallway who would take my side, and way too many people who would be happy to jump in and help pummel me into paste.

In homeroom, I keep my head down. There's a buzz of conversation and I know it's about me.

"My dad's in the Reserve," someone says, just loud enough that I can hear it. I look up—it's John Riordon, the only sophomore on the varsity football team. He's big and tough the way lions are big and tough.

"He better hope I don't catch him dissing the troops,"

Riordon goes on, talking to Samantha Riggs but watching me the whole time. "Because if I do, there's gonna be hell to pay."

OK, got it. Don't diss troops in front of John Riordon, else hell to pay. That is now filed away in my brain under the category THINGS TO REMEMBER—URGENT!!!!

The morning announcements start and we all rise for the Pledge. My stomach isn't just in knots—it's in one of those special U.S. Navy knots that gets tighter and tighter the more you try to untangle it.

I don't want to open my mouth to say the Pledge because I'm honestly terrified that my breakfast will come out. And that makes me think of Reporter Guy and his whole deal last night about people who want to ban the Pledge, and *that* makes me a syllable behind everyone else as we launch into . . .

I pledge allegiance to the flag of the United States of America, and to the Republic for which it stands, one nation, under God, indivisible, with liberty and justice for all.

Whew! Got through it. I even managed to catch up so that I finished with everyone else. Score one for me.

But John Riordon gives me a nasty look as we all sit down for the announcements, and I know that my one point means nothing. Because the opposing team has a million of them, and on *that* score, I'll never catch up.

School's a blur for me. I just can't seem to focus. I'm still sweating a little bit, still nauseated enough that I skip lunch. I don't want to be around anyone, not even the Council, so I go to the media center and find a computer tucked away in a corner and just stay there.

The computers in the media center have the school paper's website as the homepage, so the first thing I see is a story about how my ribbon-trashing has now made the *Loco*. A student reporter interviews Reporter Guy and Reporter Guy says that he plans to pursue the story "for a state and national audience. Right now, the American public thinks Kevin Ross is a hero. They deserve to know how their 'hero' thinks."

I wonder: Did he put "hero" in air-quotes or did the kid interviewing him just add that in there?

And by the way: What the hell? What's up with a reporter interviewing a reporter? Is that what you do when there's no *real* news?

I slump down in my seat. Mrs. Grant, the school librarian, comes by and sees what I'm looking at. She pats me on my shoulder.

"Don't let it get to you, Kevin. Something else will get everyone's attention in a few days and then it'll all be over."

"I guess."

"Trust me."

"Thanks, Mrs. Grant."

But I know it's not true. I'll always be the Kid Who Hates the Troops. People might stop talking about it, but they won't forget something like that.

I guess it could be worse. I mean, I guess I *could* be one of those people like Reporter Guy said—the people who want to ban the Pledge and stuff. Why would anyone even want to do that?

My curiosity gets the better of me: I start Googling around. And I learn some interesting stuff. Stuff about the Pledge.

Stuff I'd never even thought of before. Stuff no one ever bothered to teach me. Why did I have to learn this on my own?

It's weird—you do something almost every day of your life, for as long as you can remember. And everyone *else* does it, too, but no one talks about it. No one knows how it started. No one wonders. It's just a minute at the beginning of every school day, when we all get up and do the same thing without even thinking about it.

And then one day . . . you think about it. And it's like a whole new world.

As I leave the media center for my next class, Mrs. Grant says, "I hope you found what you were looking for, Kevin."

And here's the weird thing: I did. I didn't even know *what* I was looking for, but I found it anyway.

Someone has clipped today's *Loco* article and taped it to my locker with the words "LOVE IT OR LEAVE IT" scrawled across it. There's also a sticker of an American flag with the legend "These colors don't run."

I sit in algebra and I try to pay attention. I really do. But all I can think of is the look of gratitude on Leah's face when we sat together to tape that episode of *Justice!* God, it wasn't even the gratitude that got to me—it was the recognition. It was that this girl I'd been . . . I'd been *worshiping* from afar finally saw me. Knew me. Acknowledged me.

And now that's all gone. Given the news of my unpatriotic heresy, I bet I'm uninvited to her party. Great.

More than two years of yearning for her and I get my chance to be close to her and the next thing you know, I'm a . . . I'm a . . .

What did Father McKane call them in CCD? The people no one wants to—

Pariah! That's it. I'm a pariah.

A pariah and a Fool. Lucky me.

The bell rings and I slink out of algebra on my way to my next class. I brace myself for what's about to happen. I'll see Leah heading in the opposite direction—English for her on Thursday.

Sure enough, right on time, she crosses my path—with some Beautiful People in tow—and ducks her head as I pass by. Starting to regret that "Please come," aren't you? I don't know why I get a perverse tickle at the idea of making her uncomfortable. Maybe it's because if I make her uncomfortable, at least she's acknowledging that I'm alive, you know? Tell the truth, I've always been sort of invisible to her, and I guess being noticed—even by the stink of treason—is better than going totally undercover.

When you, you know, have feelings for someone.

Ugh. "Feelings"? Could I be any more girly if I *tried?*

"Hey, Kevin?"

Leah has peeled away from her friends, who have clustered at the end of the hall. Wow—here it comes: *You're uninvited to my party, you terrorist supporter, you.*

"Look, don't . . . Don't tell anyone this," she says, looking over her shoulder quickly. She has a slight overbite; I love it. "Don't tell anyone, but . . ." Her voice, already low, drops even further—I can barely hear her and I'm right next to her. "I really admire what you're doing."

You could punch me in the face with brass knuckles and not stun me half as much.

Then she walks off before I can respond, which is good because my response probably would have been something along the lines of "Abba-dabba-ga-dabba-boo." Only not so articulate.

Wow. Leah Muldoon hates America, too. Cool.

CHAPTER 16
THE UNWELCOME RETURN
OF REPORTER GUY

I DIDN'T THINK I WAS "DOING" ANYTHING AT ALL, much less anything admirable, but if Leah thinks so, maybe there's something to it. Maybe I *should* be doing something.

I start thinking about the stuff I read on the media center computer. I have this really wild idea.

If Leah was impressed by me throwing away some magnets, I bet I can *really* get her attention.

I can't start right away, though, because Flip has called a Council meeting at SAMMPark right after school. I head to the park and get there just as Flip pulls up with Fam and Jedi.

"Hail, Fool," I say, waving to them.

They hail me right back, and Jedi goes all *vvvvvvvhhhnnn, vvvvvvvhhhnnn* as Fam comes up to me. She looks concerned.

"How are you handling all this, Kross? You doing all right?"

"I'm—"

"He's fine!" Flip shouts from the park entrance. "Come on!"

"I'm OK," I tell her. She puts a hand on my arm and nods this sad little nod, and I suddenly find myself wondering: Is she *hitting* on me? Flip's girlfriend? God, please, no, let that *not* be happening. Fam is a buddy, a pal. And she's Flip's girlfriend. I mean, yeah, Flip treats her like crap, but Flip pretty much treats *everyone* like they're interchangeable parts in some model kit he's putting together. It's nothing personal.

I shake her hand off and go into the park, just in time to see Flip slapping the statue of Susan Marchetti on the ass.

"Baby, you are looking *fine!*" he says. "You are one *hard* body!"

I look over at Fam. I can't tell if she's upset or not. She just sort of looks resigned to it, right up to the moment that Flip grabs her by the wrist and pulls her close and kisses her. "And *you* are soft and squishy, just like I like it."

OK, whatever.

A few minutes later, Speedo and Tit arrive. They ride the same school bus, which takes them right past the park.

Flip leads all of us to a secluded area of the park, where we can talk in private. After a quick round of "Hail, Fool," he gets right down to business.

"OK, fellow Fools, we have a problem. One of our own has been assaulted."

Murmurs of agreement. An undercurrent of *vvvvvvh-hhnnn.* I wonder what the hell he's talking about until I realize everyone's looking at me. Oh.

"I have been applying my not inconsiderable brain power to the conundrum and arrived at an inescapable conclusion. We can't let this stand. If the pissy little bitches who run this town want to make Kross's life miserable, they have to deal with us first."

Applause.

"Uh, Flip? What are you talking about?"

He grins at me. "Can't tell you, Kross. But don't worry—I have a plan. We've got your back."

"I don't want to get into any more trouble."

"Never fear. We're going to give you the cloak of plausible deniability."

"Say what?" asks Speedo. Jedi nods, making his light saber noise the whole time.

"I mean," Flip says, exasperated, "we're gonna do it in a way that no one can tie it back to Kross. Just trust me. It's a kick-ass idea. So sublimely Foolish. It's perfect. Especially in *this* town."

"Really?" Tit asks. "What is it?"

"Did you miss the part about plausible deniability?" Flip asks him.

"No."

Flip rolls his eyes. "We already started, doofus."

"Oh." Tit's expression suddenly opens up. "Oh! You mean when we took the—"

"Shut up!" Jedi, Flip, and Speedo say it all at the same time, and Tit slaps a hand over his mouth.

"This is what the Council is all about!" says Flip. His excitement is contagious—I can't help it; I'm a little excited, too. Flip's many things, but he's never boring.

"Be conspicuous from a safe distance!" he goes on. "Shove people's faces in their own perceptions. Darken the illuminated paths so that people have to feel their way around and learn the path anew. Right?"

"Oh, yeah!" says Tit. Speedo cries out "Whoo-hoo!" while Fam nods and Jedi does his Jedi thing.

"So, get out of here, Kross. Make sure you're visible tonight."

"Visible?"

"Just make sure everyone knows you're home being a good little boy." Flip grins a wicked grin. "We'll take care of the rest."

Flip sends the others off—"You have your assignments," he tells them—and then throws an arm over my shoulder and escorts me back to the car.

"What in the *world* are you thinkin', man?" He's grinning when he says it, though. "Fame and fortune just not enough for you? What game are you playing?"

"Nothing, Flip. Honest. It just . . . happened."

"Come on, Kross. It's me." He spins me around so that we're facing each other, his hands on my shoulders. "Tell your Uncle Flipster what kind of con you're running. Why'd you pull those magnets off your car in front of the reporter?"

"Flip, I swear to God, it's not a plan. It's not a con. My dad told me to take them off—"

He interrupts me with an eruption of laughter. "Your *dad*? Your *dad*?"

"Not so loud, man!"

"But your *dad* made you do this? That's what this is all about?"

"Well, that's what started it, yeah. But I'm—"

"Your dad. I can't believe it."

He's starting to get the Flip-gleam in his eye. I have to stop it, fast. "Flip, *please* don't tell anyone I told you that, OK? This thing has taken on a life of its own and it would totally kill me if people knew. OK?"

He takes a step back and chews it over for a bit. "Never fear, Fool Kross." He puts a hand over his heart and holds the other one up high. "Fool's Honor."

For whatever *that's* worth. But it's the best I'll get.

He ushers me over to the car. "You need to get going. I have a busy night ahead of me on your behalf."

And even though I didn't ask him to do anything, I feel bad. "Thanks, Flip."

He waves it off. Now that he's got his thanks, he doesn't care about it anymore. "Don't worry about it."

I get in my car and I'm about to drive off when Flip knocks on the window. I roll it down.

"Hey, I meant to ask you—what are you going to do with the money? I mean, you'll still have some left after buying this heap, right?"

Only Flip would just come right out with it like that. It's one of the things I like about him.

"Yeah, I still have most of it. Probably put it away for college."

"You're still gonna do the college thing?"

"My dad'll kill me if I don't."

"Let him kill you." He wags a finger at me. "Better than yoking your mind to the oppressive idiocy of the academic Gestapo."

Flip's always saying things like that. About half of it is just stuff he says to gauge people's reactions. The trick is figuring out which half. I shrug and he shrugs and he shakes his head, muttering "His dad" as he heads back to the park, the Council, and whatever mischief he's got cooked up.

* * * *

I head home with a whole new plate of anxiety to dump on top of my anxiety buffet. I don't think I've ever *not* known what Flip was up to, at least not since he kidnapped Officer Sexpot.

Man, I really don't want to get into trouble. *More* trouble.

I rummage around under the sofa bed a little bit. Maybe I should get rid of the tapes. What if Flip does something that gets me arrested and the police search the apartment and find the tapes and . . .

No. No. Calm down, Kross. That wouldn't happen. Right?

I try to put the whole thing out of my mind. I let myself think back to when I was a kid, when Jesse was still around. I could do no wrong back then. No matter what I did, he would look at me with the same shining admiration in his eyes.

It wasn't just shielding him from Mom and Dad's fallout, either. I mean, we had fun. We had our in-jokes and stuff. All one of us had to say was "Pandazilla and Aquahorse" and we'd both crack up laughing. It didn't matter that we got older and that the whole thing had been stupid to begin with. It was our memory, our secret, and we loved it. I made Jesse take Pandazilla with him to California—I think it was my toy originally, but I didn't care anymore. I liked the idea of my brother carrying a piece of me—a piece of *us*—with him while he went to the other side of the country.

Ugh. It's no good. No good to think about that time. Not when I can *only* do wrong these days. I have my own "mission" tonight. I have a bunch of research from the media center. Now I need to turn it into a speech.

A speech. Good Lord, have I completely lost my mind?

Probably.

I sit outside on the porch. Mrs. Mac lets Dad and me use the porch because she almost never goes outside. I feel wide open and conspicuous here.

Occasionally Mrs. Mac passes by her living room window, which looks out on the porch. She shakes her head at me like I've done something wrong. I focus on my homework and then my speech.

The sun goes down and the streetlights come on. I turn on the porch light and keep working.

"How about that interview now?"

Yow! I was so focused, I didn't hear anyone walking up to me. I look up and there's Reporter Guy, his hands in his pockets, standing at the foot of the porch steps.

"Why would I talk to you after what you wrote in the *Loco* today?"

He shrugs. "Don't you want your side to get out there?"

Hell, I don't even know what my side *is*. "Like I trust you to report it."

He looks offended. "Come on, Ross. It helps both of us. It's win-win."

"I'm not helping you do anything."

"Fine. You want to play hardball? We'll play hardball. How'd you like me to do a story in tomorrow's paper all about your dad and what *he* did when he was in the army? Hmm? Would you like that?"

I freeze up. There's no way in the world I'm going to do an interview with this douchebag, but I can't just let him piss all over Dad, either. Can I?

He grins. "Do you even *know* what your dad did? Do you?"

And of course, I don't. Taboo. Forbidden. *Proscribed.* "Just get out of here," I tell him.

"You don't, do you?" He laughs, and it's an ugly, ugly sound. "Well, maybe you should read tomorrow's paper."

My body starts vibrating all on its own. I want to tackle him to the ground, give him a little bit of what the Surgeon got.

But even I'm not that stupid.

"Get out of here." My voice shakes with anger. "This is private property." I say it loud enough that Mrs. Mac can hear me through the window.

Reporter Guy nods and starts to back away. "You had a chance, Ross." He throws me a weak, half-assed salute before disappearing.

Now I'm rattled. He got to me. With Dad. He hit me where I didn't know it would hurt. But I'm also determined. I have Leah to impress and Reporter Guy to piss off. So I'd better be good.

CHAPTER 17
SUPPORT

I WAKE UP AND GET READY FOR SCHOOL. Today is the big day. Today I'll make my stand. I never cared about ribbons or any of that before, but now it's like the biggest thing in my life. It's like my mission. I'll state my case in a way that people will understand. Once I point things out to them, once I show them how I'm thinking, they'll get it. They'll come around. They'll see what I see. It won't be a big deal anymore that I took those ribbons off my car, because people will understand my point of view.

Last night, Flip made it sound like I would need an alibi for whatever he and the Council had planned. And now, on the way to school, I see why.

About a jillion years ago, Brookdale started building a bridge on the outskirts of town. No one can tell me what the bridge was for, but it was never finished. There are still two giant iron supports out in the middle of a field, though, like tombstones for the *idea* of the bridge. You grow up in Brookdale and you hear "Don't you go playing around the bridge" (even though it's *not* a bridge) a million times, and then you go and do it anyway.

Today one of the supports is *covered* with magnetic ribbons.

I can see it from Route 54 on the way to school, and I actually have to pull over for a second. I'm not the only one—five or six other cars have pulled over, too.

The support is almost completely obscured by the ribbons. There must be hundreds of them, thousands maybe. It's become a patchwork thing of red, white, blue, and yellow.

All I can think is, *Where did Flip get all those ribbons?* He didn't have time to order them from somewhere, and that would be one hell of an expensive prank anyway . . .

And then I see a car stopped ahead of me. The bumper is dusty and dirty . . . except for a clean ribbon-shaped space.

Oh, man!

I hustle into my car before people realize a) who I am, and b) that their ribbons are missing, leading to c) the lynching of Kevin Ross.

The prank was too late in the night for it to make the morning newspaper, but apparently it's on TV and radio and all over the Web. Flip should be giddy when I see him at school, but he's depressed. Fam holds his hand and pets it like that'll soothe him.

"No one gets it," he complains. "They're talking about vandalism and theft, but no one gets it."

"Sorry. But you know what I noticed?"

He goes on, ignoring me. "I mean, there's no bridge! Right? A support with nothing on it. Empty, pointless support."

"No one even noticed that their ribbons were missing until they saw the bridge or heard about it," I tell him. "They don't even *see* the damn things anymore."

He's totally *oblivious* to me. "No one gets it. Not a one! It's a brilliant commentary on—"

I give up trying to get through to him. "Flip, if you have to explain a joke, it's not funny."

"No, the audience is just too stupid. Cut it out." He jerks his hand away from Fam. "Subtlety is lost on these morons."

I get away from him as quickly as I can. I need to be in homeroom.

In homeroom, I bide my time, waiting until everyone is in the room and just getting settled. I still have a minute or two before the bell and then a minute or two after that before the TV comes on and the announcer of the day leads us in the Pledge.

I get up and walk to the front of the class and say, "Excuse me! Could I have everyone's attention?"

Mrs. Sawyer looks like I just kicked her in the gut. Everyone stops what they're doing and gives me the same look you'd give a guy who not only just farted in church but also stood up to announce it loud and clear.

God, I hope I can pull this off.

"Before the announcements come on and the Pledge, I wanted to say something." I'm expecting a chorus of boos (or at least for Mrs. Sawyer to tell me to shut up), but I guess I've shocked everyone into paralysis.

I clear my throat and start to talk and I'm halfway through my speech before I realize I don't even need to look at my notes—I just *know* this stuff.

"I know this all started with some ribbons on my car . . .

or, hell, off my car. But yesterday I realized that there's something that came before the ribbons, for all of us. And we don't even think about it. Just like the ribbons.

"You know, every morning in school, ever since we were all little kids in kindergarten, we come in and we say the Pledge. And I guess that's fine, but you know, I got to thinking: What *is* the Pledge? What does it mean? Why do we say it? No one has ever told us that. They just tell us to say it and we do. And if we're supposed to be pledging allegiance, shouldn't we think about what that means? For most of us, the Pledge has always just been there. But do we ever really—"

"We're supposed to say it," John Riordon calls out from his seat in back. "You don't just sit there and do nothing. You say the Pledge." There's an agreeable undercurrent.

"OK, that's fine. But why?"

"Because you do," John says, again to murmured agreement. He's not just a football stud. He's also in a bunch of the college prep classes. So people are taking him seriously. More seriously than the guy who takes the easy classes and pulls straight Cs. (That would be me.)

"It's how you show you love your country," he goes on. "*If* you do." He looks like he's about to get out of his chair and rearrange my face, but I keep going.

"So George Washington and Abe Lincoln didn't love this country?"

I get the moment of surprised silence I was hoping for. John grits his teeth and gets up.

"Sit down, John!" Mrs. Sawyer says. "You, too, Kevin."

"The Pledge didn't even exist until 1892," I go on. "The guy who wrote it was a *socialist*."

Some blank stares. Riordon starts walking down the aisle to me.

"Socialists are supposed to be, like, the bad guys," I say, speeding up. "He only wrote the thing because there was this big world's fair in Chicago and he thought it would be cool to have kids all across the country say something nice. I mean, that's it. Really. That's the only reason it exists.

"Anyway, it wasn't the same Pledge as the one we say now. So how did anyone before 1892 prove they loved their country if they didn't have a Pledge? Or, y'know, magnets to put on their, well, their horse and buggies, I guess."

My smart-assery is unappreciated, but I can tell that I've caused at least a bit of confusion in some skulls out there.

"Sit down *now*," says Mrs. Sawyer, and her voice has this note of panic in it, like she's about to pull a gun. John pauses, trying to figure out how serious she is.

"I'm not going to listen to this crap," he says.

"You both have five seconds and then I'm writing hall passes to the principal's office."

John goes back to his seat.

"You should know what you're saying and what you're doing and why," I say. I'm on a roll. I'm not stopping now. "Like, the word *equality* was originally going to be in the Pledge, but do you know why it isn't? Because the guy who wrote it knew that the people in charge of the schools back then didn't like women and African Americans. So he didn't put it in there."

Not much of a reaction there, but then again, there are only like ten black kids at South Brook, so I don't really know what I expected.

"And it originally said 'my flag,' not 'the flag of the United

States of America.' A bunch of people changed that like twenty years later even though the guy who wrote it didn't want them to. And then in the 1950s, they added 'under God.'"

That gets a couple of people stirring—no one realized that God wasn't an original part of the Pledge.

"The guy who wrote it was a minister, but he never put God into it. It was a bunch of people sixty years later who did that. Your great-grandparents grew up reciting a Pledge that didn't mention God." I look pointedly at John Riordon. "They weren't saying the real Pledge, I guess. So, like, I guess they never loved their country, huh?"

Mrs. Sawyer says, "OK, Kevin, you've made your point. Thank you for the history lesson." She's a history teacher, but I guess she doesn't appreciate the irony.

"I have more to say."

"No, you don't." She's got her pad of passes in her hand already.

"Yes, I do."

She sighs as the announcements start. Everybody jumps up and puts their hands over their heart and recites the Pledge, just like we have a million times before. I stand there at the front of the class, doing nothing, *not* saying the Pledge even though every tissue and fiber in my body wants to do it. Because that's what I've been trained to do ever since I started school, and not doing it is killing me, especially with everyone watching.

But I resist. I don't say it.

As soon as the Pledge is over, I get right back into it: "Did you know people used to salute the flag while saying the

Pledge? Like this." I demonstrate. "But during World War II, people realized it looked just like a Nazi salute, so they stopped—"

"Kevin!" It's Mrs. Sawyer. "No one can hear the announcements."

"But, Mrs. Sawyer, this is important."

"So are the announcements. You're done."

"But—"

She rips a hall pass off her pad and hands it to me. "Principal's office."

"Why?"

"You know why."

John Riordon starts clapping as I walk out the door, and a few other people join in. Mrs. Sawyer tells them to stop, but they don't, at least not right away.

And so I get to visit the Doc, not to be confused with the Surgeon. Dr. Goethe is actually a fairly cool guy. Unlike the assistant principal, the Spermling, he's pretty calm and collected most of the time.

"Why are you doing this to me, Kevin?" he asks. He's pretty straightforward, too.

"I haven't done anything."

"For a few shining, perfect moments the whole country was looking at you with pride. Now I'm hearing that the wire services might pick up the paper's cover story from yesterday. Then your stunt last night with the bridge. And now this. What have I ever done to you to deserve this?"

"I didn't have anything to do with the bridge, Dr. Goethe. I swear."

He groans and leans back in his chair. "Are you going to

sue over the Pledge? Is that it? A church and state thing because of 'under God'?"

"No. I just don't understand why we *have* to say it."

"Kevin, let's cut to the chase—why don't you want to say the Pledge?"

I want to scream! Why won't anyone actually listen to the words I'm saying instead of hearing what they want to hear? "I never said I didn't *want* to say it. I just want to know why we *have* to say it. They're two different things. Can you tell me why we have to say it?"

"Well, you don't *have* to say it . . ." The Doc fidgets.

"But everyone does. Ever since we were kids. And no one questions it. No one asks why. We just keep doing it, and if we don't, we get crucified. Like not putting ribbons on our cars."

"Is that what this is about? Trying to stir up more trouble?"

"No. I'm not trying to stir up trouble. I just . . ." And I run out of steam because I'm still trying to get it all straight in my own head, and I really wish people would get off my freakin' back while I'm doing it.

He gives me a hall pass. "I have a conference call in a few minutes. Go to class—we'll talk more about this later."

I get to go to my first two classes, which—let me tell you—are just *loads* of fun. The story of my history lesson has already spread, and if I thought it was tough being the Kid Who Throws Away Ribbons, it's even tougher being the Kid Who Hates the Pledge.

There are a few Jehovah's Witnesses at South Brook, so you'd think they'd be on my side. But I'm starting to figure out that this argument has more than two sides. Jehovah's

Witnesses don't say the Pledge because of something about not worshiping false idols.

Me? I'm just trying to make a point.

Well, OK—make a point and maybe try to impress a certain someone.

"I'm not saying you shouldn't say the Pledge." It's between second and third periods, and a group of kids has cornered me near my locker and asked me why I hate America. They didn't exactly put it that way. They actually said, "What the hell is wrong with you?"

"You can say it all you want. I just think you should know *why* you're saying it."

"I think you're a piece of shit," one of the guys says. "Who do you think you are? You think you're some kind of hero. You think you're better than everyone else."

Oh, if only he knew. If only he knew the truth, he would see that I couldn't possibly think I'm better than anyone else.

Just then, the PA blares out: "Kevin Ross, please report to the principal's office. Kevin Ross to the principal's office."

A guy ten times bigger than me and a million times meaner grabs my shoulder and shoves me from the lockers into the hallway. I stumble and trip over my own feet and go down on the floor.

"Yeah, get going to the principal's office, you faggot."

It takes me three attempts to get up. That's not because I'm clumsy—it's just because people keep knocking me down.

When I get to the principal's office, I get a nasty shock—John Riordon is there, too. He smirks at me when I come in.

"Have a seat, Kevin," says the Doc, gesturing to a chair next to John's. "Let's finish our conversation from this morning."

I take the chair as far away from John as possible.

"I'm just trying to get people to think," I tell Dr. Goethe.

"You're doing it in a way that gives me a headache," he says. "You know, a few days ago, I looked at you and thought, 'Here's a new role model for our school.' What happened, Kevin?"

He's trying to guilt me. It won't work.

"Did you know there are no other developed countries in the world that make their citizens pledge allegiance to a flag?"

"Kevin, please. This is all very interesting, but—"

"Did you know that in some churches, they teach people to add 'born and unborn' to the end of the Pledge? They turn it into like a pro-life protest thing."

John sighs a really loud sigh. "See, Dr. Goethe? It's like he won't shut it off."

"Kevin . . ."

"What if someone decided to say 'with liberty and justice for all, except for people who don't put ribbons on their cars'? Would that be cool?" I spent a *lot* of time researching this stuff—I'm gonna tell *someone*. "Everyone acts like it's this sacred oath. And no one really thinks about the words when they're saying them, or where they come from. I just want people to think. Because otherwise it's just like slapping a ribbon on your car—it's just empty-headed. It's letting a symbol substitute for thinking." And *wow*, I don't know where *that* came from. I guess some of Dad's rants and raves over the years have sort of sunk in, whether I was listening or not. He'd be proud of me right now, and it's that idea, more than anything else, that stops me in my tracks.

Dr. Goethe, though, doesn't see the tracks and doesn't

stop. "I want peace in my school for the next couple of months until summer break, OK, Kevin? Save the politics for your history class, not homeroom. We don't need any more altercations."

"Altercations?"

"Like the one you had this morning in homeroom with John."

I look over at John, but he's ignoring me.

"There was no altercation."

"That's not how Mrs. Sawyer described it. Look. Here's what we're going to do," says Dr. Goethe, leaning back and steepling his fingers. "We're going to turn this into an exercise on free speech and the power of the spoken word. Monday morning, I'm giving you three minutes during the morning announcements to state your case."

I go cold and yet somehow I'm sweating, too. The morning announcements? My face and voice broadcast to the entire school?

"Um, well . . ." Maybe this free speech stuff isn't all it's cracked up to be.

"Come on, Kevin. You either believe what you're saying or you don't."

And it hits me that he's trying to snow me. Trying to use reverse psychology. Goad me and tempt me, but make it scary enough that I back down.

Screw *that*. Besides, I can't stop thinking of Leah, of the way she leaned in close, whispering just to me, just *for* me . . .

"I'll do it," I tell him. He just nods, and I can't tell if he's disappointed or amused.

"Fine. Report to the media center first thing Monday

morning and Mrs. Grant will set it all up. Then, the next day, John will have his say."

Say what?

John grins.

"Oh, yes," the Doc goes on, as if he's enjoying my look of shock . . . and I think he is. "I said this was going to be an exercise, didn't I? Free speech cuts both ways, Kevin. You get to tell the school what you think, and then John will offer his side of the issue."

It's a long, dangerous moment. The thought of being broadcast to the student body is one thing, but then to have John come at me with the verbal equivalent of a baseball bat . . . The idea goes in like an injection of ice water and settles right in my balls. No way. Forget it.

But I can't back out in front of John. I'd be the world's biggest coward.

"I'm not sure about this, Dr. Goethe."

"John?"

Riordon shrugs. His shoulders are massive. "I'm prepared to debate my side any time, any place."

"Ball's in your court, Kevin." The Doc glances at his watch. "Let me know by the end of the day. You're both late for third period, so move it."

CHAPTER 18
I'M AN IDIOT

JOHN RIORDON. MAN. OF ALL PEOPLE! The only kid to get on the varsity football team as a freshman. As tall and broad as God, and twice as good-looking. Smart and well spoken. He's like living proof that God has a sense of humor—he makes a guy like Riordon and he makes a guy like me and then he figures we'll both survive.

So Day One would be Kross the Acned, followed on Day Two by . . . by . . .

"By the Apollonian Ideal," Flip says helpfully, like I know what he's talking about.

We're all in the janitors' office, munching on some Mickey D's that Flip scored. We're not supposed to leave the school for lunch runs, but Flip doesn't really worry about such things, as you might have guessed.

"He's really smart," Fam says. She offers me some of her fries and I stuff them in my face like it's my last meal. "And everyone likes him. Well," she considers, "all the popular people like him."

"You can wipe up the floor with him," Flip goes on, like Fam never interrupted.

"He's *smart*," Fam insists.

"Yeah, I, uh, I had social studies with him last year," says Tit. "He's no dummy."

Flip waves them off like they're bad smells. "I don't care how smart and popular he is. John Riordon never had an original thought in his life. You'll be erudite and inflammatory, while he'll be as predictable as . . . as . . ."

"Morning wood," Speedo chimes in.

"Good one! *Vvvvvvhhhnn.*"

"I don't think anyone cares who has the most interesting comments. They just want another excuse to hate me."

"This is true," Flip agrees.

Of course, I can't tell them what's *really* bothering me about Riordon, which is that he's always nosing around Leah and her friends and they're always letting him nose around them and giggling and everything, even Leah, which, yeah, is the part that really bugs me, OK?

But Tit probably gets it. He raises his eyebrows at me. God, why did I tell him? Why couldn't I just keep it a secret tucked away with all of my other secrets?

"The difference between the two of you," Flip says, "is that John Riordon only has room for football and his own repressed homosexuality in his head. You have room for big thoughts. You can't wuss out."

"Yeah, man, don't wuss out," Jedi says, and then *vvvvvvhhhnns* a little bit.

"Yeah, well, I don't like being ambushed."

Flip laughs and slaps my back. "Way of the world, Fool Kross. Get used to it."

"You guys all think I should do it?"

Enthusiastic nods from everyone except Fam. It's not that

she's *not* nodding. It's just that she's not doing it enthusias-tically.

OK, this is marginally cooler than I'd thought before. I've got my friends convinced, at least.

"That means a lot to me, guys. That you believe in me. That you understand what I'm trying to say."

Tit's the first one to look away. Speedo raises an eyebrow like he's confused, and Jedi just hums away under his breath.

The whole room's gone completely silent. Except for Jedi, of course.

"Um, Kross . . ." Tit says.

"Oh, come on! Not you guys, too!"

"Hey, look, I'm not gonna speak for anyone else," Flip says, "but I don't really care what your point is. I'm not in-terested in the cause, man. I'm just here for the fight."

Tit shrugs. "Yeah. Me, too."

No way. "Speedo? Jedi? What about you guys?"

"We're buds, Kross," says Speedo. "If you want to do this, that's cool. I'll stand by you because you've always stood by me. But yeah—I don't get it. Not really."

"Who cares about ribbons and pledges and all that crap anyway? *Vvvvvvvvhhhnn.* It's like the news and stuff. Boring." His eyes light up. "But messing with people over it? Yeah, that's cool."

Fam looks like she wants to say something, but Flip jumps up from the desk and slaps his hands together. "The Council has spoken! We support Fool Kross on his quest. You make up your mind, Kross. We'll be there for you."

Which is great, I guess. But, tell the truth, I'd rather have people supporting me who believe in what I'm doing.

For the rest of the day, though, I can't help thinking about it. I think of the look on Leah's face when she told me she admired me. It makes me dizzy. I think of Dr. Goethe calling me a "role model."

Is that what I am? What I was? What I could be?

Is it possible that I *could* be a role model, just a different kind than Dr. Goethe thought? A role model for *my* way of thinking?

Or maybe just get a chance to rub John Riordon's face in the dirt while Leah watches.

On my way to the parking lot at the end of the day, I reach into my pocket for my car keys. Much to my surprise, I find the key to Brookdale there, too. I forgot—I attached it to my key chain.

I stop dead, looking at it.

And then I go straight to the principal's office.

"OK," I tell the Doc. "I'll do it."

That afternoon, the cops come to the apartment. They're wondering about the Ribboning of the Bridge and they read the paper, too, so they figure I'm the obvious suspect.

Dad doesn't like having cops on his turf. He's tough with them. He also tells them that I was asleep in bed when he left for work at, like, two in the morning. Which would have made it impossible for me to vandalize the bridge. Which isn't a bridge anyway—it's just a bridge *support*. For a nonexistent bridge. And is putting *magnets* on something really vandalizing it? I mean, they come off.

The cops probably wouldn't be inclined to believe Dad, but when I mention that Reporter Guy was skulking around (probably hoping to get a picture of me peeing on something red, white, and blue, or molesting a bald eagle), they sort of give up.

Score one for the good guys and Flip's "cloak of plausible deniability."

For now, at least.

"So. How was school?" Dad asks once we're alone.

"You know." Don't really want to tell him about all that nonsense. Especially since he got me into it. And if I tell him about the speech I have to give, he might—ugh!—want to help me write it, which will make everything worse. I trip enough over my own words; I can't imagine what sort of verbal land mines there would be in Dad's.

He fiddles with the VCR, trying to get it to cough up the game he taped yesterday. It just makes that scary thunking sound that always convinces me it's eaten the tape.

"Might have to replace this one," Dad mumbles, glancing around at the stacks of broken VCRs in our own little consumer electronics graveyard.

"Dad, look, I was thinking . . . I was thinking that I could use the money and maybe buy us—"

He punches the wall.

No, really. He *punches the wall*. My whole body tenses up in shock, so sudden and so massive that I think a zit just popped all on its own.

"No!" He's cradling his hand a little bit and his face has gone all red and sweaty. "No, no, no!"

"Dad, let me finish. I just want to use a little bit of the reward money to buy a couple of—"

He kicks the door frame. No lie. He's really beating the hell out of the apartment.

"Stop it, Kevin! Just stop it, OK? I don't want you spending that money on things for me or the apartment. I feel very strongly about that."

Yeah, no kidding. Tell that to Mr. Wallboard, who's smarting something fierce.

"Dad, it's like thirty thousand dollars. That's a lot of money, even after I take out the price of my car."

"Look," Dad says, "I want you to enjoy that money. I want you to use it to make your life better. Go to college, maybe. I know I've messed up my own life, and I'm really trying my best not to mess up yours, too. I want that money to buy you some happiness or some peace of mind or something."

It comes out in a rush and the look on his face the whole time he's saying it isn't really what you'd expect. He looks pained, uncomfortable.

"So. Don't," he says, then retreats to his bedroom and shuts the door.

What the hell was *that* all about?

I almost go to knock on the door, just to make sure he's OK, when I spot today's *Loco* sitting on the rocking chair. I pick it up. Dad's already read it, and he's got it folded to a story on page 3.

Local "Hero's" Traitor Dad! screams the headline.

Ah, crap.

Sure enough, there's Reporter Guy's byline. And there's that same picture of me throwing away the ribbons, but this time there's an old picture of Dad right next to it. He's wearing his army uniform and he's holding up one hand, trying to shield himself from flashbulbs. He looks bewildered. He also looks *young*. He looks like I imagine I'll look in three or four years.

"Sergeant Jonathan Jackson Ross tries to avoid reporters in Qasr, Kuwait," reads the photo caption.

I scan the article. It doesn't have a lot of facts. It recaps my rise and then fall from grace, then adds on, "That young Ross would espouse unpatriotic sentiments may come as a surprise, but surely fits once one factors in his home environment. Ross's father, who served as an army sergeant, was dishonorably discharged from the military almost twenty years ago for revealing classified military secrets."

The rest of it is just more badmouthing of me.

Revealing classified military secrets.

Dishonorably discharged.

No way. I look at the closed bedroom door. No way. I don't believe it. Not my dad.

CHAPTER 19
CALI CALLIN'/CALLIN' CALI

TWICE THAT NIGHT, I COME CLOSE to knocking on Dad's door and asking him about the story in the paper. But I can't bring myself to do it.

Dad and the army. Like I said, it's the one topic that's always been off-limits in my family. It's not like someone engraved it in a stone tablet or anything: THOU SHALT NOT DISCUSS DAD'S MILITARY SERVICE. It's just that we never talked about it. I never really missed it, tell the truth. By the time I was born, he'd been out of the army already, so it's not like I ever had any memories of him being *in* the army. I found some pictures once of him in his uniform, young and thin in the bright glare of the desert sun. My parents' wedding album had pictures of a bunch of guys in their dress uniforms, including Dad. I asked about that once when I was real little—"Why is Daddy in a costume?"—and I just got "Daddy used to be an army man, like your toys" from Mom.

Even as a kid, I could tell from her tone of voice and from the way she sort of looked away from me that she didn't want to talk about it. Which was fine by me, because really, who the hell cares what their parents did ten thousand years ago?

Only now I *have* to care.

I think back. I try to remember anything I can about Dad

and the army. He would sometimes mention it in passing, but usually it didn't mean anything. Like, if I complained about not having enough room for my stuff, he would say, "When I was in the service, I carried everything I owned in a duffel bag." Or if I said it was hot and could we put on the air conditioning, he would say, "This isn't hot. *Over there*, it was hot."

Over there was as close as he ever came to talking about it.

But there was this one time . . .

Back before Mom and Dad got divorced. They were arguing because, well, that's what they did. I must have been ten, so Jesse was four or five. We still lived in the townhouse back in the old neighborhood.

I don't remember what started it. It was probably something on TV. Dad's always seeing something on TV or reading something in the paper that sets him off. He got really pissed, and when Mom tried to calm him down, he snapped at her and stalked off to their bedroom.

Me and Jesse were playing in the family room. We'd built this big Lego fort for our superhero action figures and now Pandazilla was knocking it down.

Mom looked at us and then stomped off after Dad. I'm pretty sure she said, "I'm so tired of this" under her breath.

A minute later, the bedroom door slammed. Jesse jumped and looked at me.

"It's OK," I told him. "They're just talking."

But no sooner was the word "talking" out of my mouth than I heard Dad's voice. Loud. Not loud enough that we could understand exactly what he was saying, but loud enough that we could hear him and understand that he was angry.

Then: Mom. Just as angry.

"What are they doing?" Jesse whispered.

"Just talking," I said again. "Grown-up talking."

It was crap and I knew it was crap, but what else was I supposed to say?

"Let's go outside."

Jesse nodded at me, his eyes huge as the voices kept going back and forth. But he didn't get up. He just kept nodding.

I tried to pull him up to his feet, but it's like he'd shoved a lead brick in his pants or something—he wasn't going anywhere, even though he wanted to.

"Come on, Jesse," I told him, tugging.

"Make them stop," he said.

"I can't. Come on, let's go."

Tears spilled from Jesse's eyes so fast that I couldn't believe it. There was no pause or moment where his eyes filled up or anything. One second he was totally dry, the next he was just *gushing*.

"Outside," I said. "Come on." I was tired of pulling.

Mom's voice got real clear: "You were a *hero*, John," she yelled. "And then you let them make you into a villain—"

"*Let* them?" Dad bellowed.

I gave up trying to pull Jesse to his feet. I collapsed on the floor next to him and wrapped my arms around him and put my lips right up to his ear and said, "It's OK. It's OK," and rocked him and hoped that my voice was loud enough to block out *their* voices.

". . . when it was politically expedient!" Mom said.

"That's enough. OK? That's just . . . enough!" Dad yelled back.

"It's OK," I kept telling Jesse and kept rocking him and let him wipe his eyes and his cheeks with my shirt while he cried. And he clung to me like a kitten and he was really brave and really good because he didn't make a sound, he just let me rock him and talk to him, and that . . .

That was my first experience being a hero.

I don't know what to do. I want to ask Dad about the paper, but it's like my whole life I've been trained not to talk about it. I can't make myself do it.

So I figure I'll call Flip and get his read on the situation. He's not the most sympathetic guy in the universe, but he's the smartest person I know *and* he has the Internet at home, so maybe he can find something. But I pick up the phone and find that we have voice mail.

The first message is from Dr. Goethe, asking Dad to call him at some point to discuss my behavior. I make an executive decision and determine that Dad doesn't need to discuss my behavior—I delete the message.

The second message almost knocks me on my butt.

It's Mom.

Oh, God.

Mom.

She called. She actually called.

I haven't heard from her since right after the whole mess with the Surgeon. It's been weeks. And now it's like . . .

God, chill out, Kross!

But I can't help it. I almost never talk to her. The time difference and she's always so busy and I have no freakin' privacy here and—

"Kevin, sweetheart, it's Mom. I saw you on TV, honey. Rita and Jesse and I all watched it together. I'm sorry it took a couple of days for me to call you, but I wanted to wait because I have some terrific news."

Terrific news?

"I really want to tell *you,* though, not the voice mail, so please call me back. Don't forget the time difference—three hours."

And then a dead line.

My mom *never* calls. I always call her.

Mom didn't just leave Dad and me. She disappeared off to California and lost something like fifty pounds and moved in with Rita. So, yeah, my mom is now kinda hot and a lesbian. And the world just should not work that way. It's too confusing. No one's mother should be a hot lesbian. It should be illegal or something.

And the part that sucks is that it's not like I can talk to anyone about it. If I try to talk to Dad about it, he just shuts down. And there's no way I can talk to any of my friends about it. I mean, you can't just tell your buddies that your mom is a hot lesbian. I mean, really.

I get cards on my birthday, Christmas, Easter. Send cards to her, too. The occasional phone call. Last summer, she and Dad had a huge screaming fight on the phone, which ended when they agreed to split the cost of a ticket and fly me out to California for a week.

Jesse had grown three inches by then. His hair . . . man, his hair was the first thing I noticed when I saw him at baggage claim. It used to be this ugly mop of stuff just sprouting from his head, but now it was like ten shades lighter and *golden*. Mom had lost all that weight and looked like my older sister, not my mother. She and Rita held hands and called each other "honey" and "baby."

I mostly stayed in the room that I shared with Jesse. Mom kept trying to feed me vegetarian stuff and kept giving me creams for my face. They all felt weird and icky.

In fact, the whole situation felt weird and icky. It's not like there was anything wrong with it—Mom was happy, Rita was nice, and Jesse was some new kid I'd never seen before. For the first time in his life, I couldn't connect with him. He didn't cry or seem bothered by things or anything. Pandazilla was on a shelf in his room, but there was a layer of dust on him. And that was disturbing, but not what was weird and icky.

No, the weird and icky part was *me*. I didn't fit in. I didn't belong.

So I was glad to leave, but when I got home, everything seemed darker and colder. Not just because of the weather, either. I kept looking at the pictures of Jesse on the wall. And at the picture of Mom and Dad I keep in my wallet, where Dad won't see it. There was this massive disconnect between what was in front of my eyes and the California memories in my brain. It was as if the pictures had suddenly become lies. Like someone had invented them, like *I* had invented them. I didn't believe in them anymore. I couldn't believe that Mom had ever been the slow, heavy woman who raised me. That my brother had been a tiny, shy kid with mousy hair and no confidence.

Jesse had always been afraid. Of everything. Maybe it's because he lived in a house where the two adults could—and would—suddenly start screaming at each other at a moment's notice. I don't know. But he'd always been afraid of everything—the dark, cats, dogs, you name it. And Mom was always sighing heavily and pinching the bridge of her nose and telling me to go get her some Advil.

Now they had both changed. Improved. But the worst part wasn't seeing that. The worst part was knowing that I would never change. Never improve. I wouldn't get the magic makeover and the new life. I would just be stuck in Brookdale and I would just be stuck in *me*, with the dull brown hair and the zits and the bad attitude and the snow. Because I had made my choice.

I call her back. Rita answers the phone.

"We were so happy to see you on TV!" she burbles. Rita is endlessly enthusiastic. She's like a cheerleader with her gears stuck in overdrive or something. "Jesse kept saying, 'That's my big brother.'"

"Is my mom there?" I ask. It's one in the afternoon in California, but Mom telecommutes.

"Just a second."

And then she's on. She's less burbly, but she also can't stop talking about me on TV—though she mentions I should have been sitting up straight and that she has a new face cream "that will take care of those blemishes for you."

"They're not blemishes, Mom. They're zits. Let's be honest."

"There's no need to be crude, Kevin."

"Sure."

"Kevin, I want you to come visit us again this summer."

Last year's knock-down, drag-out fight over who would

pay for the plane ticket flashes through my mind. But this year ... hey, I'm rich, right?

"That sounds ... that sounds good, Mom."

"Wait, honey, I'm not done yet. I mean for the whole summer."

My brain sort of fizzles out for a second. I must have heard her wrong.

"The whole summer?" A lot can happen in a summer. My imagination takes charge for a brief moment, imagining my return to Brookdale in the fall, a new me, as different from the current me as Jesse is from the kid who left the East Coast. It's a nice fantasy.

"And if that works out and you like it here," she goes on, "Rita and I want to have you move in with us. For good."

CHAPTER 20
I GO ON TV (AGAIN)

Moving to California. For good.

Hours later, I'm still trying to absorb the conversation with Mom, but I'm doing a lousy job of it. Going to California would totally change my life. I wouldn't have to worry about Dad's past. Or the stupid hero crap. Or the even stupider villain crap. I could start over.

Those videotapes that I shouldn't have wouldn't matter anymore. Maybe I could even get past Leah—out of sight, out of mind.

Moving. It's the kind of thing I used to talk to Father McKane about. On my own, it's too big to imagine. It's like my brain's got a quart of space open and I'm trying to pour in a gallon of stuff. And all the stuff that won't fit in is just splashing all over me and confusing me.

Fortunately, Flip calls and I get distracted. "Hail, Fool. It's only just begun," he says.

"What's just begun?" I'm not sure I like the giddy, ominous tone of his voice.

"Don't you worry about a thing. Just keep doing what you're doing. We'll handle the rest. Sunday night–slash–Monday morning. For maximum impact." He giggles. That's either a really good or a really bad sign.

I get an image of the Council of Fools spreading out across Brookdale in black ninja gear, hell-bent on wreaking our particularly ridiculous brand of havoc.

"Please don't do anything too crazy," I tell him. "You're gonna, y'know, obscure my point and stuff."

Which is the wrong thing to say, really, because Flip *lives* to obscure people's points. That's sort of why there is a Council in the first place.

I shove it all aside to work on my speech. I'm not stupid or anything, but I don't try really hard in school, so this is sort of like doing a triathlon after not working out for a long time. I'm using all these brain muscles I haven't used in, like, a thousand years.

It takes the whole weekend and a bunch of trips to the library for research. Dad asks what I'm up to and I tell him it's a project for school, which isn't a total lie.

By the time I'm done, it's late Sunday. I rehearse, say my speech out loud over and over again—whispering to keep from waking up Dad—so I can be sure it's under three minutes.

It's pretty good.

I *think* it's pretty good.

Will Leah think it's pretty good? Because not only would it be cool to have her take one step closer to me, but it would also be cool to have someone on my side in all of this. Someone who *agrees* with me, I mean. It's nice that the Council has my back, but they don't really *care* about any of this.

I call Flip on his cell so that I can read the speech to him, but he doesn't answer, which means he's probably in the back seat of his car with Fam. I close my eyes real tight and try to banish the image of their pasty, skinny bodies locked together.

So I call Jedi. I can hear his PS3 in the background the whole time I'm reading the speech to him.

"Sounds good to me," he says.

"Dude, were you even listening?"

"Uh-huh. Whoa! Damn! Almost died!"

"Jedi, help me out here. Does it suck or not?"

"Hang on. Save point." I listen to some yelling and screaming and bullets in the background and then it all goes quiet. "OK. *Vvvvvvhhhnn.* Kross, man, it sounds OK to me, but what do I know?"

"But do you think it will convince people?"

"Convince people of what? *Vvvvvvhhhnn.*"

Oh. My. God. If I could jump through the telephone line and choke him to death, I would do it. I swear.

"Dude. I'm trying to get people to think for themselves. You know? To stop doing what everyone else does just *because* everyone else does it. Or just because everyone has *always* done it."

"Why the hell do you care?"

I don't have an answer for that. I just *do*. Isn't that enough?

I try Speedo next. "You know what I've been thinking?" he says before I can even start to read my speech. "I think there should be ribbons . . . for *ribbons*."

"What?"

"Yeah. Like ribbons for your car that say 'Ribbon Awareness' or 'Support the Ribbons,' you know? Wouldn't that be funny?"

"Dude, your tightie-whities are so tight they're cutting off the blood supply to your brain."

"I started wearing boxers this weekend," he informs me. "It's very strange that everything can breathe down there."

Ew.

"You need to chill," he says. "Everyone'll forget about all of this over the weekend anyway."

OK, so Speedo's no help.

Tit's my last call. He actually lets me read through the whole thing. Then he's quiet for a while before he says, "Kross, you sure you want to do this?"

"Why?"

I can almost hear him picking his words. "I mean, I get that you're doing this to impress Leah with how fearless you are, but—"

"That's *not* why I'm doing it!"

"Man, you've got a boner the size of the bridge support for her. And she goes hanging around with Riordon and his pals—"

"Shut up, Tit."

"—and you know that you don't stand a chance against any of those guys in a fight or anything, so—"

"Dude, shut *up*."

"—you figure you'll stomp him into the ground with your mouth instead and then she's all impressed and everything and you guys go off into the sunset together, right?"

I sit there. I stare at Dad's bedroom door because it's one of the only things to stare at in this place.

"Right?" Tit says again.

"No," I lie. But he's right. I didn't realize it until he said it, but he's right.

"You really think any of that's gonna happen?"

"I don't know. I'm just trying to make a point. I just want people to get off my back about things. Show them that just because you don't have a ribbon or whatever, it doesn't mean you're a bad guy."

"Good luck with that." He sounds like he really means it.

"Thanks, Tit."

Monday morning, before school, Dad's gone and I watch a tape again. I still hate myself for doing this; I'm still powerless *not* to do it. I should destroy it, is what I should do. I should tear them up—all of them—and smash the cases like my camcorder is smashed and then I could never watch again, but I just can't bring myself to do it.

On the way to school, I listen to the radio: WHY's *Morning Madness with Skip and Skippy*. And this is how I learn what Flip was *really* up to over the weekend, and it didn't involve negotiating the clasp on Fam's size-AA training bra.

"It's gotta be kids," says Skip (or Skippy—I can never keep them straight).

"No, man," says Skippy (or, again, Skip). "Kids can't pull that off."

"Are you crazy? *Only* kids could pull it off. It's so juvenile . . ."

"You're just jealous you didn't think of it first."

"True . . . If you're just joining us," says Skip, "we're talking about the image that was spammed out to newspapers and TV stations in the area today, including our own *Morning Madness* anchor desk . . ."

"Located in the third-floor men's room, in the stinky stall."

"Right. Anyway, it's a fu—"

"Watch it, man! FCC!"

"I was going to say 'funny.'"

"Sure you were."

God, get to the point!

As if he can hear my thoughts, Skip says, "It looks like someone took a blow-up doll and dressed it up in some red, white, and blue lingerie—"

"Very tasteful," Skippy interjects. "Very patriotic."

"—and has it, uh, *her* posed with a, uh . . ."

"A marital aid."

"That's no aid. That's a marital *tower*."

Skippy starts cracking up.

"I mean, that's the biggest, uh . . ."

"Marital aid," Skippy gasps.

"I've ever seen. This thing needs its own zip code."

"And an altimeter."

"Needless to say, she's in a very, uh, *compromising* position with this thing—"

"Not that it looks like she minds." Skippy still can't breathe.

"And there's a word balloon here that says, 'Keep it UP, America!'"

"Tell them the best part!" Skippy says.

"Well, the best part is that in the background, you can see . . . Well, it looks like a car dealership, with flags and some of that red, white, and blue what-do-ya-call-it? Bunting."

"*Bunting,*" says Skippy, like it's pornographic.

"And a caller in the previous hour tells us that this is, in fact, the car dealership up in Brookdale, the one owned by the *mayor* of Brookdale. And Brookdale's where they're having all this mess with the kid who—"

I turn off the radio. I don't need to hear any more.

Speedo, as usual, is totally wrong. The weekend has made no difference at all. I get the hard looks that I've become accustomed to by now as I enter school. Leah sort of tilts her head as I walk by. I choose to interpret that as a quiet show of support.

In the media center, Mrs. Grant sits me at a table and points a camera at me.

"Are you sure you're ready for this?" she asks.

"I don't really have a choice now."

She shrugs. "There can be something wrong with the camera today."

"Thanks, but no."

Dr. Goethe announces "something special this morning," and explains that "our local hero" is going to discuss politics and free speech. You can almost hear a hiss throughout the school.

"And tomorrow morning, John Riordon will present an opposing viewpoint." This time, there's no "almost" about it— I hear cheers echoing all the way down the hall.

Great.

Mrs. Grant nods to me, and here I am, on TV for the second time in as many weeks.

"Hi, South Brook. I've been thinking about some of the things that have been said around here. The things I've said and the things that have been said to me. And you know what the best part is? That we're *allowed* to say them. We live in a country where we can say whatever we want.

"But I guess what's been bothering me is that people don't really feel like they *can* say whatever they want. Because if they say something that isn't popular, they're going to be yelled at or laughed at or beat up. And that's not cool.

"After I was on *Justice!* everyone in school wanted to hang around me. It was crazy. It was like I was some kind of hero. And then with a picture in the paper, it all changed. And no one ever came up to me and asked me why I took those ribbons off my car. No one ever wanted to know. It's like everyone was sharing one brain and one thought: 'Ribbons good. No ribbons bad.'

"Well, what's the point of freedom of speech if everyone says and thinks the same thing anyway? What's the point of freedom of speech if everyone is *forced* to say the same thing? Or afraid to say anything different?

"So here's why I took off those ribbons: because no one can tell me what they're for. It's the easiest thing in the world to spend a buck on a ribbon and slap it on your car and think that you're doing something to support the troops. But you don't support the troops by putting things on your car. That doesn't help anyone. It's not like all of the money people spend on ribbons goes to the troops. I looked around and I can't even figure out if *any* of it goes to them! I found all these places online that sell ribbons, but none of them say they donate any money to the troops.

"It's like . . . It's like someone's making a lot of money on this, you know?

"If you want to support the troops, raise money to send

them care packages and maybe try to figure out how to bring them home so they don't die. I did some research, and did you know that during World War II, people really made sacrifices for the troops? They collected scrap metal and old rubber tires to be recycled into weapons and stuff. They recycled paper for the troops to use. They rationed gasoline and food, all to help the war effort. They *sacrificed*.

"And what have *we* done? Not much. We spend a buck on a magnet and we tell anyone who doesn't that they're not patriotic or they don't love their country or they hate the troops. We don't sacrifice—we just go with the flow and don't ask questions.

"And look, about the Pledge. People say it every day, but no one thinks about it. So what's the point, then? And why is it only kids who say it? My dad doesn't say the Pledge every morning when he goes to work, and unless your parents are teachers, I bet they don't either. So why say it? If you want to say it, great. But why should you *have* to say it? I've heard some people say that it shows you love your country. Well, that's fine, but you could hate the country and still say the Pledge and no one would ever know. Nothing would blow up, you wouldn't glow or anything. And if you don't know the story of the Pledge and what its purpose is, then, well, you're just mouthing the words. And then they don't mean anything.

"I guess what I'm saying is that I wish people would think for themselves. Don't just do what everyone else does—use your own brain and figure things out for yourself. If you want to put a ribbon on your car because it's important to you, then great—just don't do it because everyone else is doing it or because you're afraid not to.

"Because freedom of speech is pretty pointless if everyone keeps saying the same thing."

And that's it. Mrs. Grant cuts away to Dr. Goethe, who thanks me and goes into the morning announcements. Meanwhile, I've got ten gallons of sweat streaming down my back and under my arms, but I feel pretty good. I feel like I've accomplished something.

Then I go to the locker room for gym class, and I get the crap beat out of me.

CHAPTER 21
CORN BREAD

WELL, NOT TOTALLY. But it's not fun. Mr. Kaltenbach comes in just as two guys have me backed up against the lockers in a little nook behind the showers.

"Think you're some kinda hot shit hero?"

Bang—punch to the shoulder. Just a warm-up punch, showing me what they could do, what they *would* do.

"Whiny little *liberal*. Your dad ought to kick the shit out of you for the stuff you've been saying."

I guess they didn't read last week's *Loco*.

I'm figuring I stand a decent chance of at least nailing one of them in the balls before they take me down when Mr. Kaltenbach wanders over.

"What the hell is this?" he asks.

"Nothing," says the guy on my left, grinning.

Mr. Kaltenbach sighs and jerks his thumb over his shoulder. "Move it."

"Thanks," I say when they're gone.

He snorts at me in disgust. "Yeah, whatever."

Oh, good. Now even the teachers hate my guts. Hero to zero in no time flat. I think I set a world record.

★ ★ ★ ★

For lunch, I don't feel like being around Flip while he crows about the magnificence of his latest Officer Sexpot scandal. Doesn't he realize his pranks are just making it harder for me?

I go to the auditorium, head backstage, and then—after a quick look around to make sure no one is watching—I scale the skinny ladder that leads up to the lighting catwalk over the stage. With the curtains down, you can't see up here unless you're actually looking for someone. And who ever looks up?

It's a shaky ladder and it always feels like it's going to crumble by the time you get to the middle (of course it would be the middle), but it's cool. And I'm skinny anyway, so I'm not worried. It'll hold. It always has.

I take a stab at eating my peanut butter and jelly sandwich, but the jelly has bled into the bread so it looks like a massive purple bruise, which makes me think of the bruise that's probably forming on my shoulder, and I can't eat. The rest of my lunch bag is some potato chips, some pudding, and a bunch of little carrots. None of it looks appetizing. Why did I pack this junk?

Flip and the rest of the Council wander in down below and head into the janitors' office. A few seconds later, Flip emerges and roams the stage for a little while, looking for me. I can hear him whispering my name loudly, poking around, but he can't find me. I hold back my arm, resisting the urge to pelt him with the carrots, just to see if I could get him. Would that be Foolish or just foolish?

Instead, I just watch him look around, and then give up, throwing his hands up in the air before returning to the office, leaving me alone.

* * * *

By the end of the day, the rumors that I'm clinically insane, on massive doses of antidepressants, or both are in full swing. My car has not survived unmolested today—someone keyed the passenger-side door pretty good.

I'm pretty sure that at least two cars from school follow me home. I slow down at the driveway, but at the last second decide not to pull in. Instead, I keep going, take a left at the light, and drive around a little bit more. They keep following me.

I lose one of them at a light by signaling left, then turning right.

I notice that the signs that praised me a week ago are all down now, except for the one at the Narc. At the WrenchIt Auto Parts store, the sign now reads, UNITED WE STAND! Good Faith Lutheran says, simply, GOD BLESS AMERICA. And so on.

And man—it kills me because I don't disagree with any of that, but I know that those signs are up now because the people who *put* them up think I don't think that way. I don't have a problem with standing united. I don't have a problem with God blessing America, should he decide America's worth blessing. I just want people to think about it and not charge into things blindly and not assume that just because I don't wear my heart on my sleeve that I don't have a heart at all or that—

OK. Cool. I'm pretty sure I've lost the second car.

I head home. Dad is actually cooking something, which is weird. He usually goes to bed so early that I fend for myself, but here he is, mixing something in a bowl.

"How was school?"

"Fine."

He nods and keeps mixing.

"Hey, Dad?"

"Hmm?"

I freeze up. I was about to ask him about his discharge. I even had the sentence all prepared: *What they said in the paper about you . . . it's not true, right?*

But now I just can't. He seems sort of happy and content standing here, mixing stuff. I can't bear to wreck it.

"What is it, Kevin?"

"Nothing, I guess."

I don't get my dad. I'm not ashamed to admit this. Tell the truth, if he was *your* dad, you wouldn't get him either. Part of it is probably that I don't see him a lot. The other part, though, is that he's a man of few words, and I'm the opposite. Once I get going, I can't keep my mouth shut, which is how I end up in situations where it's me against South Brook and Brookdale and the whole freakin' planet.

Dad can read guilt, though. It's like a second language to him. He can tell something's wrong. "You're not involved in any of that stuff the police were asking about, are you?"

"No, Dad."

"Because I told them that you've been home with me every night, but I know that once I leave for work, you could be sneaking out of here . . ."

"I'm not, Dad."

He grunts and starts spooning the mixture into a pan.

"What are you making?"

"Corn bread."

Right. I don't know whether to laugh or just stand there with my jaw hanging down to my knees. Corn bread. My dad is making . . . corn bread.

"You got a problem with that?" he asks, but it's not a *total* tough-guy tone. There's a little glint in his eye.

Once it's done, much to my surprise, it's good. Really, really good. Buttery and sweet at the same time, crumbling to melt in my mouth with every bite. We eat it with some microwaved turkey sandwiches, and the corn bread makes the sandwiches taste better somehow.

"Where did you learn how to make this?"

Dad shrugs. "Your mom."

Since we seem to be having something of a moment, I figure I'll take advantage of it.

"Hey, Dad? What was it like in the army?"

I blurt it out so fast that I barely realize I've said by the time I'm done. It's not *exactly* the question I wanted to ask, but it's a start.

"It was fine," he says. "It was the army."

"Did you have to kill people?"

He sighs. "Why is that always the first question people ask? Saved a lot of lives. No one ever wants to hear about *that*. Not scary enough. Not *sexy* enough." He gets up and dumps his dish in the sink, and the next bit comes out in a rush, like he's forcing it out, and I don't need Mom's telepathy to understand: "People should stop worrying about what I did or didn't do and start thinking about whether or not I should have been there in the first place. Violence never solved anything."

"Yeah, tell that to Leah Muldoon." It slips out before I can stop it.

But it's like he didn't hear me. "I was nineteen. And that was the average age for the guys in my squad. We were kids, not much older than you. Give us guns and bombs and helicopter support and tell a bunch of kids to make foreign policy work." He shakes his head. "Kill people to save people's lives. Blow things up to build them up. And what's the result? Ten years, fifteen years later, we're right back there again, doing it all over again. Fucking it all up."

My dad *never* curses. Never. It's like an unwritten rule of the world or something. So hearing him drop the f-bomb so casually makes me feel like I should apologize or ask him if he really meant to say that or hide under the sofa or something.

"'Blind faith in your leaders or in anything will get you killed,'" he says, and then shakes his head again.

"Is that . . . Is that why we don't go to Mass anymore?"

It's like he suddenly remembers I'm in the room. "What?"

"Blind faith—"

"No. No. That was a quote. Something someone said at a concert I went to when I was . . . God, I was your age, I guess. It doesn't have anything to do with . . . Do you miss Mass? Do you want to go back?"

I shrug. "I don't know."

He gazes at me. "Be honest with me."

"I guess I miss it."

"OK. I can see that."

"Why did we stop going?"

He purses his lips like he's trying to remember how to make words.

"You know all about the priests who were molesting kids, right?"

"Duh." I have eyeballs.

"I guess that really threw me."

"Father McKane doesn't do that stuff."

"Yeah, I know. But it's . . ." Oh, God. Here he goes. I can tell. His brain is going into overdrive and I won't understand anything he says.

He shakes his head and then his whole body shakes, like he's cold. He chews his bottom lip. And then he speaks. Slowly. With effort.

"I couldn't go and confess my sins and hear what is supposed to be the Word of God from men who are so flawed."

"But Father McKane doesn't—"

"He's just a man, Kevin. They're all just men. No better than you or me. Sometimes worse. And I just couldn't do it anymore. Do you understand?"

"But that's like judging all of them for what a *few*—"

"God, Kevin!" He makes a fist and his face goes red, but I'm not scared. He's not mad at me. He's mad at himself, for not being able to make me understand. "I'm not . . . I'm not saying they *all* do it. I'm saying it made me—made me realize they're just men. Flawed. Messed up like the rest of us. I don't need or want what they have to offer. Can't you see that?"

He lets out a long, slow breath. His whole face is slack, as if it's exhausted from the effort of saying those words, of getting them in the right sequence.

"If you want to go, I won't stop you, Kevin. Maybe it was wrong for me to pull you out of church. But I thought I was doing the right thing."

"I guess sometimes I miss it, is all. I liked having someone tell me the right thing to do."

Dad leans across the table to hold my gaze. "Remember something: You can't look outside of yourself for power. Or favor. That only comes from within."

I digest that for a moment. Then—because he won't stop staring at me—I nod.

He relaxes a little. "Anything else on your mind?"

Yeah, Dad. Like, I need to know—were you a traitor to your country? Am I following in your footsteps? Oh, and Mom called and she wants me to move out to California. How about all of that, Dad?

But I just can't bring myself to do it.

Instead, I get up and give him a big hug. He stands there for a second, surprised, not moving. But then he wraps his arms around me and crushes me to him, and for a moment I'm little again and Mom's here and Jesse's crawling on the floor somewhere maybe. Just for that moment. It's a lie, but it's a short one, and maybe that's not so bad.

But after Dad goes to bed, I sit up and think about it. I *do* miss Mass, to some degree at least. I liked knowing that every week—whether I needed it or not—I was going to be drenched in all the ceremony and goofy pomp of the Mass. I sort of wish they still did them in Latin. That way it would be this totally alien experience . . . but a good one. It's like you'd know that something good was happening to you but you wouldn't know the details. Which is sort of how I think about God, tell the truth.

But what I really miss, I guess, more than anything else is one sacrament in particular: penance and reconciliation. Non-Catholics just don't get it. They call it "confession" and they don't really glom on to the real meaning of it. It's not just about confessing your sins. It's about *apologizing* for them, telling God that you're sorry for not living up to expectations. And then you get forgiven for that.

That's all a lot more involved than just confessing.

So even though I used to have to stretch my imagination to come up with things worth confessing and even though it was nerve-wracking going up to Father McKane and talking about all the things I'd done, I always felt better afterward. You get it all off your chest, you get your penance, and all's right in the world.

Mom always hated the idea of me going to confession. "You're a child," she used to say. "Children haven't committed sins." But back then, Dad was hard-core religious, so I went. And I liked it. Mom didn't understand, but that was OK.

So the irony is that, tell the truth, I could *really* use a little penance and reconciliation right about now. I guess I could go to Mass on my own, but it would feel weird without Dad.

Instead, I just lay back on the sofa and stare up at the ceiling and tell God I'm sorry for all my sins and hope that he hears me and forgives me.

CHAPTER 22
GOD RESPONDS

NEXT DAY, LUNCHTIME, I'M UP ON THE CATWALK AGAIN. I want to die. I really, really do. I figure God didn't get my message last night. Either that, or he did and the answer was "Go screw yourself."

See, this morning John Riordon got his turn on the morning announcements.

He's a lot more telegenic than I am, but you'd have to be a burn victim with Parkinson's *not* to be. Still—the minute the TV screen lit up and there was John Riordon wearing a jacket and tie and a little flag pin in his lapel, his hair swept back, his teeth shining white . . . the minute I saw that image, my heart took on water and began to sink.

And then he opened his mouth and it only got worse.

"My father serves in the U.S. Army Reserve. Two months ago, he got an e-mail and he wouldn't talk about it for days. But it seems that some friends of his overseas had been ambushed and killed. Some of them lay in the sun for hours before they died. Don't they deserve our support?"

Every eye in the room swiveled to me for a second.

"I'm grateful for the opportunity to speak to you this morning, but I'm disappointed that it's even necessary. I don't understand why some people feel the need to prop themselves up by putting America down. Aren't we supposed to stand united, especially now, in a time of war? Why is it that some people think that the best time to ask questions and cause trouble is when things are the toughest?

"It's mystifying to me that this is even an issue. There are people in the world *right now* who are planning to kill all of us. I'm not making this up; we all know it's true. So why is it that when we're all in danger, when we're all of us—as a country—fighting for our lives . . . why is it that *now* some people choose to undermine us? And choose to undermine the brave men and women who are fighting and dying to keep us all safe from harm? Such words, such ideas, are more than merely offensive. They're incendiary. They *burn*. You might as well set the flag on fire."

At that, every single person in the room gasped. Even me. For different reasons, though. I was thinking, *I can't believe he's stooping so low.* Everyone else, I'm sure, was imagining me with a can of lighter fluid, a match, Old Glory, and a devilish look on my face. No doubt while high-fiving Osama bin Laden.

"Wartime is not debate time," John went on. "This is the greatest, freest country in the world. We have freedom of speech, but also freedom *not* to speak. Freedom to stand by our troops as they risk their lives and not question what they're doing or why. Questioning them while they're in harm's way is the most vile, reprehensible thing we can do. We owe them our support. Not our ambivalence. And if we can't give them that, well . . ."

He took a deep breath.

"Well, then maybe we should just shut the hell up."

All of South Brook High inhaled as one. "Hell" is pretty mild . . . but not when spoken over the morning announcements. Maybe I should have dropped the f-bomb in my speech or something.

John smiled. "Thank you for this opportunity. And God bless America."

I heard some people murmur it back at him as Dr. Goethe came on the screen, but by then I was already in some kind of alternate reality. An alternate reality made up of the surface of my desk and my hands, which lay there, twined together, white-knuckled. I could already feel the cold fury ramping up around me all around me.

And I realized something. I thought, *Oh, crap. Oh, man, I made a mistake. A big mistake.*

John is better *at this than I am.*

John is amazing *at this. It doesn't matter that he's wrong. He's* better.

I was dead.

But that wasn't even the worst part, believe it or not. I sat perfectly still through the rest of the announcements, totally silent, as if I could will myself invisible. Maybe even *better* than invisible. Maybe I could make myself . . . *inhistoric.* Sit quietly enough and people wouldn't just stop seeing me, but they would also totally forget I ever existed. That would be great.

No such luck, of course. The hallways on the way to first period were a smash-up derby for me—I was thrown into walls and lockers so many times (all "by accident," naturally) that my shoulders and arms and sides were throbbing and battered by the time I got to class.

I kept my head down, but I could feel everyone looking at me.

That's how the day went. And that was bad enough. But the worst thing of all . . .

The absolute worst thing of all . . .

Right before lunch.

Now, I'm not an idiot. I wasn't about to go to the cafeteria and suffer there. But on my way to the auditorium, I saw them.

Together.

Leah and John Riordon.

No, really. The two of them were standing in the hallway in this little nook created by a jutting wall from the office and the alcove for the elevator that only the kids in wheelchairs are allowed to use. They were just standing there, talking, only it was more than that, I could tell. She was leaning against the wall and he was leaning *toward* her, one palm against the same wall, leaning in, leaning.

God, it was so obvious!

She was smiling. He was smiling. He was still wearing his jacket, though he'd loosened the tie so that it hung around his neck like he'd just come home from a tough day of saving the world or something . . .

She laughed.

He laughed with her.

I made it into the auditorium and up the ladder in record time.

And, tell the truth, I'm thinking of not coming down. Or maybe going down the super-fast express.

I saved her *life!* I mean, seriously!

And what was all that crap the other day about "I really admire what you're doing"? What the hell was that?

My lunch is the usual junk because Dad never buys anything new, but I don't feel like eating anyway. I start pinching off pieces of bread, mashing them up into little balls, and throwing them down on the stage.

How can Leah admire what I'm doing and then go off with that . . .

Duh. Don't be an idiot, Kross.

All you need to do is look in the mirror. Studly and clear skin trumps goofy and pizza-face any day of the week.

I chuck another PBJ ball onto the stage and am rewarded with a familiar voice saying, "Hey!"

It's Fam. Great. My secret spot is blown.

She scrambles up the ladder like she's been doing it her whole life, not rattled at all by the way it shakes and shimmies and spazzes. I count three times when she *should* fall but somehow doesn't. The catwalk jerks and sways as she makes her way over to me.

"I was wondering where you got off to," she says as she sits down next to me. "So, this is your place, huh?" She looks around like she's admiring the space in my new apartment. "Not bad."

Well, I can never come *here* again. Great.

"At least you can't be seen with the America-hater."

I think this is the first time I've ever been alone with her. Why did she bother coming up?

Is she . . . Is she looking for a new boyfriend?

Ugh. I don't want that. I mean, Fam is . . . She's *Fam*. She's one of the guys. She's also so skinny that you could probably use her to snake a drain or something. She's got this cluster of pimples on her left temple that just never seems to go away, so she covers them with makeup, but you can still see the bumps. Maybe if we dated, we would have matching zits or something.

"Poor Kross," she says. "They're really raking you over the coals, aren't they?"

"Looks like it." Ugh. Still wondering: *Why is she here? What does she want?*

"Maybe you should . . ." She tilts her head like she's trying to get the thoughts to line up. "Flip said last night that you should use the hero thing to your advantage?" She's not sure. "You never even talk about it. You need to, like, remind people that you saved Leah Muldoon from being raped and killed by that guy. That'll shut them up."

The idea that I'm the subject of Flip and Fam's pillow talk really creeps me out.

"No. That's not the way to do it. It shouldn't matter what I did. I want to convince people because I'm *right*, not because I'm some . . . 'hero.'" But that's a lie—I don't want to talk about saving her life because I'm scared someone will ask a question that will lead to the truth.

She nods like she's glad I don't agree with her. Then again, it wasn't *her* idea—it was Flip's.

"I get it." She reaches out and pats my hand, once, then twice. Then . . .

Just . . .

Leaves . . .

It . . .

There.

Uh, what? Fam is holding my hand. Kinda.

It's like someone's shoved a steel rod down through my spine; suddenly I can't bend my neck or my back at all. I'm sitting upright like I'm in a posture class from hell.

"I want to help you, Kross," she says.

"I don't need help from a freshman."

She jerks her hand away. When I look over at her, her face has become a map of hurt.

"I'm not an idiot, Kross. I can help."

I don't say anything. She still wants to help me? After what I just said?

"I have the Internet at home. I know you don't. I can look things up for you. You know. If you need me to."

So now I feel like the worst person in the world. "I'm sorry. I shouldn't have said that. I'm just all . . ." All what? I don't even know. I don't know why I'm doing any of this.

I tell Fam that, saying it before I've even really decided to. It feels good to say it out loud.

"Maybe because it helps you?" she says. "Or takes your mind off of something else?"

And damn—she's right. For the most part, when I'm thinking about the ribbons and the flag and free speech, I'm *not* thinking about Leah and the damn videotape and the horrible truth.

She strokes my shoulder for a moment. "It'll be OK, Kevin." It's the first time she's ever used my real name as opposed to my Fool name. It sounds strange coming from her lips.

"Why are you even here?"

"I like you, Kevin." Kevin again.

"But . . . you're dating Flip."

Her face freezes except for her eyelids, which blink rapidly. Then, without warning, she barks out a loud, high laugh.

"Not like *that*, Kross! As a friend. A *good* friend. You were always the one who was nice to me. God, why do you have to be one of *those* guys?"

"What guys?"

"One of those guys who worship women."

I can't help laughing. "Yeah, as if."

She rolls her eyes. "Oh, puh-lease. I've seen you around girls. It's like you're way down here"—she holds a hand as far down as she can go—"and we're way up here." She stretches so that her other hand is up over her head. She looks like she should be saying, *No, I swear to God, that fish was* this *big!*

"I don't . . ." But I can't finish it because . . . Is that real? Is that me?

"It's like . . . It's like . . . " She stops stretching out and returns to normal and fumbles for words for a second like Dad. "It's like girls aren't real people."

"Hey! That's not fair. I know girls are—"

"They're *more* than real people," she says. "That's why we're way up high. It's like a girl is a treasure to you. Something to win or conquer. Or something so high up you can never get it. Untouchable. So it's like they might as well be nothing if you can never have one."

She folds her arms across her chest and nods triumphantly, which is a neat trick. I wish I knew how to nod triumphantly.

I don't want to answer her. Because, really, there's a grand total of two women in my life: Mom and Leah. One of them is three thousand miles away and untouchable and might as well be nothing. The other is right here and *still* untouchable and I *want* her to be like a treasure I could win or conquer, but in the end, she might as well be nothing, too.

Wow.

"You're, uh, you're pretty smart, Fam."

"For a freshman?"

"No. Period."

She grins at me. There's this part of me that wishes her smile made her beautiful, but it doesn't. And then I wonder if that matters at all. I think of my own smile, the one I hate.

"—treated me differently," she's saying.

"What?"

She rolls her eyes. "Come on. I'm not stupid. I know how everyone else reacted when Joey brought me into the Council." It takes me half a second to remember: Joey=Flip.

"Jedi was really pissed," she remembers. "Speedo never once looked in my eyes when he was talking to me—he was always looking at my boobs."

What boobs? I think. Which is mean, but true.

"Tit would hardly talk to me at all. But you were nice, Kross. Even nicer than Joey, if you want to know the truth. And when you saved Leah, I knew you were a good guy." She smiles at me, and it's really not a bad smile, but it just makes me feel worse.

"Fam, what if I told you . . ." I stop. No. No way.

"Told me what?"

What if I told you the truth? That I'm no hero. That on that day, I . . .

"Nothing." I can't do it. I change the subject: "If Flip isn't nice to you, why do you stay with him?"

"Oh, he's not so bad. All boys are jerks in high school."

"Not me."

"Oh, yeah? What about what you just said a minute ago?"

"Right. Sorry."

She leans in and for a second I'm afraid she's going to kiss me. And then she *does* kiss me, but it's just a light little brushing of her lips on my pockmarked cheek.

"Stay strong, Kevin. You're a good guy, and you're doing the right thing."

She scampers down the ladder and disappears.

I wish I could be sure she was right.

SELF-LOATHING #3

No one understands. But how *can* they understand? They don't live my life. They don't think my thoughts. My damn thoughts.

If I could somehow *purge* my brain, just flush it out . . . That would fix everything. I need something like that stuff you use when the shower is clogged and the water won't go down, only for my brain. I need to flush out Leah and then I need to flush out Mom and Jesse because Leah is what I used to flush out Mom and Jesse in the first place, right?

I feel terrible about it all. I can't help it—being Catholic means you feel bad about pretty much everything all the time.

Here's how we deal with guilt in my family: We pretend the thing we feel guilty about doesn't exist anymore. So Dad has no pictures of Mom anywhere in the house. I have one in my wallet, but that's it. And there's one picture of Jesse on the coffee table, but Dad never looks at it.

I try not to look at it either. I don't call Jesse a lot. We e-mail or IM sometimes when I'm at school or the library, but that's it.

It's just that . . . I mean, I was his hero. I was his big

brother, his defender. I took care of him when Mom and Dad were too busy fighting to do it.

And then I let him down.

I messed everything up. That's my life, really—one long string of messing things up. Even saving Leah. Even that was messed up. I didn't even do that right.

These days, I have to struggle to figure out exactly how bad a person I am. Because there's the secret I keep, the secret about that day with Leah and the Surgeon. And that's pretty bad. I mean, that one alone is sending me to hell.

But then there's what I did to Jesse.

Poor kid. He was only seven. He worshiped me. I was his hero.

I don't think he really got it. He knew that he'd packed up all of his stuff and that big burly guys had come and put it on a truck. Mom had showed him the map on the computer and how they were moving all the way to California. But I don't think it really clicked with him that *I* wasn't going. That *Dad* wasn't going.

And it didn't help that my parents were so damn clueless. They just made it worse. They weren't real smart about it. I guess they weren't thinking . . .

See, they had all of us go to the airport together. The moving truck had left a couple of days ago and now Mom and Jesse were flying together out to California. Dad and I drove them and walked them to the security gate and Dad gave Jesse this big hug and said, "Be good for your mother." And I wouldn't hug Mom—even though she held out her arms and waited patiently, I wouldn't do it, and I didn't want to hug Jesse either because then it was real, but he was my little brother. I had to do it.

So I hugged him and I said, "Bye, Jesse. I love you."

And that's what did it.

As I pulled away from him, I could see it in his eyes. He suddenly got it. He was going away. Three thousand miles away. And Dad and me weren't going with him. He might never see us again, for all he knew.

He started screaming. I mean, he was wailing and bawling like you wouldn't believe. It was mortifying. He wasn't a little kid, you know? He was seven, almost eight, but he didn't care. He screamed and cried at the top of his lungs. For me. For Dad. Even for Mom, which was weird because he was going with Mom.

Mom and Dad jumped into action. It was the first time I'd seen them do something together in a long time. They were trying to calm him down, trying to distract him or at least get him to quiet down a little bit. But nothing was working. He was just out of control, a little scream machine with the volume cranked all the way up.

There had been some kind of terrorist threat recently, so there was all kinds of extra security there. They were watching us. And people were slowing down to look. And the people in the security line had nothing better to do than stare, and my little brother was just determined to give them all a hell of a show. Nothing my parents did could stop him. I tried to get in there to help, thinking that maybe that dumb-ass story about Pandazilla and Aquahorse would work one more time, but Mom just pushed me back and Jesse kept putting out the decibels.

Finally, I couldn't take it anymore. I don't know where it came from, but I just screamed at him: "Jesse! Just shut the hell up and get on the plane!"

They were the magic words. They didn't just shut up Jesse—they shut up the whole world. Everyone just stopped talking and looked at me. Mom and Dad stared. Security guys, random people—they all watched.

And my little brother hitched all his sobs back into his chest. He had snot running out of his nose and tears streaming down his face and he was now suddenly completely silent as he looked at me like I'd kicked him in the head.

I felt like the lowest form of life on the planet.

Mom wiped up his face. She took his hand and led him to the security line. He didn't fight it.

He kept his head turned the whole time, though, watching me. Watching me until I finally turned away and made Dad take me home.

CHAPTER 23
THEY BUILD YOU UP

AT THE END OF THE DAY, BEFORE I ESCAPE TO MY CAR and to the relative safety of home, I go to the media center. Mrs. Grant is cleaning up some books and papers at the circulation desk. All the lights are off. She gives me a look that's a modification of Fam's dog-to-the-vet look. It's worse because it's an adult doing it. When adults pity you, you know you're screwed.

"Can I help you, Kevin?"

Yeah, can you cut my head off and file it somewhere where future generations of idiots can learn from my example?

I don't say it, of course. Duh.

"No, I just . . ." I stop because I don't want to finish what I was going to say. It's so pathetic. I came here to ask her how she thought I did compared to Riordon. When I decided to do it, it seemed OK—she was impartial and nice and maybe I did better than I thought.

But now, standing here, with her giving me that dog-to-the-vet look . . . I'm doing what Mom calls "fishing for compliments."

"Never mind," I tell her, and I turn to go.

"Wait." She comes around the desk. "Stay for a minute."

"I don't want to keep you."

"I'm not rushing off anywhere. What's on your mind?"

I can't ask her how I did in the debate. That's just sad. But I *can* ask her what she thinks about the issue itself, right? That's not pathetic. That's just getting information.

So I ask her. Who did she agree with—me or John?

She gives me this nervous little laugh. "It doesn't matter what I think."

"Come on. Please?"

She sighs. "Look. My generation messed up a lot of things. We did a lot right, but we messed up a lot, too. But here's the thing—we tried. We marched and we protested and we complained until things changed. We didn't always change the right things and we didn't always get our way, but we tried. And I'm glad to see you trying, Kevin. *That's* what matters."

Um, no—that's the same old adult bull they sling when they're trying to avoid bad news. *Hey, Dad, I went 0 for 4 at the plate and dropped an easy fly ball!*

Well, you tried, son. That's what matters.

No, what matters is I *suck.*

"Tell me the truth: Do you think I'm right or do you think John's right? Just tell me. I can take it."

"Well, look. I probably shouldn't say, but . . . I think you're right."

I can't help it—a happy little "Yes!" slips out.

"Don't go celebrating," she warns me. "I was predisposed to agree with you in the first place. You didn't convince me of anything. I felt the same way from the start."

"But I'm right, right? I mean, I'm not losing my mind or anything—John's wrong."

"Well, *I* think so."

"Then why is everyone listening to him instead?"

She leans against the circulation desk. She looks really, really tired. "People—especially young people—can be swayed pretty easily by something attractive. A slick presentation. A sophisticated message. If you make a complicated issue seem simple, you can get a lot of people on your side, even if you're wrong and even if it's not true."

"That sucks."

"That's what I try to teach you in Media. Just because something looks professional or has high production values or is nice and shiny and neat doesn't mean that it's right."

"But the shiny stuff will always have an advantage?" Man, that's depressing.

She echoes my thoughts: "As depressing as it sounds . . . yes. Sorry, Kevin."

And on that lovely note, I head home.

I flip around the radio stations, stopping to listen to a story on NPR. I learn how many soldiers have died or been wounded recently, about the threat level, about the things the president says we need to do to defeat "the evildoers." Which is such a weird and wimpy way of describing them, really. It makes them sound like goofy-ass mad scientists, rubbing their hands together and cackling . . .

Make a complicated issue seem simple . . .

Maybe that's the point.

Most of the cars I see on the way home have new ribbons on them, replaced almost immediately after the Council's theft. As if people couldn't bear the thought of *not* having them for even an instant. As if they feared *other* people would judge them. I do see one homemade bumper sticker that gives me a chuckle, though: COURAGE IS BEING A LIBERAL IN LOWE COUNTY.

But that's the only thing that makes me feel like maybe the *whole* universe isn't against me.

Well, what did I expect—the world to change just because I gave a speech on the morning announcements?

My key chain dangles from the ignition. The key to Brookdale clings and clangs and makes me feel even worse. Why do I keep it? It's like a reminder of all my lies, all my fears. God.

I keep thinking about Riordon's speech. It's better than thinking about Riordon macking on Leah and Leah just lapping it up. There are so many weaknesses in his argument it's ridiculous. But now I think that's my own fault. I went into this with the wrong attitude. I mean, I *know* that I'm right. Which means that the other side is wrong.

My mistake was thinking that if they're wrong, they must be stupid.

Man, *that* sends a chill right up and down my spine. I always thought that the wrong side was wrong because they were too dumb to get the truth. But Riordon proved that the wrong side can be *smart*. And that's worse than them being stupid. Because it means that they can convince the people who *are* stupid that they're right.

Jeez. What a tool. Burning a flag. Like I would do that.

At home, Dad's not making corn bread today, unfortunately. He's watching a ball game that he taped last night instead. I try not to disturb him. We've never talked about that stuff Reporter Guy published about Dad, and it's like I've been tiptoeing around it ever since.

And I'm sick of it.

I wait for a commercial and then make my move: "Hey, Dad?" Before he can say anything, I plunge on in: "I'm really sorry."

"What? Why? What did you do?"

My throat goes dry, just like when Leah came up to me in the cafeteria.

"About the . . . You know, Dad. The paper. The *Loco*."

He stares at me so hard that I imagine I can feel him pushing me away just by force of eyesight.

"What are you *talking* about? That wasn't your fault."

"But—but he wouldn't have written that if he wasn't writing about *me* . . ."

"No, no, no." Dad gets up, shaking his head. "No. Listen to me: He's writing about you because you got rid of those ribbons, which is what *I* told you to do. But if it wasn't that it would have been something else because that's what these people do—they build you up and then they tear you down."

"But—"

"No. That's all ancient history anyway." He gets a soda from the fridge and returns to his chair just as the game comes back on. "Don't worry about it. It's done and over with."

OK, that *totally* isn't what I expected. After a lifetime of being told never to talk about Dad and the army and all that, suddenly it's just, like, "Don't worry about it" and "It's my fault." Which it is, because he *did* make me get rid of those ribbons.

I flop on the bed and watch the game with him for a little while. Maybe he's not as messed up in the head as I always thought.

Or maybe I'm just getting messed up enough that he's starting to make sense to me.

Either way, though, I have to admit he's got more experience at . . . well, just about everything. So I might as well use it.

Another commercial comes up. Dad reaches to fast-forward the tape, but I jump in:

"Hey, Dad. How do you stop people from being stupid?"

He grunts and rolls his eyes. "You don't."

"Really?" You're kidding me. I thought for sure that at some point someone must have figured this out.

"I've tried to explain to people when they're being stupid," he says, "but then I realized something: Most people *like* being stupid."

"I don't get it."

He pauses the game as it comes back from commercial. "Some people just prefer it. It makes their lives easier if they let other people think for them."

"But that doesn't make any sense. That's just stu . . . Oh."

He nods in satisfaction and starts the game again.

"Hey, Dad?"

He does one of those hiss-y inhales that makes me think I've bugged him one too many times, but then he pauses the game. "Yeah?"

"What, uh, what do you think about flag burning?" Riordon's jab is still bugging me.

"You planning on burning a flag?" he asks with such stern disapproval that I feel guilty for something I've never even contemplated doing.

"No."

"Well, good. I mean, it would be a stupid thing to do. You'd get people so riled up that they'd miss the point. There are better ways to get your opinions across."

"But what about the people who *do?*"

He shrugs. "Who cares, really?"

"But the flag's, like, a *symbol* of our country. People died for it."

"When I was only a little bit older than you . . . There was a picture, OK? *That* picture . . ."

He shakes his head. Clears it. It's a good talking day for Dad, I guess. "I remember seeing a picture. In the paper. The collapse. You know, the collapse of the Soviet Union. A Russian soldier, burning a Soviet flag. You see? If *he* can . . . I remember thinking to myself, 'If he's free enough to do that over *there* . . .' Isn't that what it's all about, Kevin?"

Well, OK. Tell the truth, I'm not 100 percent sure what the Soviet Union is or was. But anyway, I get his point—if people in other countries can burn their flags, then shouldn't we be allowed to, here in this, "the freest country in the world" according to John Riordon?

"Thanks, Dad."

He nods sort of dreamily, like he's glad he doesn't have to talk anymore. Did he always know this kind of stuff, back when I wasn't listening to him? It's tough to know someone's smart when they don't talk. Mom always said he was smart, but Mom also said she loved him.

I stay up late thinking about it all. Dad's right: People will stay stupid if they can. And in being right, he confirmed what I was thinking before, so that's cool.

What people don't get is that symbols may be great, but they're just *symbols*, right? And the problem with a symbol is that you don't always know what it means, or what it means to someone else. So you think you're on the same page, but you're not. If it took us hours of arguing in English class and we still couldn't agree on what the moors symbolize in *Wuthering Heights,* how the hell can we assume we all agree on what the *flag* symbolizes?

I saw a guy on TV once who said that the flag didn't symbolize freedom—it symbolized years of slavery and oppression. I don't really agree with that, but who am I to tell him he's wrong?

So it's like everyone can dump whatever meaning they want on a symbol, which means that you can't really rely on it. You can't be sure it means what you think it means, so it's better to go to the truth of the matter, to the meanings themselves.

Right?

My head hurts. This stuff is complicated. I'm not used to it.

OK, here's the thing—no one died for the flag, for the symbol. That's stupid. They died for what the symbol *represents*.

I mean, the flag represents freedom. To me, at least. And that's fine and I'd probably be willing to die to protect my freedom.

But would I be willing to die to protect the *flag*? Duh—no! It's just a flag. It's just a piece of fabric. *No one* would die for that. Even the people who think flag burning is wrong—if you put them in that position, I bet they'd choose their own lives instead.

In fact, around about midnight, I have something of a revelation, which is very cool. The right to burn the flag is the greatest possible symbol of our freedoms. That's what I realize.

So, I consider burning a flag at school. Just to make my point. Leah couldn't *help* but be impressed, right?

Only it wouldn't be a *real* flag. It would be one with forty nine stars. Or one with a single off-white stripe. Or something like that. Some tiny, minuscule difference, just to show how stupid it is to get upset about it. Because, like, burning that extra star somehow makes it terrorism or what Father McKane used to call "apostasy"? (I love that word. It sounds cool when you say it, but how often do you actually get to use it? *Apostasy*.)

But two things stop me: One, Dad's right. The act of burning the flag would get everyone so pissed off they would miss my point.

And second of all—I don't know where to get a flag with just forty nine stars or a single off-white stripe.

So, I settle for a rebuttal. It's not fair that Riordon got to critique everything I said but I didn't get the chance to bash him back. I'll take up Fam's offer to help and I'll go to the Doc and demand a rebuttal.

I drift in and out of sleep. I've got Dad and Fam and Leah and Dr. Goethe and Reporter Guy all yelling and screaming and cajoling inside my head, and who can sleep with *that* kind of racket going on?

Mom joins in the chorus, too. I still haven't told Dad about her offer. I need to, but I can't for some reason. I mean, I'm definitely going. There's no question about it. I'm going. I need to get away from Brookdale, away from the whole hero/villain thing, away from Leah, because . . . Because it's not good for me to be around Leah.

I think of what I *really* wanted to ask Dad: Is it true what they said in the *Loco*? Did you betray your country? What happened, Dad?

I mean, I *need to know*. Because I feel like I'm following in his footsteps, in a way. And I need to know if it's the right thing to do, or if I'm gonna end up pissed off and depressed and just plain messed up, emptying garbage cans for a living.

So after Dad leaves for work in the armpit of the morning, I start snooping through his stuff.

It takes longer than I figured it would. Dad's bedroom is tiny, but, like the rest of the apartment, it's piled high with all kinds of un-garbage. Three broken vacuum cleaners, one of those powered mop things with a cracked plastic case, the guts of a computer monitor, and two different nightstands with the drawers removed and stacked up in a corner.

I go pawing through all the junk, looking for hidden stuff, then go through the dresser. Dad's clothes, in total opposition to the surroundings, are folded and stacked all military-like. I'm very careful handling them—for all I know, Dad has memorized exactly how everything is positioned.

Nothing in the dresser, so I move to the tiny closet. There's boxes of my stuff in there, things I haven't looked at in years. I don't let myself get caught up in it, though—I have a mission.

At the bottom of the closet, way in the back, I find a shoebox that doesn't look all that sexy, so there's gotta be *something* in it for Dad to have kept it. I sit there for a second, holding the box, and I'm sure that when I open it it's going to actually *be* shoes, because that's the way my luck seems to run.

Instead, there are two smaller boxes inside, and some papers. I try to read the papers, but it's all military gobbledegook and my brain gives up because the boxes are much more interesting.

I open them.

Wow.

Medals.

CHAPTER 24
VERY ACTION-MOVIE-HERO-ISH

NOW, MY DAD HAS TOLD ME IN THE PAST that the army gives out medals at the drop of a hat. They have medals just for being in the army during a time of war, for example, whether you fought in that war or not. (Dad calls that one the "CNN Medal" because you get it for watching the war on TV.) They give you medals when you pass certain tests. So just having medals doesn't necessarily mean anything.

But I recognize one of them—a Purple Heart.

The other one is shaped like a stop sign. It has an eagle on one side and says, SOLDIER'S MEDAL FOR VALOR on the other.

Valor. That doesn't sound like something they give to guys who betray their country.

I sit there on the floor for a long time, staring at those medals. I have a lot of trouble imagining my dad as a guy who would do something that would be medal-worthy. He's just, you know, my dad. Everyone has a dad. Most of them are nothing special. Mine hauls garbage and is surly a lot and can never finish a thought when it's a really important one and can barely cook enough food to keep himself alive. What could he have done that's so great that the army would give him two medals?

And what did he do that was so bad that they kicked him out?

I put everything back where I found it and go back to bed, but now any chance of sleeping is totally shot.

I have to know.

It's three in the morning, so in California it's only midnight. Mom and Rita are probably already asleep, but I can't help it—I watch my hand pick up the phone, watch my fingers punch the number in.

Mom picks it up on the third ring. Her voice is clotted with sleep. "John?" she says. "Did something happen to Kevin?"

"It's me, Mom."

"What are . . . Do you know what time it is?"

"Yeah."

"Is something wrong, honey? Is your dad OK?"

"Yeah, Mom. Look, I'm sorry I woke you up, but I have to ask you something."

"Wait. Hold on. Can't this wait until morning?"

"It *is* morning."

"I know. I just meant . . .'

"*Please*, Mom."

A long sigh. And then I hear her say something that's not meant for me. Talking to Rita, I guess. And then: "Hold on. I'm switching phones."

And then she's on a different line and Rita hangs up the bedroom phone. "What is it? What do you need to know? Is this about coming out here?"

"No. Mom, why was Dad kicked out of the army?"

She doesn't say anything for a little while. I sort of expect her to explode at me, to be all like: "You woke me up for *this*?"

Instead, she says, "Honey, I don't think we should talk about that."

"Come on, Mom. Don't I deserve to know?"

"You don't need to know about this. Really. Maybe when you're out here we can sit down and talk about it. You know, face to face. But I just . . ."

"Come on, Mom. Please."

It takes some time, but she's tired and I'm persistent and I wear her down and she tells me.

She tells me everything.

I hang up and I manage to get a little bit of sleep before I have to leave for school. When I grab my keys in the morning, though, I can't help looking at the key to Brookdale hanging there. It's like my own personal medal, I realize.

They build you up and then they tear you down, Dad said.

And he would know. He would know.

I head to school with a sort of righteous fire burning in my belly and run off to the office before the bell can ring for homeroom.

"I want another chance," I tell Dr. Goethe.

He looks at me from behind his desk, his eyes weary and his face a little flushed. I think of all the trouble he went through last year when Flip hacked the lacrosse team's grades and I feel a little bit sorry for him, but no one's keying *his* new car and following *him* home from school and cornering *him* in the locker room, so the sympathy doesn't last very long, tell the truth.

"Kevin, this is over."

"The debate on free speech is *never* over." It just kind of spills out of me, but I like the way it sounds. Very action-movie-hero-ish. There should be music playing in the background.

"You had your say. John had his say. Let's put an end to this, OK?"

"But, Dr. Goethe—"

"But nothing. You're here to learn, Kevin. Not to take potshots at each other on the morning announcements. I let you and John have some time and some fun because I felt it was an important lesson for your classmates. But it's time to get back to the business of learning."

Fun? He thinks this is *fun?* I want to know what he's smoking and if I can have some of it, because I could *use* a good dose of fun right about now!

"But he made it sound like I—"

The bell rings for homeroom. Dr. Goethe sighs and scribbles out a hall pass for me.

"Get to homeroom. If you want to discuss free speech and the flag and the war, that's what social studies classes are for."

I stand there for a second, trying to marshal up some truly awesome, Dad-worthy comment, something that will twist Goethe's brain in his shiny chrome-like head and make him rethink everything.

But all I can think of is "Blind faith in your leaders or in anything will get you killed."

Which doesn't impress him, even though it should.

"Get going, Kevin."

SELF-LOATHING #4

I SULK THROUGH HOMEROOM because there's nothing else for me to do, not with everyone glaring at me.

Last night, apparently, Flip Photoshopped up a picture of Officer Sexpot linked arm in arm in a chorus line with the president (from his photo op in an air force uniform) and Hitler and an old picture of Saddam Hussein, with a word balloon coming out of Officer Sexpot's mouth that said, "I just LOVE a man in uniform!" The picture was blasted out to every e-mail address Flip could get his hands on, as well as hacked into the *Lowe County Times* website and the Lowe County Board of Education website. It was scrubbed pretty quickly, but not before everyone saw it. The *Times* described it in the morning edition, but they didn't show it, which is weird because Flip had OSP dressed up in her police uniform, so it's not like she was naked or anything.

I keep my head down in the halls and in classes. It's Wednesday, and I always see Leah on her way to trig. I usually love these glimpses, but now Riordon's ruined them, like a thumb covering part of a photo. He's always with her, making moves on her and she just eats it up. She's all giggly and flirty and batting her eyelashes-y, and tell the truth, there's a moment—just a little moment, a moment*let*, but it's there—when I think to myself that I wish I hadn't done something that day at the library, that I'd looked over and thought to myself, *This is none of my business*, and moved on.

Is that mean? Does that make me unlikable? I don't really care. It's real and it's honest and it's true, and I guess *you've* never had a single cruel or unpleasant thought in your life, huh? Get off my back.

Tell the Truth

CHAPTER 25
THE KEY OPENS SOMETHING

BACK UP ON THE CATWALK AGAIN, but this time I eat my lunch because I figure that I'm pretty much at war at this point and Dad is fond of saying, "An army travels on its stomach." Which, when I was little, I took literally and I imagined a hundred thousand guys crawling along the sand on their bellies.

So I eat my gross lunch, reminding myself that it's just fuel for the mission. I have to think of a way to get my side of the story out. I have to think of a way to counteract what Riordon said. I know Dad thinks that people like to be stupid, but I can't believe that. I have to believe that if you shake people hard enough, they'll eventually wake up.

Yeah, wake up. Wake up to the truth. But the truth's a funny thing. People think they know the truth about me, for example, but they don't. And maybe that's the problem. Maybe I don't deserve to be right. Maybe God is punishing me for my sins. My lies.

The ladder rattles; the catwalk shakes. Fam pops up.

"Hey."

"Hi." Since she hasn't told anyone about my little hiding place, I don't mind so much sharing it with her.

"How'd it go with the Doc?"

I had told Tit I was planning to demand a rebuttal. Word spreads fast in the Council.

"Not so good."

She sits down next to me, dangling her chicken legs over the side. I'm skinny, but Fam is anorexic. If I hadn't personally witnessed her inhaling an order of hot wings at Cincinnati Joe's on more than one occasion, I would think she was *literally* anorexic.

"That sucks," she says. "What are you gonna do now?"

I hadn't really thought much beyond being an army and traveling on my stomach. "I don't know. If the Doc won't let me talk, I don't have many options. I might have to do something big and stupid." I tell her my unformed plan to burn a pseudo-American flag.

"Where would you get one?" she asks.

"Yeah, that's what stopped me, too."

We sit in silence for a little while.

She kicks out her feet like she's on a swing. "Man. I was all excited. I thought he'd let you talk again for sure. I even started some research for you." And then she starts babbling something about Sweden and Norway and other countries and stuff like that, but I'm sort of distracted and I'm only half listening.

". . . quotes from *Colin Powell*," she babbles. "I mean, that's pretty cool, right? And there was this Supreme Court justice who said that—"

"Hey, Fam, can we cool it for, like, five minutes?" I snap it out and I didn't really mean to. I just need to clear my head.

She looks like I smacked her in the face. My inner Catholic starts yelling at me.

"Look, I'm sorry. I didn't mean it like that. I'm just really stressed, is all."

She shrugs. "I get it. OK. I'm sorry. I was just trying to help."

"No, no, it's cool, and I appreciate it and all. I just needed to open up the safety valve for a couple of minutes. Is that cool?"

Fam nods and I feel this sudden, insane urge to hug her. I turn, and I guess the urge is contagious because she leans toward me. Before I can stop myself, I put my arms around her. It's all weird and awkward because we're sitting with our legs dangling over the catwalk, so we're sort of twisted and it's not comfortable and besides, it's *Fam*, so what the hell am I thinking?

And then—thank God—there's a stabbing pain in my thigh.

"Ow!" I pull away. Fam's confused.

I sat on my keys. I dig into my pocket for them and show them to her. She gets it.

The key to Brookdale dangles there. Reminding me: Hero. Zero. Liar. And worse.

Damn. I'm starting to hate this thing.

After school, the truly bizarre happens: Leah marches up to me in the parking lot. I look around quickly—there aren't many people around, and most of them are seniors, who have better things to do, I guess, than watch me.

"Are you still coming Friday?" she asks, and I can't read what's in her eyes as she asks it. Which is no big surprise. If I was able to read her eyes at all, I would have known enough to ask her out a couple of years ago. Or just plain given up.

"Do you still want me to?" I say it *really* mean, with every last ounce of mean in my body. I load it down with mean. She deserves it, Miss Flirty-with-Idiot-Riordon.

The meanness goes right over her head, because she looks at me kinda shocked. "Of course I do! Why wouldn't I?"

And then, before I can point out *exactly* why, she says, "I really admire what you're saying. What you're doing. So please come."

"Leah . . ."

"Look, I know you don't necessarily get along with all of my friends. I'm not stupid. But I don't let my friends tell me who to hang out with or who to like. Besides, you owe me a favor."

My jaw drops. Oh, crap! What is she talking about? What does she know?

She laughs, and it's this great, innocent, friendly laugh. "I'm joking! I owe *you*, Kevin. I owe you everything. So let me start by making sure you have fun Friday, OK?" She hugs me quickly, so quickly that I don't even have a chance to register fear or excitement over it, and then she traipses off to her car before I can come up with a response.

I'm now officially weirded out. It was unofficial before, but now all of the papers have been stamped.

I don't get it. She hangs on Riordon's every word, worships the ground he walks on, flirts with him . . . But she admires what I'm doing? What I'm saying?

What world am I living in, and do the trees grow upside down here?

Gah! I kick my tire just because I can, and it makes me feel better. Then I drive to the Burger Joint. It's one of the restaurants that offered me free meals for life. Tit and Speedo wanted to meet there and chill.

As soon as I walk in, though, I'm nervous. What if Carl has changed his mind after my recent, you know, *apostasy?* Late afternoon, the place is almost empty before the dinner rush. Carl spies me and comes around the counter, wiping his greasy hands on the once-white apron that covers his enormous belly. "Hey, hey, it's Batman!" he says. He snaps his fingers to one of his wage-slaves. "Batman here gets whatever he wants, on the house. These guys, the Robins"—he points over my shoulder at Tit and Speedo, who've just come in—"gotta pay."

We sit down. I feel bad about all the free food I scammed from Carl when I worked here a couple of summers ago. But not *too* bad—I order more food than I can eat and share it with Tit and Speedo.

They both know about being shot down by the Doc already. Speedo hoists his Coke for a toast. "You had a good run, Kross. You tried. *L'chaim.*"

"*Skol,*" says Tit, and downs his Dr Pepper.

"I don't want this to be the end, though, guys. I want to keep it up."

Speedo laughs. When he laughs, he gets a double chin. We call it his face flab. "Oh, yeah. Good idea. No offense, but you weren't exactly raking in the converts, you know?"

"I had one." I say it under my breath, but they hear me anyway.

"Who?" says Tit.

"Yeah, who?"

"No one. Never mind." I'm not going to tell them about Leah. It's useless.

"Come on. Who?"

"Who?"

I'm resolute. But it's tough to keep things from a Fool, because, basically, we're really damn annoying. Five seconds later, Tit is singing "Who?" at the top of his lungs and Speedo is making like an owl.

"Whooooo? Whooooo? Ah-whooooooo!"

"Who-who-who! Who-who-who!"

We start getting looks from the few people here. "Guys, cut it out."

Tit accompanies himself with a drumbeat on the table. Speedo leans back and owl-calls to the ceiling at the top of his lungs.

"Whooooo?" Bum-bum-bum. "Whooooo?" Bum-bum-bum. "Ah-whooooooo!" Bum-bum-bum*bum!*

"Who-who-who! Who-who-WHO!"

"OK, OK! I give! Jeez!"

"Spill." Tit's eyes shine. As soon as I say Leah's name, they widen.

Speedo's shocked, too, but only Tit can truly understand how big a deal this is.

"So is she gonna say something?" Speedo asks.

"I doubt it. She's not getting involved." *Because she's got the hots for Riordon,* I don't add.

Speedo whistles. Tit hasn't said a word. He just looks at me like . . . I don't know.

When Speedo goes to the bathroom, Tit leans over the

table, leans in close. "Kross. I'm just gonna say this once. All this stuff you're doing and you've been doing: Are you sure you're doing it for the right reasons?"

I almost give him a serious verbal smackdown, but here's what stops me: No. I'm *not* sure.

An hour later, stuffed to the gills with way more food than any three people should be able to eat at one sitting (paid for with way less money than is reasonable), we split up in the parking lot. I pull my keys out of my pocket and stand there for a second, mesmerized by the key to Brookdale.

I remember looking at it before, when I was with Fam. *Listening* to Fam. Listening while she prattled on about . . .

About . . .

Sweden . . .

And then, amazingly, the key opens something. It opens my brain right up and it hits me: The perfect idea. To wake people up, to make a point that they can't ignore. It's scary and it's genius.

So I stand there for a minute, just totally buzzing—*vibrating*—with this great idea and no one to tell it to. I need to tell Flip. And Fam. They're probably together and I would call them on their cells . . . if I had a cell.

(Well, actually, I have thirty-seven cell phones back home. But none of them works. Thanks, Dad.)

Terrific. Here I am, busting with a great idea, and there's no one around to tell it to. I clench my keys in my fist until my fingers scream in pain, and then I have no choice but to get into the car and drive away.

CHAPTER 26
THERE'S THIS GIRL . . .

STILL PSYCHED ABOUT MY IDEA, I cruise over to the mayor's car dealership because I have to fill out some final paperwork. The mayor isn't happy to see me. I know this because when I get out of the car he shakes his head and says, "I can't say I'm happy to see you."

I get some lecture-y talk about respect and such, about how he bent over backwards to give me such a great deal on the car and would it really hurt me to leave the ribbons there, and you know, Kevin, my name is on that car, too, right here on the little plaque on the bumper, so when you drive it, you speak for me, too, and look at this, it's all scratched up already and I don't know, Kevin, I really thought you were different, I really, really did.

In the end, there's some kind of paperwork snafu and he claims that he needs to hold on to the car for a day or two to process some kind of warranty information, which I think is total bull, especially since he's got this smarmy grin on his face the whole time, but what am I supposed to do about it?

So now I'm car-less.

The car people let me use their phone to call Flip.

Flip, fortunately, has a lot of free time on his hands. Which is why he's in charge of the Council. "Idle hands are the

Fool's playthings," he's said to me a million times, which is kind of annoying because I know what the saying is *really*, and it makes me wonder if some of the other stuff he says that sounds so smart and so original is really just gakked from other people.

So anyway, he's cool with picking me up and chauffeuring me around a little bit. He comes over in his beat-up orange coupe. Fam's riding shotgun, but Flip makes her get in the back so that I can sit up front.

I don't really like that. I don't know *why* I don't like it, but it bugs me. Always has. Why can't she sit up front? But because I'm me, of course I don't say anything.

"So, I've got this great idea for a Council prank," Flip says as we pull out of the lot.

"Hold on. Me, too."

Flip frowns. *He's* the leader, after all.

"That's great, Kross. My idea is that on Friday we go to SAMMPark—"

"I can't do Friday."

"Council meeting Friday," Flip goes on, as if he hasn't heard a word I've said. "Officer Sexpot is going to take things to the next level, and your presence is requested."

"Flip, I can't do Friday. Really. And *my* idea—"

"Dial it back to chill, Kross. Everything else has merely been a prelude. This is going to be the *true* return of Officer Sexpot. Up till now, we've been dicking with national issues. But that doesn't really hit people where they live—Friday we're gonna wake Brookdale up."

"That's great, but listen, Flip. If you do *my* idea, you'll get a lot more attention."

"All this patriotic crap is boring," he goes on. "There's only so much humor in it, you know? Besides, it's too easy. There's nothing sexy about it. No imagination. 'Oh, boo-hoo! Someone doesn't love America! Oh, woe is me!' Whatever."

I grit my teeth. Flip just hates it when he's not in control, and right now he isn't. He's not in charge of anything. I'm tempted to tell him that, but I still need him. "Look, there's a lot we can do with the patriotic stuff. There's a lot of good points to be made."

"We make mischief, not points."

"I thought we were supposed to do both at the same time. Isn't that why we do *any* of this?"

He shrugs. "We do the things I *say* we do."

I can't win. "I'm telling you, my idea is better. And seriously, I can't do anything Friday anyway."

It finally sinks in. Flip glances over at me and raises an eyebrow, something he thinks makes him look very adult but actually only makes him look very lopsided. "Excuse me, Fool Kross? Are you really bailing on the Council and the ultimate triumph of Officer Sexpot?"

"I have a party to go to." Ugh. As soon as it's out of my mouth, it sounds ridiculous. *I have a party to go to.* Like I'm a starlet or something.

"A night with Dionysus or a night with Loki. It's your choice, Kross."

Man, I hate when he does that. "I don't know what you're talking about."

"A party happens and then it ends." Now he sounds like a professor somewhere. "You go, you drink, you potentially get laid"—he looks over at me again, as if appraising my chances and wondering what's lower than zero—"and then the next day it's over and that's it.

"But a night with the Council lives in infamy. This latest exploit of Officer Sexpot's will be the pièce de résistance, the tête-à-tête, the crème de la crème of Foolish behavior."

I believe him. I really do. Flip doesn't do anything halfway, and if he's got something new worked up for Officer Sexpot, then I'm sure it's better than the other Officer Sexpot pranks we've pulled this year. But it's Leah. How do I explain that to him?

I give it a really lame shot: "There's this girl . . ." And I stop because Fam's in the back seat and you don't talk about chicks when other chicks are present. That's pretty high on the Guy Rule List. And besides, where do I go from there? *There's this girl and she doesn't give a crap about me, but I follow her around like a stupid puppy dog anyway* . . . I'm an idiot.

"Ah! Are you in love, Kross? Are you? Because that would be a supremely foolish thing to do at your age." I hear no capital letter that time. And by the way—oh, please. He's only a year older than I am. "You should be thinking of many, many girls, dancing wenches garbed for your pleasure. Don't let yourself be nailed down to one chick. Not only are there plenty of fish in the sea, but dolphins and other mammals as well."

Maybe compared to a male porpoise I'm somehow desirable, but I don't think that's what he's aiming for.

"Look, Flip, that's all great, but can I just tell you my idea?"

He nods. "If you must."

So I lay it all out for him. I've got it all figured out, even where to get the materials. Flip follows along, saying nothing.

". . . and everyone will think I did it," I tell him, "but I'll be at the party with tons of witnesses, so no one will know."

He pulls the car into my driveway. "I don't know, Kross."

"Flip! Come on, man. It's genius."

"Well, sure. But I don't get it. How is it funny?"

"It's not *supposed* to be funny. It's making a *point*."

"So . . . how is *that* funny?"

"Flip!" I'm gonna rip my hair right out of my head.

"Seriously, Kross. There's no joke there. It's a fine idea, but—"

"Joey."

Fam. From the back seat. She's been so quiet this whole time that I almost forgot she was even there. Flip must have actually forgotten, because he jerks like someone just cattle-prodded him.

"What?"

"Joey, listen to Ke—to Kross. This is what the Council *exists* for, right? To mess with people's heads. To show them that the world they see isn't what they *think* they see."

He leans back in his seat and drums his fingers on his steering wheel.

"You have a point, Fool Kross. Your idea has merit." He says it like he just knighted me. Never mind that I'm not the one who said it—Fam did. I glance in the back seat and she grins at me and gives me a thumbs-up.

"So you'll do it?" I ask Flip.

"Indeed. But you have to help me with *my* plan. We'll push

it back. Yours will take some time and planning. We'll do it on Friday instead of mine, then do mine next week."

"Fine. Sure. Great!"

I rush into the house before I realize that I never asked Flip what his idea is.

That can't be good.

CHAPTER 27
I GET MY PARTY ON

BY THE TIME FRIDAY NIGHT ROLLS AROUND, I'm totally ready for another weekend. I could use a month of weekends at this point.

Before I can relax, though, I have the party to go to. I *have* to go to it now. I have no choice. The Council is prepared to pull my prank tonight ("All systems are a-go-go," Flip told me) and I have to be far away when it happens because *everyone* will assume I did it.

I get dressed and I'm digging under the sofa bed for a videotape without even really realizing it. What's going through Leah's mind, I wonder. What is she thinking? Why does she keep flirting with John Riordon but then tell me that she admires what I'm doing?

Speaking of which: What *am* I doing?

Am I trying to change people's minds? Am I trying to keep people from being stupid? Am I really going to accomplish anything by pointing out some of the stupidities and hypocrisies of the world?

I'm not even sure, tell the truth. I don't even know why it matters so much to me. Except that . . .

Except that everyone called me a hero. Everyone looked up to me. And I know the truth—that I'm not a hero, never was.

I put the tape in and watch it. I hate myself for it, but I can't help myself. I'm going to be seeing Leah in less than an hour. I'll be in her *house*. Around her *things*. And yet here I am.

I bought into the hype, even just a little bit. For a little while there, I thought I was a hero. But I'm not. The fact that I'm sitting here, watching this tape, proves that I'm not.

It's not the Burger Joint tape. It's another one. A different one.

I'm no hero. I'm scum.

I shouldn't go to the party. I shouldn't be around decent people.

But who am I kidding? I'm going. I can't help myself.

The mayor has my wheels, but there's still Dad's car.

"You're on your provisional license, so I want you back before midnight," he reminds me as he hands over the keys.

I tell him that's not a problem and then I throw a towel and my bathing suit into my backpack.

I know the way to Leah's house. It's a gigantic rancher out in one of the exclusive developments in Breed's Grove—owning the Narc must pay well for Mr. Muldoon.

I can't help it—coming out here makes me think about Susan Ann Marchetti. Killed by a kid from Breed's Grove and she gets a park named after her and a nice statue. Is dying heroic?

The last time I was out here, there were two big trucks out front—a makeup truck and a satellite rig so that *Justice!* could broadcast live. Now there's half a dozen cars parked in the big circular driveway. I park Dad's heap where it will be tough to box me in—when it's time for me to go, I don't want to have go begging people to move.

I sit out in the car for a minute for one final pep talk with myself. I ask myself for the billionth time: Why am I doing this? Why am I going to the house of the girl I'm, y'know, interested in, when all of her friends will be there? Friends who don't know me but know enough not to like me.

Well, in this case, I have no choice, so I take a deep breath and go ring the doorbell.

Mrs. Muldoon answers the door. Her face lights up when she sees me, which is one of the best things to happen to me in a long time. Then again, I *did* save her daughter's life and I guess that buys me some affection despite the whole hating-America thing.

"Hi, Mrs. Muldoon."

She gives me one of those one-armed hugs and a little kiss on my cheek, then ushers me into the house. It looks pretty much the same as it did before: The living room (where *Justice!* shot its episode) is bigger than my entire apartment.

I didn't really look around much when I was here last time. There were so many people running all over the place and big lights and TV equipment set up that it looked more like a sound stage than someone's house. But now that I can actually see it, I gotta admit: I feel like an idiot for ever thinking I had a chance with Leah. She lives in a palace. I live in a basement.

"Everyone's out back by the pool," Mrs. Muldoon says, gesturing down a hallway that's wider than Dad's bedroom. I look down at my shoes. It's like they're not worthy to walk on the hardwood.

"Oh, of course," Mrs. Muldoon says, mistaking my hesitation for something sensible. "You need to change. Go ahead and use Leah's bathroom. Down the hall, your first right, then left. It's right across the hall from Leah's room."

I spend the minute or two it takes to get there thinking how bizarre it is that Leah has her own bathroom, much less that I'm about to go into it.

On the way, I see the backyard through a big picture window. There's something like twenty kids out there, running around the pool, doing cannonballs off the diving board. They're all having a good time. All of the guys are shirtless and the girls . . . Lord, the girls are unbelievably hot, whether in bikinis or one-pieces. Jedi was right—it's wall-to-wall hotties.

I hustle down the side corridor. The bathroom's to my left. It's incredibly clean and almost as big as Dad's bedroom.

Her bedroom is to my right.

I tell myself, "No." I even mouth it, my lips moving silently.

But my feet have different ideas. I go to the right.

SELF-LOATHING #5

I STAND THERE, QUIET. I'm in Leah's bedroom.

The first thing I think is this: I wish my camera wasn't broken.

That summer two years ago, when I first taped her. When it all began. I tried so long to figure out what it was about that tape. Why it drew me in so much. Why I obsessed over it.

Leah was my safety valve for a while. She helped me not think so much about Mom and Jesse leaving. And then . . . Then, somehow, my safety valve became dangerous. Somehow, thinking about Leah became as bad and as painful as thinking about Mom and Jesse—only I couldn't stop.

It took breaking the camera and the end of my taping to make me realize it. It took standing here right now in Leah's room, looking at her things, at her private things. The bed she sleeps in, piled high with pillows of different shapes and sizes. The full-length mirror where she sees herself every day, looking at her clothes. Sometimes naked, here, in private, where no one else is supposed to be.

My knees go weak. I make myself walk across the plush, lavender carpet until I stand before the mirror. She has photographs taped all around it—a collage frame of her life and her friends. The mirror reflects . . . not me. Not to my mind's eye. No, to my mind's eye, I see Leah. In her solitude. In her privacy.

Here's what it was about the camera.

It was being able to *watch*. Without having to worry.

The rest of that summer, I kept the camera on all the time, even though it killed the batteries and wasted lots of tape. I loved the idea of letting fate or whatever determine what I would see.

But I kept coming back to that first time. To Leah.

She never came into the Burger Joint again. At least, not that summer. But when high school started a few weeks later, guess who was in my English class? And my science class? And my history class? And guess who had the same lunch period as me?

It was like the universe was trying to tell me something. I had to decide if I was going to listen to it.

And I did. I listened to it. For two years. Until that day.

I wasn't studying. At the library. That day. *The* day. I didn't go there to go to the library at all.

I was . . .

I was following her.

Leah.

Following her, and—

God.

God, I'm a terrible person. I'm such a . . .

The mirror shows me the worst person in the world.

I was stalking her, OK? I used to do it all the time. I'm quick and quiet and no one notices me and I would follow her around and . . . would videotape her. Everywhere she went.

Through a hole in my backpack.

And then watch the tape later. A stupid, jerky, out-of-focus—

It wasn't just the one time. It wasn't just the one tape.

It was almost *two years*. Two years of following her everywhere. Memorizing her class schedule. Memorizing everything I could, taping everything I could.

Piles of tapes. Leah's high school life, documented in shaky-cam.

Leah going to gym.

Leah coming back from gym, her hair still slightly damp from the shower.

Leah at lunch with her friends, laughing, yelling, eating.

Leah with the Dance Club in her tights.

Rehearsing with the Drama Club—*The Crucible*. She played Goody Proctor and it was the one time I was able to videotape her without having to hide it. I convinced the school paper to let me tape the show with a tripod.

My pride, my shame: an up-skirt shot from the Home-coming pep rally last year.

A day when I ran into her at the Narc, in the cereal aisle, and followed her to the deli counter and then to frozen foods before she disappeared through swinging doors labeled "Employees Only."

All those and more. More and more and more.

OK? There. OK? You know now.

The only difference between me and Michael Alan Naylor is that he got caught.

CHAPTER 28
NO POINT IN TRYING TO BE GOOD

THE REFLECTION OF ME IN THE MIRROR has tears running down its cheeks. He wipes his eyes, and the motion draws my attention to one of the pictures. Leah, in a black and pink striped top with black skirt and boots. God. Just standing there. Sort of gazing at the camera like she's not sure *how* to gaze at the camera. Not smiling; not scowling. Not doing much of *anything*. Just . . . *there*.

Not particularly beautiful. I guess that's why Tit was surprised when I mentioned her. I have to tell the truth—she's not the hottest girl at South Brook. Not even the hottest girl in the sophomore class. She's a little too plump, probably, and her face is a little crooked, and she doesn't really do much with her hair.

But here's the thing—I don't care. I just don't.

I'm holding the same backpack I used to tape her. It took me a while, but I eventually figured out how to position the camera and how to hold the backpack so that I could tape her while looking like I was just carrying the pack over one shoulder.

The same backpack. My hand finds the hole, the carefully positioned hole.

No camera anymore. And let's all thank God for that, you know?

I'm no hero.

I say it silently to the monster in the mirror.

He gives me a look that says, *If I had a new camera tomorrow, I'd do it all again.*

He says, *If I had a camera right now, I'd hide it in her bedroom. I'd see everything.*

I force myself to turn away and cross the hall to the bathroom. I close the door and sit down on the edge of the tub because suddenly my legs are too weak to hold me up.

God, what is *wrong* with me?

This isn't even my second time here. It's more like my fifth. I couldn't drive until recently, but I've known her address almost since the beginning. A couple of weekends, I walked all the way out here to Breed's Grove. Walked here and scoped out the neighborhood. Snuck around in the dark, making endless circuits of the house, trying to figure out . . .

Oh, God. Trying to figure out which window was hers. And what . . . ? What would I have done if I'd known?

I let myself cry in Leah's bathroom. I've sullied her so much already, what's the big dif if I get some tears on her bathroom floor?

After a few minutes, I figure Mrs. Muldoon might think I've died in here. I change into my bathing suit and splash cold water on my face to cover up the redness of my eyes.

Then I go back down the hall and turn and go out through some French doors to the pool, like I never did anything wrong. I'm good at pretending.

I feel out of place immediately. The guys are the ones who

shove me around. The girls are the ones who ignore me. No one even bothers to look over at me.

There's a table with drinks and snacks on one side of the pool and a DJ is playing old eighties music really loud. They don't notice me, or if they do, they don't show it. I don't know what the hell to do. But I know this: I'm going to try to be good. I'm going to try very, very hard to be good.

Leah sees me and comes running over. *Now* everyone notices me.

She's wearing a green and lavender two-piece. It's modest by bikini standards and Leah isn't even in the top five of the hottest girls at this party, but it's *Leah* and I devour her with my eyes.

"Look! Kevin's here!" she calls out, so of course everyone looks and it's like a stalker's worst nightmare—everyone watching *him* as *he* watches.

She throws her arms around me, and I'm way too aware of the stretches of naked flesh on both sides of the equation—my torso bare, her belly and arms. I pray to God—please, *please*—not to let me get an erection. Please.

"You came!" she says. "I'm so glad." And then she kisses me on the cheek and gives me an extra hard squeeze before letting me go. "Drinks and snacks are over there. Mom's getting pizza in, like, an hour."

She grabs my hand and pulls me closer to the pool and the other kids.

"I think you know everyone, right? Great!" She goes off to pour herself something to drink. Yeah, I know everyone. By sight, at least. It's not like we're all chums or anything. And they all sure as hell know me—I'm the guy who saved Leah's life, but they don't remember that. All they know is I'm the guy who hates America.

"My brother's over there," says one guy. "Extended his tour. Again."

Great. I don't need this.

"Not tonight!" Leah says, coming back out of nowhere. "We're not talking about stupid politics. We're having *fun*. We're celebrating. Kevin saved my life and the DA called my parents today and said their case is so strong that they'll probably look for the death penalty."

This is news to me. Some of the guys nod grudging respect my way. They're all thinking, *He's such a wuss we could kick his ass easy . . . but he* did *stop that guy.*

Yeah, I did. And you all saw it on TV. I watch Leah and I remember sitting next to her on her sofa while *Justice!* taped us. At one point, she said, "You know, I never believed in destiny or fate. And then Kevin saved me. He was in the right place at the right time. What are the odds? It had to be fate."

I wish that were true. I wish it had been fate and not just me.

And then what I've been dreading happens: John Riordon shows up from around a corner, carrying a Frisbee. "It went into the garage—" he says, before breaking off.

There's a tension in the air. The DJ keeps playing music, but no one's listening. They're all watching. Riordon is more intimidating the less clothes he wears. When he got all dressed up for the morning announcements, you couldn't see the massive shoulder muscles, the six-pack abs. He could crush me like a walnut.

"Tell ya what," he says, sauntering over to me. "I'll make you a deal. You don't be a dick tonight and I won't call you on it, OK?"

I grind my teeth to keep myself from saying, *Shouldn't I be saying that to you?*

"Sure, John."

He wings the Frisbee at someone who's just gone flying off the diving board. The guy catches it in midair and flips before crashing into the pool. "Six points!" Riordon yells, and charges to the pool, and everyone forgets about me.

And what do I do for the next infinite number of hours? Well, as the sun goes down and the Muldoons' outside lighting comes up, I do what I've always done: I watch.

I actually behave myself; I watch people other than Leah. I'm the outsider here. I'm the ugly duckling—there's no way around that. So I just watch and I try to stay uninvolved. I'm only here because Leah wants me here . . .

And because the Council is, right now, doing something that I can't afford to be involved in. Because everyone will come to me, assuming I did it. Which is close—it was my idea, but . . .

Just then—as if it's magic—my backpack rings.

I left the backpack near the door when I came outside. I dig inside for Fam's cell, which she loaned to me.

Flip's voice comes through, more excited than I've ever heard before—and that's saying something.

"Hail, Fool. Dude, it's done."

"Hail, Fool. How did it go?"

"Awesome." He giggles.

"Did you call the fire department?"

"Yeah, right before I called you."

"From a pay phone?"

"How stupid do you think I am, Kross?"

"Sorry. Cool. I'll see you Monday."

"Don't forget—you owe me now."

"I know."

I put the phone back, suddenly worried that someone has overheard both ends of the conversation. But no one is even looking at me. No one's paying attention. Good.

Right about now, the Brookdale Fire Department is rushing to South Brook High. What they will find there—planted in the grassy pad in the middle of the bus turnaround, visible from the main road—is five jerry-rigged flagpoles, each one bearing a burning flag.

Five flags, all aflame.

Norway. Sweden. Canada. Australia. Denmark.

If Flip did everything right, he also videotaped the burning flags before calling the fire department. He'll hack and spam the video to the usual suspects, with superimposed text:

GUESS WHAT THESE FLAGS HAVE IN COMMON WITH THE FLAG OF THE UNITED STATES?

That ought to get some attention. I think Dad would be proud, sort of. If I ever dared tell him it was my idea.

"Hey! Hey, you! Goofy-ass!"

I realize whoever it is is calling out to me. I must have a hell of a grin on my face.

"Me?" I ask. It's some jock, pointing to me from the pool.

"Yeah, you. Go get the Frisbee."

Why me? I frown. I'm not his slave.

"Come on," he says. "It went right around the corner there."

Oh, what the hell. It'll give me something to do.

I get up and go around the corner. It's darker here. No one can really see here from the party. I have a moment where I wonder if this is a setup, if someone's gonna jump me . . .

But then I see the Frisbee on the ground. I stoop to pick it up and then I hear a breath, caught fast.

I peek past some bushes.

And that's when I see it.

See *them*.

Leah and Riordon, off in their own little world.

Only this time it's worse than it ever was in school. She says something like, ". . . have to get back," but he's holding her by the wrists.

And I can't turn away, of course. I just can't. Because I watch. That's what I do.

Do I jump over the bushes? Do I rescue her again?

She's pulling away, but he tugs a little bit and she comes back and groans and presses herself against him and I've read this all wrong and she kisses him right on the lips. Hard.

My heart's hammering. I turn away, hiding in the darkness halfway between the bushes and the corner that turns back to the pool. God, I was so stupid! Did I think she was going to fall in love with me or something? With her "hero"? Was I that stupid?

Yeah. I'm dumber than I thought. I'm a complete moron.

I'm a drooling retard. I kept telling myself I didn't think that, but deep down, I did. Deep down, I wanted it. What an ass I am.

So screw it. Just screw it. There's no point in pretending.

No point in trying to be good anymore.

Before Leah and Riordon can come around the bushes, I dart back to the pool area. I toss the Frisbee to the guy in the pool, but it's a terrible, wobbly throw that gets everyone laughing. I ignore them and go straight back into the house.

I take a deep breath. I congratulate myself for not staying to watch Leah make out with Riordon even more. *That's been the cure all along, Kross. Just see her with another guy.*

But it's not the cure, and I know it. Because I know what I'm going to do before I do it.

"Are you guys OK for punch out there, Kevin?" It's Mrs. Muldoon. She came right up to me while I was lost in my thoughts.

"I think they need some more," I lie. I'm not sure, but I need to get rid of her.

"Is everything OK?" she asks, her brow all wrinkly with worry.

"Yeah, I just need to go to the bathroom."

But as soon as she disappears outside to check on the punch, I'm down the hall and turning *right*, not left.

I don't even hesitate. I just grab the picture. The one I saw before, of Leah in her pink and black outfit. My heart hammers.

I shove the picture in the pocket of my bathing suit.

A minute later, I'm back outside like nothing's happened. I grab my backpack.

Leah comes from around the corner, holding Riordon's hand. She sees me with my pack and comes over.

"Are you leaving already?"

"Yeah, I, uh . . ." I don't want to look at Riordon, but he's right here, so I have to. "I'm on my provisional license, so, y'know . . ."

Riordon smirks. He's my age, so he's on his provisional, too, but I guess he doesn't care.

"Oh!" Leah looks at her watch. "I didn't realize it was that late. We're gonna watch movies soon, if you want—"

"No, I really have to go." The picture is burning against my thigh.

"OK." She disengages from Riordon long enough to hug me. "Thanks for coming, Kevin."

I'm afraid she'll feel the picture in my pocket somehow. I break the hug early, hating myself. "OK. Thanks for inviting me. Bye, John." I wave at him weakly.

He just shakes his head and drags Leah back to the pool.

I go inside and return to the bathroom. I change into my clothes. I take the picture out of my pocket.

OK, Kross. You still can change your mind. You can put this back in her bedroom and leave.

Yeah, right. Like *that's* gonna happen.

CHAPTER 29
I TELL A LOT OF LIES

WHEN I GET HOME, DAD IS STILL UP. I give him his keys. "How was it?" he asks.

The picture of Leah is stashed in my backpack. I hear my voice—clear and unwavering—lie to Dad and say, "Fine."

"That's good."

"Anything interesting on the news?" I ask, all innocent and calm.

"Nothing."

Perfect. That's because Flip waited until the last possible minute to call the fire department. The news shows were over by then, or close to it.

But tomorrow's papers should be very interesting.

Now that he knows I'm home safe, Dad retreats to his bedroom. I get dressed for bed and then lie on the sofabed, holding the picture of Leah.

I've crossed a line. You know that old saying "Look, but don't touch"? It's like something they teach little kids. I mean, God! Even little freakin' *kids* can understand that!

I touched. I *stole. Thou shalt not steal.* It's, like, a commandment. It doesn't matter that I just stole a picture. *It's not mine.* It belongs to her and I crossed the line and took it.

It feels wrong. It feels right.

I can't tell the difference anymore.

In the morning, Dad frowns and shows me the front page of the *Loco*, which screams, VANDALISM AT SOUTH BROOK HIGH! along with a picture of the burnt flags and poles, dripping water, a fire engine in the background.

"Was this your idea?" he asks.

"I was at the party last night, Dad. And then I was here."

If he notices that I carefully tiptoed around his question, he doesn't show it. He just nods, then looks at the story again and says, "Someone's being a smart aleck."

"I guess so."

There's a tense moment when I figure he'll bust me, but then he notices something in the story and mutters, "An ordinance to prohibit flag burning in Brookdale? Idiots!" and starts scrutinizing the paper with a manic gleam in his eye.

I kill time around the apartment. I go help Mrs. Mac move some boxes into her attic. Anything to keep myself from thinking about the flag burning and the picture of Leah I've got hidden with the remains of my video camera.

Around noon, Flip pulls up in his coupe, Fam-less. I slide into the passenger seat and he hands me his laptop.

I watch a Quicktime movie of the burning: a slow pan from left to right, capturing the flags as they burn. Flip even dropped "The Battle Hymn of the Republic" in the background, which is a nice touch. It ends with a pull-back to a wide shot of all of the flags, and then the text superimposed perfectly.

"Awesome."

"Give me Fam's cell."

I hand it over. "Where *is* Fam?"

He shrugs. "Who knows?"

"Well, thank her for letting me use the phone."

"Whatever." I realize then and there, he won't tell her I said thanks.

"Well, thanks, Flip."

"No worries. We're gonna have fun on Wednesday. Officer Sexpot's ultimate triumph."

Yeah, yeah, whatever.

I go back inside to help Mrs. Mac some more. I can barely think, I'm so excited. No one can ignore this. *No one.* I made my point.

It keeps me giddy and happy for most of the day. And it keeps me from thinking about Leah. And the picture.

Saturday night and Sunday, the picture starts to haunt me again. I keep expecting the phone to ring—the police, calling to say Leah has reported stolen property and I'm the prime suspect.

But, no. Nothing.

The Sunday paper is filled with letters and editorials about the burning. The paper's editors are "horrified and sickened" by the "outrageous display of disrespect." It is, apparently, "one step away from burning an American flag," which is what's really got them in an uproar.

Most of the letters talk about how "clearly" and "obviously" the people who "perpetrated this heinous act" *wanted* to burn an American flag but were afraid to. "And so they simply settled for the next best thing—burning the flags of our allies."

Wow, talk about *not* getting the point.

At least I've got people talking.

Dad reads the paper and gets so worked up that he can barely get a syllable out, much less a coherent thought. Since Mom isn't around to yell at anymore, he takes a long walk around the neighborhood even though it's started raining.

While he's gone, I slip one of my tapes into the VCR. Why am I doing this to myself? Why do I keep giving in to this sickness?

But I watch it anyway.

CHAPTER 30
BUS RIDE OF LOSERS

ON MONDAY MORNING, THE BUS IS HELL.

I mean, really. Hell. I smell brimstone and hear the screams of the damned, or maybe those are just *my* screams.

It's the first time I've ridden the bus since the whole free speech thing started. The bus driver sneers at me as I get on. And hits the gas before I'm in a seat, knocking me back and forth and almost making me fall over. As it is, my hand brushes against someone, who jerks back and slaps it away like I've got the plague.

An undercurrent of hissing fills the bus as I lurch my way back through the aisle. All the kids start rearranging their backpacks and stuff to avoid having me sit with them. There's nowhere to go.

The driver slams on the brakes and I almost go flying backwards through the windowshield.

"Sit down! I can't drive until you're sitting down."

You jackass. No one will let me sit down.

But saying that out loud would be whining. And I won't whine.

You'd think someone would hear the bus driver and shove over a little bit so that I could sit down, but no. I approach a few seats and nothing.

"Come on, sit down!" the bus driver calls out, and some kids pick up the chant, like it's my fault somehow. I grit my teeth and keep looking. My face is burning and I feel like I could cry at any second, but no way—*that's* not gonna happen. I keep going back, then realize that I've gone too far and I'll need to turn around, but I don't think I can handle turning around to see the entire bus glaring at me.

Out of the corner of my eye, I catch the barest sliver of a seat. I pounce for it. I can only get half my ass on the seat and I'm turned out into the aisle and I can barely stay steady as the bus revs up and is thrown into gear, but at least I'm sitting, even though the guy in the seat with me presses himself as far against the window as possible, like I'm contagious, and says, "Asshole," in a very loud, very clear voice.

I really miss my car.

I walk into homeroom and I'm not there five seconds before Mrs. Sawyer says, "Kevin, go to the principal's office."

Everyone goes silent, except for a huff of muted laughter from John Riordon.

"What?"

She holds out a hall pass. She had it written before I even came into the room. "Principal's office."

"I haven't even *done* anything! I haven't even *said* anything!"

"I was told to send you down as soon as you got here."

Man! I grab the pass and go to see the Doc. He's in a *bad* mood. He doesn't even ask me to sit down.

"This has gotten entirely out of control now, Kevin. What on *earth* possessed you to do this?"

"Do what?"

His whole head flushes red, even on the very top, and he stands up to loom over me. "Don't play games with me! You could have burned this school down!"

Hey, Doc—bet you wish I was still "flying under the radar," huh?

"Dr. Goethe, I didn't set fire to those flags. I was at a party Friday night. All night."

His jaw locks in place. He leans on his desk with his fists, and I *really* wish I were in with the assistant principal, the Spermling, right now. Because the Spermling may be eleven million pounds of blubber, but the Doc looks like he could come across that desk and rip me to shreds before I could take a step toward the door.

"A party."

"Yeah. Seriously." I throw on my best "earnest" face. I have no idea if it's working or not, but what the hell. "Ask Leah Muldoon. She'll tell you." Ooh! Brainstorm! "Heck, ask *John Riordon*. He'll tell you. I was there all night."

He snorts like a bull.

I see my life flash before my eyes. It doesn't take long and what I see is pretty pathetic.

Then he sits down.

"OK, Kevin, have a seat."

Saved!

"So, you had nothing to do with this? This wasn't some misguided strategy to win the hearts and minds of your class-mates?"

"I'm telling you—I was at the party all night." Not a lie.

He picks up his phone. "Miss Channing? I want John Riordon. Now."

Oh, boy.

"I've been leaving messages for your father to call me and talk about all of this," the Doc says, gesturing as if "all of this" is some kind of gas in the air. "He hasn't gotten back to me."

"He's a busy guy." That's not really a lie either, is it?

"Tell him he needs to call me. Got it?"

"Sure." I'll have to make sure I forget that at some point.

John comes in a minute later with a look on his face like he's disappointed there was no trumpet fanfare for him.

"Sit down, John. Look, you two, this has gotten completely out of hand."

"I'm not the one who set fire to a bunch of flags," John says.

"Neither did I!"

The Doc holds up a hand. "I'm not blaming *either* of you. But clearly you guys have managed to kick up a ruckus, so I'm looking to the two of you to help put an end to it."

"I didn't start this, Dr. Goethe," John says, "but I'll be happy to help end it."

Brownnoser.

"What's wrong with talking about free speech?" I ask. "Why does it have to end? Don't we have the freedom to discuss these issues?"

Dr. Goethe gives me a stern look. "People are setting *fire* to things on school property, Kevin. That's not free speech. That's arson."

"That wasn't anyone from *my* side," John says like the sissy-boy he is.

I shrug. Because it's not like I can say the same thing.

"We need a safety valve," I say.

"What was that, Kevin?" The Doc's eyebrows shoot up on his smooth forehead like big furry caterpillars on speed.

"A safety valve. Like in history class. When things got rough, people would migrate west. We need something like that. Something to let the steam out."

John laughs. "That's the stupidest—"

"Hold on, John." He holds up a hand to silence John, who was about to whine and pout and cry. (No, not really, but it makes me feel better to think it.) "I let you guys on the announcements and you both whipped people up into a frenzy. So now I'm going to let you guys settle them down."

For the first time *ever* John Riordon and I look at each other in agreement. Because we're both thinking, *What the hell is he talking about?*

"We're going to do another debate," the Doc says. "This time it'll be in the auditorium. With the entire school there. On . . . uh . . ." He looks at a calendar. "On Wednesday. You'll both have your say and you'll both tell your groupies to cut out the shenanigans."

Another debate! A rebuttal. That's all I've ever wanted.

"I'm in!" I say. "But I get to go last this time."

The Doc looks a question at John, who shrugs. "I don't care. I'll debate him any time, any place."

"Then it's settled." The Doc pauses for a second and gives both of us a significant look. "It had *better* be settled, boys."

★   ★   ★   ★

I've missed first period, so I head to my locker to reload my backpack and hey, great, someone has written "I H8 TROOPS" on my locker in marker. Very original and crafty.

But as stupid and as juvenile as it is, it bothers me and here's why: because it's just bull. I mean, I think of my dad out there in the hot desert, not much older than I am now, with a gun and orders and not much else. How do ribbons contribute to that? They aren't magical. They don't accomplish anything. You know what I think? I think they're not for the troops; I think they're for *us*. Those of us at home. The ones who feel guilty for sending troops out there in the first place.

Because it seems to me that the best way to support the troops is to not send them off to die in the first place. And the *second* best way to support them is only to send them off to die when you absolutely have to. And the only way to know that you've done that is to talk about it, debate it, examine it, and make damn sure.

Because the world changes every day and maybe the circumstances change, so you keep talking about it so that you don't make a mistake and send someone off to die for the wrong reason or for no reason.

So I tell Fam all of these deep thoughts when she comes over to my house at night. We sit out on the porch and go through ten billion Web pages she printed out for me. It's like a free speech gold mine.

"Why didn't you just say stuff like that before?" she demands. "It sounds a lot better than what you *did* say."

Ouch. "I don't know. I guess I didn't think of it. I didn't

really put it all together until *after* I did all this stuff. I feel like I'm always playing catch-up. It's like, I do something and *then* I figure out why."

"Poor widdle Kwoss." She pats my hand and I get that whole uncomfortable feeling again, thinking of our hug on the catwalk. "Don't worry—we'll have you ready for the debate. Look at this stuff." She leaves her hand on mine as she hands over some more papers.

And all of a sudden, I'm thinking of King Arthur. No, really. Follow me here. We read about him last year in English class. Like, Arthur was married to Guinevere, see? They were hot and heavy. And then Arthur's top dog, Lancelot, showed up. And the next thing you know, he's getting busy with the queen!

I'm no genius, but is it possible that Flip=Arthur, Fam=Guinevere, and Kross=Lancelot? Is that what's going on here?

Oh, man. I don't *want* to be Lancelot! But let's face it—Fam might be the only girl I ever get to kiss, if my luck keeps running the way it's always run.

I wait for a break in the conversation and then I say, "Am I supposed to kiss you now?"

She freezes. Almost as an afterthought, she takes her hand off mine and puts it in her lap. "What?"

"Uh, never mind."

"No, I think we'll go right on minding, Kross. Did you say you wanted to kiss me?"

"That's . . . that's not what I said. I was . . . Jeez, Fam. I don't know. Am I supposed to kiss you?"

She stares at me. It's like being called on in class when you don't know the answer.

"You were just . . . Fam, you were being nice to me, and I thought you wanted me to—"

"I'm nice to you because I like you. Not because I want to jump your bones."

OK, it's official—I know absolutely nothing about girls. I was pretty sure before, but it's nice to have confirmation.

And wow. Have I *completely* screwed up the one decent relationship I have with a member of the opposite sex or *what*?

"I'm really sorry, Fam." I mumble it while looking down at my feet. That doesn't mean I'm any less sincere. I just can't look in her eyes.

"I'm with Flip," she says, frosty. "I can't believe you would even make a move—"

"I wasn't making a move. I swear."

"Then what *were* you doing?"

Oh, God. "I thought *you* wanted me to kiss you."

There's a long pause. I finally work up the courage to look at her. She's all stony-faced. Then a little crack in the stone.

"Are you saying," she says slowly, "that you don't want to kiss me at all, but you were going to do it because you *thought* that's what I wanted?"

"When you put it like that, it sounds really pathetic."

"Kross!" And she laughs. Thank God. "It *is* pathetic! What *is* it with you and girls?"

"I don't know. Please don't tell Flip what I said. I'll tell you something only Flip knows."

Her eyes light up at this. "Oh? What?"

"You have to promise not to tell anyone."

"About what you're about to tell me or about kissing me?"

"Uh, both."

"This better be good."

I take a deep breath. "OK. Look. This whole thing. All of it." I gesture to the sky. "*All* of it. My dad started it."

"Huh?"

I tell her about Dad making me throw away the ribbons. And how I told Flip, and his reaction.

"So I guess that's even more pathetic, huh?"

She thinks about it. "Actually, I think it's pretty amazing."

"What do you mean?"

"I mean, you could have gotten out of this a long time ago. Yeah, people would have made fun of you for your dad making you do it, but that wouldn't have lasted. Instead, you went with it. You made it your own. And that's amazing."

God, when you put it that way, it sounds like maybe I'm not a total and complete waste of space.

"I'm so proud of you, I'm gonna give you a hug, Kross. Try to resist the urge to propose marriage or throw me down and ravish me."

I hate her.

CHAPTER 31
STUPID FANTASY TIME

I STAY UP WAY LATE AFTER FAM LEAVES, so I decide to skip school on Tuesday. I've had enough of the nasty glares and all of that. Dad will sign a note for me if I ask him to. When he says, "Why didn't you go in?" I'll just say, "I needed a mental health day. I needed to opt out of the opt-in society."

I should be prepping for the debate, but instead I spend most of the day watching the tapes. And looking at the picture. My trophy.

I imagine what it would be like to tell Leah the truth. Well, *part* of the truth. Telling her how much I . . . how much I like her.

You could have told me, she would say, and the words are like a spear through me, but the tone of her voice is gentle.

You could have just asked me for a picture, she would say, laughing, when I confessed to stealing hers.

I would have given it to you myself, she would say, putting a hand on my arm. *It's OK. You saved my life that day. I truly believe that. If you want a picture, that's fine.*

And she would grin at me, a beautiful grin that makes me warm and—

Ugh. What the hell is *wrong* with me? That's not happening. That's not *going* to happen.

* * * *

Halfway through the day, the phone rings. Someone frosty and too polite from the car dealership tells me I can pick up my car.

Right after that, I get a call from Fam. "Hi, secret lover," she says. "I'm e-mailing you a bunch of research I did during study hall. Can you go to the library today and get it?"

"Yes."

"Glad to hear it, babycakes." Thank God I didn't tell her my King Arthur theory. I'd be "Lancelot" from now until the day I die.

"Hey, Fam. Do you think Flip is jealous of all the attention I'm getting?"

"Flip doesn't know how to be jealous."

"Maybe he should learn."

Funny—I can almost hear her smile over the phone.

I decide to walk to the dealership. It takes me about an hour, but the rain has tapered off for now and I don't really care. The mayor isn't around—he's off mayoring, I guess. But two more ribbons have been slapped onto the back of my car, and this time they're actual sticky bumper stickers, not removable magnets. Great. Revenge on a teenager must be *so* sweet, Mr. Mayor.

I consider what it would take to remove the stickers with minimal annoyance, but then I get a better idea.

I go to the library to pick up the e-mails, but I also spend ten minutes researching something else on the 'net. Yeah, it's possible. And cheap, too. I place my order and feel oddly powerful and satisfied.

When I leave, the rain starts up again. Perfect.

CHAPTER 32
THE DEBATE (DUH)

IT'S STILL RAINING ON WEDNESDAY MORNING when I wake up. I guess that's appropriate. I'm extra careful driving to school—I don't need to wreck my car along with my life.

It is—to use Flip's favorite word—*surreal* that this is actually happening. Dr. Goethe has actually canceled first period for the entire school. After homeroom, everyone goes to the auditorium. Mrs. Sawyer guides me backstage, along with John. What would she say if she knew I had the key to the janitors' office back here? Or that I spend *way* too much time up on that catwalk?

I made a decision yesterday.

Yesterday, while I put the finishing touches on my opening statement, I decided that I was going to push this as far as I could. My mom used to say, "In for a penny, in for a pound," and I never really understood that until recently. But it's like I've stepped partway into the quicksand and I might as well see if I can swim in it now. Even though I might drown.

Then again, I just might reach the other side.

After all, what do I have to lose? Leah is never going to be my girlfriend. The people who don't like me aren't going to suddenly change their minds. So I might as well just keep pushing.

I go to the auditorium and look out front before I go back backstage. The big screen they show movies and stuff on is lowered into position from the ceiling. I wonder why?

Backstage, John and I wait for Dr. Goethe with Mrs. Sawyer. I wore a tie today, mindful of how professional John looked the other day, but he's just wearing a blazer (with his flag pin, of course) and a shirt open at the throat. He looks way cooler and more relaxed than I do. I'm tempted to take off my tie, but I don't want to give him the satisfaction of knowing that he's gotten to me. And let's face it—no matter what the situation, Riordon's *always* gonna look better than I do.

One of Mrs. Grant's media helpers shows up and talks to John and I hear John say, ". . . hook up my laptop."

"What?" It spills out of me before I can stop it. John looks over his shoulder at me and smirks and says absolutely nothing.

His laptop? He's hooking up his laptop?

Dr. Goethe joins us backstage. "Um, Dr. Goethe? Can I talk to you for a second?"

He looks at his watch. "We don't have time for this."

"I didn't know we could do presentations . . ." God, it sounds weak and pathetic. John laughs as he hands a laptop bag to the media guy.

"You don't *have* to do a presentation," Dr. Goethe says, totally missing the point. "Just talk. You'll be fine."

Before I can protest any further, he gathers John and me together to explain the rules: He'll go out there first and talk a little bit. Then John and I will come and stand at our podiums. We each get a couple of minutes for an opening statement. Then we each get to rebut the other guy and ask questions of each other. Then we each get a closing statement. And then, best of all, the audience—the entire *school*—will vote on who won the debate. I'll lose. I mean, there's no question about that. The only question is by how much.

"As we agreed, Kevin," the Doc goes on, "you'll get the last word. And remember, you two." He looks at us sternly. "Remember: You're using your closing statements to tell everyone to calm down and stop this nonsense."

"Yes, sir," says Riordon.

"Right," I manage. My brain is still on Riordon's laptop. I'm gonna get creamed again.

"And nothing personal, you guys. Keep it clean."

It takes the Doc a while to calm the crowd down. Eventually, though, he does and he goes into a little spiel about the Power and the Promise of Free Speech and how it's at the Heart of our Democracy and it's a Gift Between the Generations, starting way back with the Founding Fathers and blah blah blah. I'm totally prepared, but I'm terrified anyway. I mean, I was prepared *last* time, too, but that didn't stop Riordon from scoring points.

So after a million years, the Doc reminds everyone to hold their applause until closing statements and then introduces us and everyone ignores him and applauds anyway as John goes onto the stage.

There are boos when I come out, but the teachers in the crowd cut them off pretty quickly.

I walk across the stage, amazed my legs can actually work. Bright lights shine down on me and every freakin' kid at South Brook is out there in the audience, watching.

Other than that day at the football field—which seems like

it happened a million years ago to someone else—I've never in my life had so many eyes on me. Still not used to it. John is fine with it—he *is* used to this. He gets crowds screaming and cheering for him all the time at football games.

I get to the podium and grab it like it's a life preserver. I can't lose it now. I have to do this.

Dr. Goethe explains the rules to the crowd and then asks for John's opening statement.

"Hi, there, South Brook. I can't believe that we have to go through this again. I really can't. But that's OK. This is important. Important enough to explain more than just once."

John clicks a little gadget in his hand and the movie screen lights up with a video.

The video.

"The Battle Hymn of the Republic" echoes throughout the auditorium. The flags of Sweden, Denmark, Australia, Canada, and Norway burn.

Hissing from the audience. I guess I should be freaked out, but there's this part of me that can't help being impressed—the video looks pretty good up on a big screen. Flip did a great job.

The video ends. John leaves it frozen on the last frame.

"So," he says. "*Someone* burned flags this weekend." He doesn't exactly turn to look at me, but he jerks his head a little bit in my direction, and people get the point without him actually, y'know, *pointing*. "I guess *someone* thought that was funny. I don't. Oh, don't worry—I get the 'joke.' I talked about burning a flag last time, so someone decided to burn a bunch of them. But none of them were American flags, and then this person decided to make a very unpatriotic point: that all flags are equal because all flags burn the same. There's nothing special about our flag, we're supposed to believe—it burns like everyone else's. The implication was clear: 'It's just a flag,' they say. 'What's the big deal? Chill out. Relax.'"

He clicks again. An American flag fills the screen.

"But you know, I can't relax. Because I don't buy it. Put yourself in the position of someone from one of those countries. Don't you think that if you heard about this, you'd be mad? Why should someone have the right to do that to you? Why should someone be able to trample on a beloved symbol, just to make a point? There are *many* ways to make a point. You can give speeches. You can write books or newspaper columns or essays. You can even do a debate." He gestures to the entire auditorium.

"This is America. You can say anything you want, as long as people listen to you. So why burn a flag and just enrage people? What possible point could you be making?

"And get this: It's not just disrespectful and pointless. It's also *illegal*. That's right—there have been laws protecting the flag for decades. I didn't realize that until I was preparing for this debate. For a very long time, there have been laws to protect the desecration of the flag."

More clickety-click. There are animated words and letters swooping and diving on the screen, forming into bullet points, including "Uniform Flag Law of 1917."

"Here's something else that I learned while preparing: The flag is older than the Constitution. I didn't know that. I'm sort of ashamed I didn't, honestly. But it's true. Our flag came into being in 1777"—click-click, another bullet point—"a dozen years before the Constitution. So when people trot out the First Amendment to defend burning a flag, I have my answer ready for them: The flag was here *before* the Constitution. It should be respected. It should be protected. And it should definitely be pledged to in the morning!"

There's a burst of applause that dies quickly when the Doc grabs a microphone: "I'm going to remind all of you to save your applause for the end so that we can get through this."

He gives them a couple of seconds to calm down and then: "OK, Kevin. Your turn."

John's PowerPoint presentation is still up on the screen. I want to tell him to turn it off, but I don't trust myself.

I take a deep breath and look out over the crowd.

"Well . . ." Whoa. My voice *explodes* from the speakers. I can *feel* it in addition to hearing it.

I almost give up right there. I'm sweating already and my hands are shaking on the podium.

But I'm here, right? Already in the quicksand. Time to swim for all I'm worth.

"Well, I find it interesting that John seems to think that we shouldn't have the right to make people mad. Because he's doing nothing *but* making me mad."

This goes over like rare steak at a vegetarians' convention.

"He's making me mad because . . . because . . ." Oh, God, I'm losing it. Too many eyes on me. And there's Leah, third row, watching me. She's on my side, but it doesn't matter because she won't tell anyone. So she might as well be on Riordon's side. So . . .

I risk a look over at him. Riordon's smirking.

Well, that was a mistake on his part. Because now I'm more pissed off than I am nervous.

Come on. You can do this, Kross. Stop trying to ad-lib and

stick to what you wrote last night. To the bombshell Fam discovered.

"Last week, John said that America was the freest country in the world. Well, I'm sorry, but that's not true."

I get *exactly* the reaction I thought I'd get: Massive outcry. Boos. Hisses. Shouts. John has an expression on his face like, *Is this guy even trying to win the debate?* He looks shocked and a little bit disappointed that I'm making it so easy for him.

Dr. Goethe takes almost a minute to calm everyone down.

"No, really," I continue. "It's not. By any objective measure. Man, I wish . . ." I look longingly at the screen. "I wish I had a computer, too. So I could show you this, but I guess you'll just have to listen instead. The World Bank did this study, where they ranked every country in the world based on how much freedom its citizens have. And guess what? The United States wasn't number one."

I let that sink in for a second.

"It wasn't number two."

Another second.

"It wasn't even in the top ten. Or the top twenty. It was number *thirty-three*."

I get some more gasps for that one. John shakes his head, so I aim the next bit right at him:

"The freest country in the world, John, is actually *Denmark,* which got a score of one hundred percent. The U.S. got a score of eighty-three point seven percent, after Sweden, Australia, Canada, and Norway . . . Oh, my." And here I stop like I've just realized something. "Oh, those are the countries whose flags were burned the other day, aren't they?"

I give everyone a second to let that sink in.

"See, John, you say you got the 'joke' about those burning flags, but I'm not sure. Now, we both know that I couldn't have set those flags on fire, but I've been thinking about them a lot. And here's the thing: It's legal to burn the national flag in *all* of those countries. In every single one. In Norway, Sweden, and Denmark, it's only illegal to burn *another* country's flag. We don't have a law like that here. So it seems like those countries—those *freer* countries—have a different set of priorities than you do. They understand that a flag is a symbol. But here's what *I* think the point of that prank was, and it's not that they all burn alike. It's that they're all just symbols. And burning them shows that symbols are not actually things. I mean, symbols exist so that you can talk about an idea. So that you can reach out and touch it. You can't touch freedom or see it, but you can see a flag.

"But here's the thing: When you burn a flag, you don't see the flag anymore, but that just means that the flag is gone. *Not* the freedom. The freedom is still here.

"And guess what? The answer to that question at the end of the video, what do those flags have in common with ours? It's this: It's legal to burn the flag in this country, too. It's protected. It's free speech.

"American flags are burned *all the time* in this country! Every single *day*. And you know who does it? Well, most of the time it's people in veterans' organizations. It's, like, the American Legion and the Boy Scouts, even. That's because when a flag is dirty or damaged from being used, the only *approved* way to get rid of it is to burn it!"

John explodes. "You can't compare—!"

"You'll get your turn, John," the Doc says.

"But—!"

"No buts."

"Thank you, Dr. Goethe," I say. I'm calm on the outside, but inside I'm jumping up and down and cheering. I rattled Riordon. I did it. I made him snap.

I have to look down at my notes for the next part. "John Howard recently said that flag burning shouldn't be illegal because 'I do not think we achieve anything by making it a criminal offense—we only turn yahoo behavior into martyrdom.' He's the prime minister of Australia. It's pretty sad that you have to go all the way around the world for sense like that. Oh, wait. No, you don't. Right here in the U.S., Colin Powell said, 'The First Amendment exists to insure that freedom of speech and expression applies not just to that with which we agree or disagree, but also that which we find outrageous. I would not amend that great shield of democracy to hammer a few miscreants.'"

Deep breath.

"OK. Now I'm done."

Now it's time. Questions. And I have only one question I want to ask John, really. Just one.

"Now it's your turn, John," says Dr. Goethe. "Your first question to Kevin."

"I don't even know where to start," John says. "I don't really care about laws from other countries. I care about *our* flag and no matter what you say, there are laws protecting it."

"A question, John?" Dr. Goethe prods.

"Fine." John jabs a finger at me. "Are you *really* comparing someone burning a flag to dispose of it properly with someone who's burning it out of disrespect and hate?"

And that's it. He's just walked into a trap. I shrug. "Why not? It's the exact same act, right?"

"No, it isn't!"

"Wait!" Dr. Goethe says. "Wait! I'm going to let you keep going, John, because technically Kevin asked a question when he responded to *your* question, but let's try to be orderly here. Go ahead."

Riordon's really hot under the collar. "It's *not* the same thing. In the one case, the person is doing the right thing by getting rid of an old flag. They're different."

"How? What if I have an old flag and decide to burn it as a protest? I'm doing the *exact* same thing as the guy burning that *exact* same flag to get rid of it."

We're supposed to be waiting for questions, but we're just jumping all over each other too fast.

"No, you're not!" He actually makes a fist and hits the podium. "It's not the same!"

"The only difference is what I'm *thinking*. But the whole point is this: It doesn't *matter* that they're different because it doesn't *matter* what I'm thinking. They're *both* protected. Unless you're saying we don't have freedom of *thought* in America?"

"No, you . . ." He stops. "Of course not. You can think whatever you want. But burning a flag isn't speech. Speech is when you talk."

"Then that means that pictures and photographs and websites aren't protected. None of them are speech."

"That's different."

"How? And who decides what's different?"

"The government," Riordon says triumphantly, because it's a question he can answer.

"But it can't be the government!" I tell him. "Congress *can't* decide these things—it's right there in the First Amendment. Have you even *read* it?" And I realize something—I've been talking to John this whole time. I shouldn't be. I don't care about him. I should be talking to the audience. So I tear my eyes away from John and force myself to look out at the scary, scary depths of students sitting out there in the auditorium.

"I spent a lot of time reading the First Amendment to prepare for this. And you know what? I didn't find the word 'unless' in there anywhere. Here's what the First Amendment says." And I have to look down at my notes, and then I don't because I realize I've memorized it.

"'Congress shall make no law respecting an establishment of religion, or prohibiting the free exercise thereof; or abridging the freedom of speech, or of the press; or the right of the people peaceably to assemble, and to petition the Government for a redress of grievances.'

"Again, there are no exceptions in there. It doesn't say 'unless it makes someone angry.' Or 'unless it's hurtful.' Or 'unless someone doesn't like it.' Or 'unless it's burning a flag.' It says Congress shall make *no law*. Now, I admit I'm not the smartest kid in this school. Heck, would I be up here otherwise?"

That gets me a little laughter from the crowd.

"But even *I* know that 'no law' means, well, no law. Right? There's not a whole lot of elbow room in the First Amendment. In fact, it doesn't look like there's *any* elbow room, as best I can tell."

"If Congress—"

"Wait!" the Doc jumps in. "We're getting a little freewheeling here. Everyone take a breath. John, I'm going to let you ask a question. Let's try to stay on target, OK?"

Whatever, dude.

John nods and takes the mandated breath, but he's clearly eager to jump me. "OK, John, go ahead."

"If Congress can't make those laws, then how do you explain the laws against desecrating the flag?" Riordon asks, and then nods smugly. "The government circumvents the Constitution and the law when it serves its own purposes. It happens all the time."

Wow, I can't believe he just said that! As soon as Dr. Goethe gives me the OK to answer, I go for the throat: "Dude, laws can be *wrong*. And when the government circumvents the Constitution, that's wrong, too. That's why we have courts. The government is supposed to be *under* the Constitution, not *above* it. The Constitution created the government, not the other way around.

"Besides, I read about those flag laws, too. But I actually bothered to look into them. What—did you just go to Wikipedia and stop there?"

I want to go on, but the Doc stops me. "That's your question, Kevin."

This is a little more complicated then I thought. I need to focus so that I can ask my one, important question.

"Those laws exist," John insists. "I read about them." He fumbles for a second, then goes all clicky again, cycling back through his presentation until he shows his sexy little bullet-pointed list of laws and stuff. "It's right there, in print. How can you deny cold hard facts, Kevin?"

Oh, good—he asked a question. My turn.

"I know they exist, but do *you* know what they're for? They say things like 'the flag can't be used for advertising purposes.' So I guess we should go arrest the mayor, because he's got flags all over his car lot."

"That's not what they meant!" he says.

"Hey, it's my turn right now. And sure it is." I have to cheat here and look at my notes because I couldn't memorize the line: "Justice John Marshall Harlan said that these laws are needed because advertising tends to 'degrade and cheapen [the flag] in the estimation of the people.' So maybe you should stop worrying about the flag burners and start worrying about the car salespeople and the people who use flags on TV to sell stuff on Memorial Day and Flag Day and Veterans Day and July Fourth. Maybe you should even worry about the sports teams that sew flag patches on their uniforms and get them dirty. That's desecrating the flag right there."

And I stop and realize I'm looking at John again, so I turn back to the audience instead. Nothing happens for a little while. I look back at John. He's like a dog on a leash who could get to the cat if he had just another inch of slack. The Doc watches me. Finally, he says, "Your question, Kevin?"

Oh. Right. Crap. I made an awesome point and now my mind's totally blank. I have my one question, but it doesn't really fit in with what I just talked about. I suck.

The Doc gets tired of waiting for me. "John? Your response to Kevin's comment?"

Riordon grits his teeth. "I did my research, too, Kevin." More clicky-click. He's getting agitated looking for the right screen. "There. See?" He reads off the screen. "Justice Hugo

Black said, 'It passes my belief that anything in the Federal Constitution bars . . . making the deliberate burning of the American flag an offense.'"

"Yeah, but—"

"I listened to you," John says. "Now you listen to me. Justice Black said that. Even Thomas Jefferson and James Madison were against flag burning." Clicky, and their quotes appear on the screen. "And Norman Schwartzkopf said, 'I regard the legal protection of our flag as an absolute necessity and a matter of critical importance to our nation.' So maybe until *you* serve in the army, you should just keep your opinions about this stuff to yourself. What do you think of *that*?"

Wow. Did he really *say* that? The whole crowd *oohs* like I've been burned, but I'm totally ready for this one. "You know something? There's nothing in the First Amendment or in the whole Constitution that says that you only have your rights if you've served in the military. But if you really think that way, then I guess the president should just shut up from now on, because he never went to war. And you know what? It's one thing to be against flag burning. It's another thing to make it illegal and to punish people for doing it. I'm against people saying racist things, but I'm not going to throw them in jail for it. Are *you*?"

"That's not . . . Goddamn, that's *not* what I said!"

The Doc steps in as the crowd takes a collective deep breath. Awesome! I really rattled that pain in the ass. I scan the audience quickly, looking for Leah. She's not reacting at all. Damn.

"Let's move on, guys," the Doc says.

"No!" John's *really* hot now. He's all flustered. He realizes he just lost his cool, but he can't help it. "He's making it sound like I don't support free speech."

"That's because you *don't*," I say. John's getting red in the face and I can't help it—I just want to laugh at him. I bite my lip to stop myself.

"You're lying!"

"I don't know what else to call it."

Dr. Goethe keeps trying to jump in, but we just keep going. We're like gladiators. Except we're yelling at each other and not hacking away with swords. But otherwise, *just* like gladiators.

"Why don't you support the troops?" John yells, and I yell right back at him that I do, I *do* support them. I just don't have to announce it to the world on my car, for God's sake, and then he's all over me about the Pledge and I'm right back at him and then—

"That's *enough!*" the Doc thunders. He glares at me as he walks past my podium, then gives John the same look as he takes up a spot between us on the stage. The auditorium has gone dead silent except for the echo from the Doc's bellow.

"One final question," the Doc says. He looks down at a notepad he's been carrying the whole time. "Before things got out of hand, it would have been . . . Kevin's turn. Kevin, you can ask John the final question."

Oh, you're kidding me. This is just too perfect.

I take a deep breath. It's a risky question because John could have the World's Most Awesome Answer, but I have to take the chance.

"My question is this: John, what have you—you, *personally*—done to support the troops?"

It takes a second for everyone to realize what I've just asked. The auditorium doesn't fall silent all at once—it happens in a few seconds, as people figure out the question and what it means and turn to look at John.

Even Dr. Goethe looks a little surprised.

John opens his mouth to speak. He suddenly looks really, really silly with his PowerPoint presentation all blown up behind him. He half turns to look at it, but the answer isn't there.

Not this time.

"Well," he says at last into the scary silence of more than a thousand people.

"Well . . ." he says again, after a second.

"I have . . ." he says. And stops. Maybe he was going to say *I have ribbons on my car* or something like that. Something that he realized was really, really lame.

He just stands there. In the silence. I stand there with him, but I'm enjoying it a lot more than he is.

And finally he turns to me, his face twisted into anger and outrage, and says, "What have *you* done, Kevin? What have *you*—"

"No!" says the Doc, stepping between our podiums, holding his arms out like we're two boxers trying to hit each other after the bell. "That was the last question. That's it. This has been a very . . . spirited debate," he goes on. I think he's regretting this whole thing, which for some reason makes me totally, completely, obscenely happy. "I think everybody has learned some very interesting tidbits on *both* sides. But things are getting a little heated and time is short, so we're going to move on."

John protests, but the Doc cuts him off. Me? I look down to see that my hands have sweated so much that my notes are covered in it. But I'm still standing upright. I got under Riordon's skin. That's the biggie for me. I made him realize he can't just punt me around like a football.

And I know I'm *right*, too. That's the big victory. Even if no one else out there knows . . .

I know.

"Both gentlemen have prepared some closing remarks." He gives each of us very significant looks. I wonder why for a second, but then I look out at the crowd again.

Man. There's a *vibe*. People are worked up. You can *feel* it, even from the stage.

Wow. I helped make that happen.

"John, you'll close first."

And the Doc steps back to let John talk.

John shakes his head like he's waking up. I'm close enough to him that I can see he's gripping the edge of the podium like he's strangling it. Probably thinking of my throat.

He clicks a few times and then there's a shot of a guy in an army uniform. I guess it's his dad. He takes a second and then—somehow—manages to start talking very calmly.

"I'm glad that I had this opportunity. Like I said in my opening, I'm sort of surprised that it had to come to this. I think these arguments are fine, but I also think they're old. Old and done with. We have freedom of speech in this country, but like I said the other day—we also have the freedom to recognize when we're not accomplishing anything and just shut up.

"I want to talk about my dad a little bit. Because he's

where I learned all of this. He joined the army right out of high school. He served at a listening post in Alaska for six months at a time, during the winter, when it was dark twenty-three hours a day. It wasn't fun, but it was necessary. He didn't like being away from my mom or his parents or my uncle and aunt, but his country needed him and he answered the call.

"See, that's what this all comes down to, in the end. His country. Your country. My country. *Our* country. It's about loving our country. That's the very definition of patriotism. Love of country. And if we love our country, then why would we *ever* want to cause it harm? Why would we ever want to hurt it or insult it or not support it? In a time of war, why would we want to disrespect and not support our troops?

"That's what my dad taught me. He taught me by exam-ple. After he got out of the army, he went to college and got married and had me. But he still had that thirst, that love for America. So he joined the reserve. And like I said last week— he's lost some friends along the way. I guess it would be easy for him to be cynical. To be angry. To be so angry that he would do something stupid, like burn a flag.

"But he's not. Because he's a patriot. He's a true American. He loves his country.

"Shouldn't we all do the same?"

He pauses here for a moment. Just a moment. And then: "The last thing I want to say to you today is this: These debates are great. They're part of a tradition of American free speech. But we're done, and that's fine. We're finished. Both sides have— Well, in a minute or two, after Kevin speaks, both sides will have had their say. So let it rest there, South Brook. Thank you."

There's wild applause for John Riordon, All-State Stud and Suppressor of Free Speech.

The Doc thanks John. Says it's my turn.

The world swims in my vision. I feel faint. I can't remember what I was going to say.

I look down at my notes.

"Uh, Kevin?" The Doc clears his throat. "It's *your* turn."

Riordon. He just *had* to talk about his father again, didn't he?

SELF-ACCEPTANCE #1

"John's talking about the Pledge and ribbons and flag burning. I'm not. I'm talking about the big picture. About liberty and free speech. And you know what? Compared to those things, who cares about a pledge or a ribbon or a flag? They're nice symbols, but they're just *things*.

"I'll take a second to answer that last question of yours, John. I *do* support the troops.

"But not with ribbons. A ribbon is meaningless. The ribbons are for *us*, not for them. Support is *action*. It's too easy to put a ribbon on a car and then forget about it. You know, I said the other day that during World War II, people made sacrifices to support the war effort. These days, we're not asked to sacrifice anything. They just tell us to shut up instead.

"Supporting the troops isn't just a slogan. Jeez. It's *doing* things. Sending care packages. Donating money and blood. Maybe instead of all those American flag pins people wear, they should wear pins with two numbers instead: the amount of money they've donated and the number of pints of blood they've given.

"So here's what I'll do, what I've *done*: I'm giving what's left of my reward money to a veterans' group, so maybe the guys coming home can have some decent health care for a change.

"Which brings me to . . . I'm glad John talked about his dad. Because I'd like to talk about mine.

"If you read the *Loco* last week, you might have seen my dad mentioned in the paper. The story said he was a traitor to his country. That wasn't true.

"Like John's dad, mine joined the army right out of high school. But that's where the similarity ends. Because John's dad went to Alaska and mine was shipped out overseas, serving in a front-line infantry combat unit.

"While he was over there, my dad got some medals. I bet John's dad got some, too. The army gives out a lot of medals. But two of my dad's were special. One was the Purple Heart. You only get that if you're wounded or killed in action. A lot of guys get them because a lot of people get hurt. My dad was hit by shrapnel from a roadside bomb. He was pretty messed up. To this day, he's not . . . he's not totally better. No one at any of the VA hospitals can figure out what's . . .

"Funny thing, though. While my dad was recuperating in the hospital, some cook dropped the wrong spatula or something. Started a fire. The whole kitchen went up in flames. My dad was in the mess hall at the time, and even though he was still recovering, he ran into the fire twice to pull soldiers out.

"For that, they gave him something called the Soldier's Medal of Valor. *Not* a lot of people get that one. It was a big deal. They called him a hero. They wrote him up in *Stars & Stripes*.

"I didn't know any of this. Unlike John's dad, mine doesn't talk about the army all that much. I had to find out why from my mom.

"See, it turns out that some guys in my dad's unit were

killed in what's called 'friendly fire.' Which means that other Americans did it by accident. Only the army was pretending it didn't happen that way. They were telling everyone that it was enemy fire. And my dad knew that that wasn't right, that the families of those dead soldiers deserved to know the truth. So he went through channels and he tried to get the army to tell the truth, but they just kept telling him to butt out and do his job like a good soldier.

"So my dad got fed up and he went to a reporter who was embedded with a nearby unit and he told him the truth. And the army said my dad had given away military secrets, like where the deaths happened and things like that. Things that they claimed could help the enemy. So they kicked him out of the army."

I stop for a second. My throat is raw. I thought I would feel bad saying all of this, like I betrayed Dad or something, but instead . . . instead I feel good.

"So my dad didn't teach me the same lessons that John's dad did. My dad never talked about any of this, so I had to learn from him by watching and just trying to figure it out on my own. Just like *he* had to figure it out on his own, out there in the desert.

"And this is what I've figured out: Yes, John, we've always had the freedom to shut up, but here's the thing—America was founded by a bunch of loudmouths. They started complaining and they didn't shut up until they won.

"You can love your country *and* still want it to improve. It's like loving someone who smokes. You tell them to quit—you *want* them to quit—because you don't want them to die of lung cancer. So you badger them and you criticize their choices, but you still love them more than anything in the world.

"I look at the Constitution . . . I look at it and I see . . . Look at it this way: There are people who want amendments to ban flag burning or gay marriage or whatever, but look at the Bill of Rights—it's about the rights we *have,* not the rights we *lose.* The Constitution doesn't exist to restrict freedom—it exists to *expand* it."

I can't stop myself now. I'm going to do it.

"So you can be as slick as you want. You can have fancy computer stuff and be better-spoken than me and better-looking and all of that, but none of that changes one simple thing. None of that changes the words 'Congress shall make no law.' No matter how much you try, you just can't change those words.

"Just because John is slicker doesn't mean he's right. I know I'm not polished, but that shouldn't matter. You can't change those words. They're still the same, whether it's John speaking them or me.

"So, you know what, John? I'm tempted . . . If you *really* don't have anything new or original to say, I'm tempted to give you your own advice from the other day and tell *you* to just shut the hell up."

I look out at the audience. It's totally silent. I run the last foot of the marathon.

"Instead, I'll just say: Keep talking. I support your right to do it, and besides, you're just digging your own grave."

What happens next isn't quite a Hollywood ending, but I guess I'll take it.

It starts with a raucous catcall that I recognize as Tit. Followed by a piercing whistle the likes of which only Flip can produce. And then applause from different spots all over the auditorium.

Flip spread out the Council. To make it sound like there's more people applauding than just a concentrated section.

And it works. Because some other people join in. Not a lot. Not even anything approaching a majority.

It's a minority. But a *loud* minority.

Not bad. We can start with that.

CHAPTER 33
CLARENCE DARROW?

BACKSTAGE, I CAN STILL HEAR THE CROWD GOING NUTS. Both sides are going at it now, trying to outdo each other. It takes the teachers a good ten minutes to calm everyone down enough to collect the ballots.

The Doc is furious. John's pissed, too.

"Kevin," the Doc says, barely controlling himself, "your job at the end was to calm them down, not get them all excited again."

"Yeah!" John says, sounding like a pathetic child.

I don't rise to the bait. "Look, Dr. Goethe. You can't do this once and expect it to let off all the steam. You need to do it all the time. You should make these things a regular occurrence or something. That's how safety valves work. You don't just use them once and then forget about them."

"I'm disappointed, Kevin."

"I'll be happy to talk about this issue any time, any place," I say.

"We're *not* doing this again, Kevin. Your Clarence Darrow days are over."

"Yeah," John chimes in. "This was supposed to be it."

"Do you only stand up for what you believe in when you

have permission?" I ask him. I don't know who Clarence Darrow is, but you can bet your ass I'm going to find out.

If the Doc wasn't standing right here, I think Riordon would drag me down to the ground and stomp me into paste right there.

Mrs. Sawyer comes back. "Voting's done," she says.

The Doc has us join him back on stage to read the results. I don't know why he's even bothering. There's no way in hell this crowd gave me the victory.

"The votes are: six hundred and thirty-eight to John Riordon, four hundred and twenty-seven to Kevin Ross."

John's side goes nuts. I can hear boos from *my* side, and there are more of them than I'd ever dared hope for.

Wow—638 to 427. I thought he would blow me out of the water. I thought it would be a total landslide.

As the teachers start to wrangle kids and get them out of the auditorium and off to second period, I turn to John and grin. "Remember: any time, any place."

CHAPTER 34
THE LAST DAY IN THE LIFE OF OFFICER SEXPOT

I SHOULD BE FLYING HIGH. I should be insane with triumph. But I'm not. I don't get it. I still feel like the same old loser I've always been.

It's one in the morning and I'm at SAMMPark, waiting for the rest of the Council to show up. Flip said to meet near the statue right inside the park entrance, so that's where I'm standing.

The Council shows up after a couple of minutes. Flip gets to me first and surprises me with a hug.

"Tough loss, man," says Tit.

I break away from Flip. "Was he that much better than me?"

"Nah," Tit says, throwing an arm around my shoulder. "People are just idiots. They vote for the guy they'd want to have a beer with instead of the guy who knows what he's talking about."

Flip adds, "The good news is, people don't outgrow it. Adults are just as stupid."

"How is that good news?"

Flip shrugs. "It's all Foolish, baby. It's all Foolish."

"Yeah, well . . . I don't know, guys. I think I prefer things quiet. It's been . . . It's been kinda chaotic, you know?"

Flip laughs. "The world is *dominated* by chaos. Except for the human race, which tries to impose order everywhere it goes. Despite the evidence around us—soil erosion, climate change, statistical variances in the gene pool—we still try to make nature walk in a straight line when it would rather zigzag." He sighs. He's on a roll.

He turns to the Council. "Sounds like Foolish behavior to me, boys. I hereby nominate the human race for membership in the Council of Fools!" He raises both arms and shouts to the sky. "Humanity! Join us! Join your masters! All opposed, say 'Nay'!"

And then nothing but silence and Flip's panting as he strains, listening.

"There are no dissenting votes!" he cries. "I hereby admit humanity to the Council of Fools!" He punches the air in triumph. "Dude," he says, grinning, "I just upped our membership by six billion. Not bad, huh?"

I look around. "Where's Fam?"

If he's disappointed that I didn't join him in his revelry, he doesn't show it. He just holds up his cell. "Standing lookout, in case the cops come by and try to interrupt."

"Interrupt what?"

He just snaps his fingers. The guys rush out of the park, then come back. Speedo and Jedi have Officer Sexpot, who's tastefully decked out in some barely there bondage gear. Tit is carrying another set of similar clothing.

"The plan, dear Kross, is sublime in its perfection. Designed to drive a stake through the heart of that which is held most sacred in this shitty little town. If you thought people were in an uproar over the ribbons and the Pledge of Allegiance and that shit, just wait until they see what we do . . ." He pauses and grins a wicked grin, as if he wished that a drumroll would start up right now. "To Susan Ann Marchetti!" He points to the statue and steps back.

"Boys, you know what to do!" Flip grabs my arm and pulls me back to watch with him as the Council guys close in on the statue and start to climb up the pedestal.

"What . . . What are they doing?" I ask, but even as I ask it, I realize—the statue is lifesize. The same size as Officer Sexpot.

"Oh, the torment!" Flip mock-moans. "Oh, the weeping, the wailing, the gnashing of teeth that will ensue in fair Brookdale when it's revealed that the town's patron saint and perfect little girl is actually a lesbian bondage fetishist locked in a classic sixty-nine with an officer of the law!"

"You can't be serious." But already I can see the guys putting some of the bondage gear on the statue.

"This is going to be classic," Flip says. "This won't just piss off one group or another; this will piss off *everyone*."

I watch it happen for another few seconds. "Flip, dude, don't do this. It isn't cool."

He blinks and pulls back from me. "What?"

"She never did anything to us. She's just some poor kid who got killed. Why are we doing this to her?"

"Poor, deluded Kross—we're not doing *anything* to her. We're doing it to her statue."

"No. Look. It's her memory. It's . . . Think about her family. This isn't right."

"I can't be nailed down to such mundane concepts. We've transcended right and wrong and ascended to the realm of intellectual mischief. You understand that. Besides, this has a nice little side benefit: Once word about this gets out, people will stop talking about all of the crap with you and the ribbons and everything."

"This isn't Foolish, Flip. It's just mean. It's wrong."

"Wrong? Who are *you* to decide right and wrong?" For the first time since I've known him, I see a glimmer of anger in Flip's eyes. And I don't like it. "Daddy's boy. Big goddamn *hero*," he says, quirking his lips into a grin at the very last moment to take most of the sting out of it.

Daddy's boy. Reminding me that he knows. Is he jealous of all the attention I've gotten?

No. Fam's right; Flip doesn't get jealous. It's impossible to be jealous when you assume you're better than everyone else around you.

"I'm tired of the patriotic stuff. It's old hat. It's been done before."

So he's bored with the flag game. He wants to move on. But here's the thing—I don't.

"This is tradition," he goes on. "The role of jester is an ancient and honorable one. Speaking truth to power has always been the province of the Fool."

"Yeah, I remember that from English class, too." And I've realized something—Flip isn't a genius after all. He just pukes up stuff from school with a swagger and a cigarette and everyone falls all over themselves. "But it has to *mean* something. You can't just be a jester for the sake of being a jester."

He looks at me with a blank expression and a little tilt to his head. "Says who?"

"Jesus, Flip! Come off it! Jesters didn't act in *secret*. They acted in *public*. Like I'm doing. Not from the shadows. You just keep spouting all this intellectual crap, but we're talking about real people and real—"

Just then, Flip's cell phone beeps. It's a special ringtone for Fam, the lookout.

"Cops!" Flip hisses, and everyone falls silent. The park isn't well lit; we're all in shadows.

The guys jump down from the pedestal and get behind the statue. The whole place goes quiet except for the crunch of gravel from the parking lot, where a police car minces along the ground. I can see its headlights from here.

I look over at the statue of Susan Ann Marchetti. Over her permanent nurse's outfit, she's now partly clad in a leather bra with spikes sticking out of it and some boots that are strategically slit to wrap around her legs all the way up to her thighs. Officer Sexpot is sort of hanging half off her, upside down.

I yell. Like I'm being gutted.

I don't even know I'm going to do it until I do it. Flip jerks back and looks at me in shock, and believe me—the look on my face must be just as shocked, because I can't believe I just heard that scream come out of my mouth. But there it is, there it goes, there it went—it's past tense now and there's the sound of a police car door opening and closing.

SAMMPark's frozen in a moment in time as we all look at one another through the dark.

And then, as if we've all heard the same silent, telepathic command, we break and run like hell.

I'm fast. Not join-the-track-team fast, but fast enough. I run away from the park entrance and the cop who's no doubt about to come through there. The rest of the Council has the same idea and now there's a pack of kids racing like the devil's on their tails toward the other end of the park.

"Wish . . ." Flip puffs next to me, "I could see . . . the look . . . on his face!"

And he starts laughing while he's running until the motion makes him cough.

I put on a burst of speed and outpace him, making it to the wall near the soccer field before anyone else. I've been climbing this wall forever—I know where the handholds are. I launch myself onto the wall and scramble up and over.

My car is waiting for me a hundred yards away in a gas station parking lot. I make for it and hop in. I resist the urge to gun the engine and floor the gas and roar off like a getaway man at a bank robbery; that would just make me look suspicious.

Instead, I force myself to wait until I've caught my breath before I crank the engine. Other Fools are spilling out of the park, running like hell, heading for Flip's car. Like I haven't got a care in the world, I drive home.

CHAPTER 35
FEAR

DAD'S UP FOR WORK WHEN I GET HOME. If he's pissed that I've been out after midnight on my provisional license, he doesn't show it.

"Who's this?" he asks.

He's pointing to Leah's picture. I left it out on the table. Oops.

"A girl."

"Isn't this the girl you saved?"

"Yeah." Of course, it's more complicated than that. I consider asking Dad for advice, but maybe not. He's not the best guy to ask about women, after all, having turned Mom off to penises for the rest of her life. "Hey, Dad?"

"Hmm?"

I almost say to him, "What would you think if I moved to California for the summer? Or forever?" I almost say it. But something stops me. I don't know what. I don't know why.

And now I have to say something, because he's looking at me expectantly and I can tell that "Never mind" just isn't going to cut it.

"Did you ever run away?" I don't even realize I'm going to say it until I actually say it.

"Run away? Like, from home?"

"No. No. I mean, in the war. Did you ever get scared? And run away?"

I feel like I've stepped over an invisible line. Accusing my dad.

"I was scared the whole time. All of us were. That's what war is like. You're afraid. You *have* to be afraid; otherwise you'll get killed." He shrugs like it's no big deal. "And we ran away, sure. In the army, it's called 'strategic withdrawal.'"

"Really?"

"Sure. The trick isn't not being afraid and not running away. The trick is dealing with your fear and running *back*."

Fear. God, that's what it all comes down to. Somehow everyone believed I was a hero when they couldn't understand how terrified I was. Somehow people looked to me as some sort of fearless rabble-rouser when they couldn't see the scared, confused kid inside.

Are we ever truly brave? Or do we just adjust our fear for a little while and mistake it for courage? How can fear on the inside look like bravery from the outside?

"Dad, Mom wants me to come visit her this summer and maybe live there permanently."

Oh. Oh, God. There it is. It's out. It's *out*.

I expect him to be angry. To punch the wall again. Or to go into his weird little trip-over-his-tongue phase.

Instead, he just looks at me. Nothing changes in his face at all. He doesn't move his lips or his jaw. He doesn't wrinkle his nose or widen his eyes or arch his brow. I don't even know if he's *breathing*—that's how still he is.

But his eyes change. Completely. Totally.

He's sad.

"Well, Kevin," he says at long last. "Well, I guess that makes a lot of sense."

And now I wish it *didn't* make sense. I wish it was the dumbest idea in the world so that I could say, *No, Dad—you're wrong. It's a bad idea. It's a bad idea, and I'm not gonna do it.*

I've seen my father angry. I've seen him outraged and confused and stern and in shock.

But I've never seen him so sad.

I hate that I'm the reason.

"Dad, I don't have to go—"

"Your mom's made a good life for herself out there," he says with a little sigh. "She's doing really well. She's happy. And I'm happy *for* her. You would be with your brother. You'd . . . You'd be in a better *place.*"

We both look around the apartment.

"Your mom misses you."

"But if I left . . ." I can't finish my thought. The words just won't come out.

Dad takes a step toward me. He hesitates, and then he hugs me. It's like before, only better because this time it was *his* idea.

"I would miss you so much," he whispers. "But you have to do what you think is best, Kevin. What you think is *right.* That's what I've always taught you, right?"

And it is. It *is* what he's always taught me. Stopping Flip from defiling Susan Ann Marchetti's memory . . . That was my *dad.*

"I don't know what to do, Dad."

He tightens his grip on me. "Welcome to my world."

CHAPTER 36
REVELATION

I MANAGE TO GET A FEW HOURS' SLEEP after Dad leaves. I toss and turn a lot. No one answer seems better than any other one.

The phone rings just as I wake up for school. I jerk into a frozen sitting position.

OK. It could be...

1. The cops
2. Flip, pissed at me
3. The cops, really

I consider not answering at all. But by the fourth ring, I grab it up. Better to know, I guess.

And the answer is... none of the above. It's Jesse.

"Hey," he says, and I can almost hear the wind and surf and the grains of hot sand in his voice.

"Hey," I say back. We have deep conversations, my brother and I.

Silence on the line.

"So, what's up?" he asks after a while.

"You called me," I remind him.

"Yeah, I know. I woke up extra early to catch you before you went to school. What's up?"

It's weird. It's like we've switched places and I'm the younger brother all of a sudden.

Used to be that me and Jesse talked all the time, about everything. We were like our own little secret society in the house while Mom and Dad yelled and screamed at each other. Then he was gone and there was this long silence of miles between us.

"What's going on, man?" I ask him. "Is this whole deal legit?"

"What whole deal?" Ever since he moved to California and became Total West Coast Guy, my little brother sounds like everything in the world is both too boring for him to deal with and too annoying for him to care. I don't know how he pulls it off. It's like yawning and glaring at the same time.

"Me coming to live with you guys."

"Sure. Why wouldn't it be?"

Because Mom disappeared and barely contacted me. Because she's a different person now. *You're* a different person now. I don't fit in, so why would she want me there?

Or because if it's *not* legit, then I don't have to make the decision. No matter what I decide, I'm a hero to someone . . . and a villain to someone else.

But I don't say any of that to him. Because he's my little brother, yeah, but he's also a stranger. He's not the kid who used to worship me, used to follow me around all the time, annoying me but also, I have to admit, sort of flattering me, too.

And now, well, things have changed. He's younger than I am, but he's more confident. He would never understand how I could be afraid that Mom doesn't *really* want me.

Then again, he's the one she took.

"I guess I just don't get it," I tell him, which is more honest than I'd intended on being. "Why now?"

"I don't know."

"And does she really want me to live out there?"

"She was talking to Rita and they were going on about stuff."

"What kind of stuff?"

"Like fixing your skin. You really need to do something about that, bro." He says it like he's an indulgent parent gently scolding a child.

"Yeah, I know." It just doesn't seem all that important. There's always something else, and besides, even without the zits, I'm still no prize. So why go through all the effort of polishing crap? It's still crap at the end of the day.

"Hey, Jesse?"

"Yeah?"

"You remember that time when we were little and we wanted Reese's peanut butter cups at the store, but Mom wouldn't buy them, so when we got home we went into the kitchen and we squirted half a bottle of chocolate syrup into the peanut butter and ate it with spoons?"

There's a pause and I wonder if we're still connected, and then he says, "Mom says peanut butter is loaded with fat. And Rita's allergic to peanuts anyway."

"Oh."

We wait in silence. I try not to think about how much it's costing Mom to have Jesse and me sit on the phone and not say anything.

"Hey, Jesse?"

"What?" Like he'd wait forever for me to talk.

"I'm, uh . . . I'm sorry. About that time. At the airport."

Long pause. "What?"

"At the airport. When you moved to California. How I yelled at you." It feels good to finally do it.

"I don't know what you're talking about."

"Come on."

"No, seriously. What are you talking about?"

Isn't that just the way? You stress and kill yourself and guilt yourself and it turns out to be nothing.

"So are you gonna do it?" he asks.

"Are we talking about my skin again?"

"No. About you moving out here."

"Is that really why you called so early?" It's like four in the morning out there.

He waits so long to answer that I think—again—we've been disconnected. Finally: "Kev? Do you remember what it was like when Mom and Dad were married?"

The yelling and screaming? Sure. Who could forget? "Well, yeah."

"Because I don't."

"And that's why you called me this early? Because you don't remember . . ." And I stop.

Jesse sounds *sad* that he doesn't remember.

It hits me then—he doesn't know what it was like. He has a

good life out there in California, but he doesn't know if his life used to be better. As far as he knows, it's always been this way.

I try to remember back to when I was six or seven. It's tougher than I thought it would be. I remember little bits and pieces, but nothing major. Maybe that's because I don't have anyone to talk to about those memories, so they just fade. Is that how memory works?

"What's wrong, Jesse?"

"I don't know. I just wondered what it was like."

"Do you remember Pandazilla and Aquahorse?"

"Of course." He laughs a little. "I remember *you*, Kev. I just don't remember *them*."

Maybe that's for the best. But we talk some more and I try to be fair, try to tell him the good stuff and the bad stuff. We start filling in each other's gaps a little bit and that's cool, even if some of the gaps are painful.

After a while, call waiting beeps, which is probably good. I don't know how much of this remembering we should do at one time.

Jesse hangs up after saying, "I hope I see you in a couple of months," and I click over to the other line.

"Did you see the paper?" Flip asks, his voice bouncing.

I go get the newspaper from the doorstep. It's raining and the paper's a little soggy, but I can still read the headline: Vandals Desecrate SAMMpark. There's a picture of cops milling about the statue, and you can actually see the statue just the way we left it.

"It's even better this way," Flip says, all giddy. "I didn't even have to hack anything this time. They did the work for me. Of course, we lost Officer Sexpot, but that's no big deal. She went out at the top of her game, God bless her."

I tell him I need to go, even though I don't have anything to do before school. I look at the mess of my camcorder, at the picture of Leah, at the newspaper. My life is a mix of some really weird stuff and I don't know what any of it means.

But maybe I don't have to. Maybe I just have to keep running back to it.

If Flip thought that the attempted desecration of the SAMM-Park statue would somehow take the heat off me at school, he was wrong. Even the mayor's new stickers on my car don't inoculate me.

There is a slightly different vibe, though. I'm not crazy enough to think that I changed people's minds, but maybe I gave them something to think about, at least. And if Dr. Goethe takes my idea seriously, there will be more opportunities to do that.

One inch at a time. One *mind* at a time.

I feel . . . OK. But I *should* feel great, tell the truth. I mean, I stomped all over John Riordon, verbally speaking. I got some people to applaud for me. Just this morning, Mr. Wistler, the guy who runs the school paper, asked me if I would write an editorial.

I fought the good fight for Susan Ann Marchetti. I finally told Dad about Mom's offer.

But . . .

But even though I try to avoid seeing Leah or Riordon in the halls, I end up catching them repeatedly, almost as if God is shoving them in my face. *See what you don't get, Kross?*

It bothers me up until around lunchtime, when I go hide out on the catwalk and then kick myself for being a complete idiot.

How can I be pissed at Leah for not returning my, y'know, my *emotions* when she didn't even know about them? Is she supposed to read my mind? Until I saved her life, I hardly ever even talked to her. Even *God* likes us to remind him we love him—how can people be any different?

It's tough to admit, but Riordon *deserves* her. He had the courage to talk to her, to go after her. Me? I just . . . I never did. I had the courage to save her life, but not to ask her out. I don't have any right to be pissed at either of them.

Man, that sucks. No matter how bad things get, you can make 'em a little bit better by getting angry at *someone.*

I hear Fam on the ladder before I see her.

"Hey, Kevin."

"Hi, Jules." It just feels right. I don't feel like a Fool right now. "Thanks for letting me borrow your cell the other day."

She plops down next to me. "You're welcome."

"And thanks for, you know, for everything else." She says nothing, so I keep going. "For the research. And for keeping my secret. And for, you know, not telling Flip about me being an idiot. And . . ."

And we sit in total silence for a little while.

"You OK?" she asks.

"I guess."

"Is this about . . . that girl?"

Something in the way she says it . . . It's that hesitation. I realize that she knows "that girl" is Leah.

"Yeah. I don't . . . I don't know."

"Don't know what?"

I sigh. *"Anything."*

She laughs. "Have you tried *talking* to her?"

Now it's *my* turn to laugh. "Not a chance."

"Why not?"

"Because . . ." *Because she's perfect. And I'm scum.* "There's just no point. She's better than me. She's out of my league, OK?"

Fam snorts. "I don't know what's worse—when guys treat us like sex objects or when they treat us like . . . like . . . *goddesses.* I mean, we're just *people,* Kevin. We stink up the bathroom like anyone else. We're not magic."

Not much to say to that, so I just nod and sit there.

"It doesn't have to be all or nothing. You can be friends with girls, you know."

"Like you?"

"I'm a good role model," she says, preening. I laugh.

When the bell rings, Fam gets up and heads to the ladder. "Aren't you coming?"

"Nah. I'm sitting out gym today."

"Take care of yourself, Kevin."

"I will."

So I stay there for the next period. Away from everyone. I just sit there and look at Leah's picture and wonder what the hell I'm doing with my life, with myself, with any of it.

And I think about what Fam said. And about how stupid I am. She's right: Why do I think girls are either goddesses who can't be bothered with me or not good enough for me? Why am I always on the extreme end?

Well, Kross, it's simple: You miss your mommy.

Ugh. That's stupid. Flip's voice in my head. I don't know where that came from.

I do miss my mom, though. I miss feeling like I matter, like I belong.

Gee, Kross, and here you've been moving heaven and earth to get all kinds of attention. Go figure.

My own voice that time. I tell it to shut up anyway because I don't feel like listening.

Back in the real world, I get busted for skipping gym and sent to the office. Figures. I've blown off enough classes that I guess it was inevitable.

Which, really, isn't that bad, since I want to talk to the Doc about more debates anyway.

Today I rate—I get not only Dr. Goethe but also the Spermling.

"This is very disappointing," says Dr. Goethe. The Spermling sighs heavily.

I shrug.

"You could have been a wonderful role model for your classmates," Goethe goes on, and the Spermling nods righteously. "You could have been an inspiration. Instead, you've . . ." He trails off, as if he's not sure exactly what I've done.

"I what? I spoke my mind? I encouraged other people to think for themselves? Is that a crime?"

"You didn't go about it in the most mature fashion, Kevin."

"Well, I'm sixteen—what do you want?"

That shuts him up for a second; I don't think he expected that.

"And now, uh, skipping classes . . ." Goethe goes on.

"Just gym."

"Physical fitness is very important," the Doc scolds.

Just then, the Spermling does something that could be a grunt or could be a snort—who knows? He's so fat that he snores even when he's awake. I can't help it—I grin like a smart-ass. Yeah, physical fitness is *real* important. Exhibit One—the Spermling.

"Oh, yeah, totally. *Clearly.*"

The Doc catches my drift, but he just says, "Nonetheless."

Silence. I don't really have a smart retort to "Nonetheless." What a lousy, conversation-killing word.

So I get some chewing out and some detention and I get dismissed.

But then something bizarre and amazing happens.

When I emerge into the murky halls of SBHS, Tit comes up to me, breathless, before English starts.

"Kross, where have you been? You missed gym and you—"

"I was meeting with the Doc and the Spermling."

"You missed it! Oh, man, everyone's talking about it! I was *there*. You missed it."

"Missed what?"

"Crazy J beat the crap out of Mr. Kaltenbach in gym!" His eyes dance like someone's flashing a strobe light in his face.

"Really? Are you sure?" Crazy J has beat up just about everyone in the senior class at some point. He's a really screwed-up guy, but I've never heard of him beating up a teacher.

"I was *there*," he says again, as if that explains everything.

"Mr. Burger had us inside because of the rain, so we were doing chin-ups. Kaltenbach had the baseball team doing laps around us. And then out of nowhere—wham!" Tit smacks a fist into his palm to make the point. "Crazy J hauls off and punches Kaltenbach. *Hard.* Knocked him right on his ass. He hit his head on the bleachers, man!"

And then . . .

And then a tiny miracle happens.

By the time I'm out of English, it's like my life's been reset to the day before the library and the Surgeon, and the ribbons, wiped off the South Brook radar screen by Hurricane Crazy J. The hallways are abuzz with talk of Josh Mendel's latest and greatest affront to civilization.

All traces of my celebrity and notoriety have been swept away in the most recent tide of teen scandal. At the end of the day, I head to the parking lot, unnoticed and alone.

How weird.

Of course, *I* haven't been reset. I still did it all, still said it all. I still have two bumper stickers on my car that I don't want there.

Fortunately, they're not going to be an issue much longer. When I get home, there's a package waiting for me. Two *new* stickers inside—the perfect size to cover the original stickers.

But I put down the box and look at the picture of Leah. And at my broken video camera, crushed when I dropped my backpack to tackle the Surgeon.

I think of what I said to Flip in SAMMPark. How he was doing something wrong. Not something clever.

Is that what I've been doing all along, ever since this hero stuff started? Have I been doing clever things to cover up my own sin?

Yes. Yes, I think so.

OK, here's the truth. The last and final truth, the thing I've held back. I can't hold it back any longer, because I'm tired. I'm not that strong and it's just too heavy.

That day at the library.

It's not just that I was following Leah.

It's not just that I was taping her.

It's that . . .

When he attacked her . . .

I didn't run back into the alley because I heard her scream. I was *already there*. I knew her routine. I knew she cut through the alley. I was *waiting for her. Just like he was.*

I saw it. I saw him moving toward her. From behind a Dumpster.

I jumped him just as he was about to grab her and stick her with the needle. I did that.

But . . . but you see . . . I *saw* him. I had maybe a minute. A *full minute.* Do you know how *long* a minute is? It's *forever.*

A minute when he didn't see me. When no one knew I was there.

And I just *watched.*

I watched him approach her. I saw the needle. I knew what he was going to do, what was going to happen.

And I did *nothing.* For a full *minute.*

I watched. And when Leah screamed, it was like I suddenly realized that this was *real.* This was *live.* It wasn't on one of my tapes. It was happening. Leah was about to be drugged and raped and murdered.

And I just stood there! Watching it!

It would have been so easy just to stand there and keep watching. To keep *taping*. Just let it happen. Take no action. I mean, that's what I've always done—nothing. So it would have been easy to keep doing exactly that.

And end up with a videotape of Leah's abduction to go in my creepy, screwed-up voyeur's collection.

I am actually *worse* than Michael Alan Naylor. At least he had the balls to act on his own. Me? I didn't move a muscle until Leah screamed.

And I have a videotape to prove it.

CHAPTER 37
PENANCE AND RECONCILIATION

IT'S NOT ENOUGH TO FEEL BAD about what I've done. It's not enough to hate myself for it.

As long as those tapes exist, I'll always be tempted to look at them, to watch those stolen moments of Leah walking the halls at school, sitting at lunch—any place and any time I was able to catch her.

"Stolen moments" is the perfect way to put it, actually. Because she didn't know. She didn't say it was OK. I just did it.

I break my own cardinal rule about never throwing away anything incriminating at home. I just can't bear another *second* with those damn tapes in existence. Every time I look at them, I think of me, skulking around, in the shadows. A damn stalker. I can't handle it.

So I crack the cases under my foot. I pull out the tape and crumple it up and then make sure to break it in several places. It's several twisted messes by the time I'm done with them all.

Dad asks about them, of course. Sees them in the trash. Of course.

"The machine ate them," I lie.

He's holding up a handful of tape like it's a dead cat. "Did the machine break the cases, too?"

"I got pissed." I shrug.

"What was on here?"

"Old Ravens games."

Dad regards me for a second, then tsks. "Watch your temper, Kevin."

When I'm alone, I sit there for a long time, looking at the new stickers, the broken camera, the picture. And this is what I realize: You can't go forward until you've dealt with whatever's behind you. It would be the easiest thing in the world to run to California, but that would accomplish nothing.

I don't know what to do next. But I think I know where I can find out.

It's weird being back at Sacred Heart after so long. It's been at least a year since I've gone to Mass. I slip in just as the evening service is starting and slide into a pew way in the back so no one sees me.

And, man! It's funny how it feels so familiar. Like I never went away. Father McKane starts off with the greeting and I'm doing the ole north-south-east-west like I never stopped.

"The grace of our Lord Jesus Christ and the love of God and the fellowship of the Holy Spirit be with you all," he says, and I don't even need to look down at the missal because I'm already saying, "And also with you." Like no time has passed at all.

I think about that night at SAMMPark, when I told Tit about Leah. Maybe God *has* been watching me. Maybe it's just that I couldn't understand what it meant. That I was *supposed* to tape Leah at the Burger Joint and become obsessed. And then I was *supposed* to follow Leah to the library. Maybe it's like I was *sent* or something. All so that I could become a hero and then fall from grace and learn a lesson about real heroism. All to protect her, regardless of what came next.

Or maybe it was all coincidence and accident, but maybe coincidence and accident is how God works. Maybe those are his tools.

"Let us acknowledge our failures," Father McKane is saying, "and ask the Lord for pardon and strength."

And the words spill out of me:

"I confess to almighty God, and to you, my brothers and sisters, that I sinned through my own fault, in my thoughts and in my words, in what I have done, and in what I have failed to do . . ."

And that's the kicker, really. It's the stuff we *don't* do that kills us, in the end. It's when we don't tell people things, like me not telling Leah how I felt for so long. That's what led to the rest of it.

I let the readings and the Gospel wash over me. Always liked this part—the part when stories are told. And then the sermon, where Father McKane ties it all together and makes all of those stories relevant somehow. With Easter coming up, he talks a lot about resurrection, about renewal, which is cool with me because I feel like I've been resurrected, in some ways. If not reset, then at least given a new lease on life.

And here's the thing about resurrection—it's not a chance to start over. You don't come out of the tomb and say, "Great! Forget all of that stuff I did before; now I'm a whole new person." No, you're the same person—you just have a chance to be *better*. You get the chance to fix the things you screwed up, the things that would have stayed screwed up if you hadn't come back. Like, when Jesus came back, he didn't go off and play piano in a bar somewhere, right? No, he picked up where he left off and kept teaching, just in a different way.

And I realize that this is what *I* need to do. I can't let Crazy J's temper tantrum sweep away anything I might accomplish. People—especially high-schoolers, but people in general, really—have short attention spans. But that doesn't mean that I should stop talking. It just means I have to keep getting their attention.

So that's what I'm going to do. My argument, my debate, my *fight*, didn't end when Crazy J decked a teacher. It just moved into a new phase. I'm not sure what that phase is yet, but I know it's there.

I'm one guy, and look at what I stirred up just by asking questions about these things. Imagine what two people could do. Or three. Or ten.

Or four hundred and twenty-seven.

And then Father McKane snaps me back to the present by saying the prayers over the gifts and then we're all giving each other the sign of peace. There are startled looks as people realize it's me, that I'm right here, right here in church. But no one turns away.

And then we're lining up for communion. When it's my turn, Father McKane's eyes crinkle as he grins.

"The body of Christ," he says.

"Amen."

I take the wafer and slip it into my mouth. Walking back to my seat, I'm suddenly aware of how everyone is watching me. But that's OK. I've dealt with worse.

At the end of the Mass, I wait and watch as everyone files out, shaking hands with Father McKane and chatting with him before going on. It's an evening service, though, so it's not that crowded and pretty soon everyone's gone except for him and me.

"Kevin." He smiles at me. "Good to see you again."

And he's like the only person to say *that* to me in a while.

"Do you have time to hear a confession, Father?" Better get it out before I lose my nerve.

He nods. "Of course, Kevin. Of course."

And so here I am in the confessional, that little box that Mom used to call the "outhouse of sins" when Dad wasn't listening.

"Bless me, Father, for I have sinned. It has been . . ." And here's the ironic part about confession—it really tempts you to *lie*. To lie about what you did or didn't do. Even to lie about how long it's been since your last confession. I figure that's why you start off saying how long it's been—to confront the temptation to lie right up front and get it out of your system.

"It's been fourteen months since my last confession." I feel really, *really* bad saying it. Fourteen months is a *long* time and I can't even remember all of the many sins I'm sure I've committed since then. I tell this to Father McKane.

"I remember the big stuff, sure, but I'm sure there's a lot of stuff in there that I'm just not remembering. So I can't confess to it, so I can't be forgiven, which means I'm damned, right?"

"If you're truly sorry in your heart, God will forgive you *all* your sins, Kevin. Let's hit the big stuff, OK?"

"OK."

Deep breath.

Second temptation to lie.

Avoid it.

I tell him about California. About Mom's offer, about how I wanted to take it. About uncharitable thoughts toward Dad—that's a commandment right there, not honoring thy father and mother, you know?

I'm stalling, I realize.

I tell him about the pranks with Officer Sexpot. (I don't call her Officer Sexpot to *him*—he's a priest!) He makes a little strangled sound that I think is a laugh, but I don't know.

Yeah, stalling.

What's the point?

So, I tell him . . .

"There's this girl . . ."

And I tell him everything. *Everything.* Right down to the videotape and the stalking. This is the big stuff—you've got multiple commandments, here, from lying ("bearing false witness") to stealing to coveting. *Bigtime* coveting. I'm in the Hall of Fame for Coveting, tell the truth. They build statues to me there. Which—crap!—is like a false idols thing. Damn, another commandment!

"And you destroyed this tape?" Father McKane asks. He's very serious now. Usually he's a pretty happy-go-lucky guy, which is one reason why I've always been cool with confession. Then again, I've never confessed to anything truly horrible.

"Yes, Father. All of them."

"And you have no intention of making another one?"

"I couldn't even if I wanted to. The camera's busted."

"I . . . see."

"But even if it wasn't," I say in a rush, "I wouldn't do it anyway. I've learned my lesson. I've figured it out. It was wrong. I didn't think I was hurting anyone, but that doesn't mean it was OK to do it. And I see how it can lead to other stuff that's not so cool."

And then there's a long silence. So long that I start to think he's fallen asleep or something, so I press my face real close to the screen between us and try to make out his face, but of course I can't, which is the whole *point* of the screen in the first place. This is all supposed to be anonymous, but it never is.

"You've had an interesting fourteen months since the last time we spoke," he says suddenly.

"It's been the last month or so that's been *really* interesting."

"Yes. I follow the papers."

More silence. Is he waiting for me to confess to the magnets? The bridge support? The burning flags? All of that stuff? Because I won't. No way, no how. Most of it I wasn't involved in, but the stuff I *was* involved in, I believe with all my heart. No way in the world I'll apologize for it. Not to him. Not even to God.

"I can absolve you for most of this, Kevin. But you know . . . you can't look outside of yourself for authority. For forgiveness. God forgives, but first we must forgive ourselves. Before this has all been made right in God's eyes, there's something you need to do. Think of it as your penance. It's the only way you'll ever feel better about this again."

I know exactly what he means.

CHAPTER 38
REVELATION (AGAIN-LUCKY ME!)

SO HERE I AM, SITTING IN MY CAR at the end of Leah Muldoon's driveway. My stomach's a mess of acid and grinding. It's like I've swallowed rocks and my gut is doing its best to digest them, but they won't break down, so they just keep colliding against each other and churning and rolling.

The picture of Leah is like a hot coal in my pocket.

I close my eyes and try to make it better. I try to imagine a happy ending.

I give her the picture and she says, *I don't understand. You... Of all people, you could have had this. All you had to do was ask me.*

And then ...

And then she rushes into my arms ...

Throws herself at me ...

Peppers my face with kisses ...

But probably not.

That's what I'd *like* to have happen. What I fantasize, what I dream. But let's face it, the world just doesn't work that way. And it has nothing to do with anything. It just *is*.

So I'm going to walk up the driveway. I'm going to ring the doorbell. I know Leah's home because her car's in the driveway. But if she doesn't answer the door I'm going to ask her mom or her dad or whoever *does* answer to get her for me. And then I'm going to hand her the picture and I'm going to say *nothing*. I could spout out stuff about how I've been watching her for years and how I've adored her from afar, but what would be the point? Nothing would change. Nothing would improve. Not for either of us. I've confessed to God and that's cool. I'll give back the picture, which is a confession all its own. But she doesn't need to know the details. They would just disturb her. Hurt her. And I don't want to do that.

Father McKane just said I had to make amends with Leah. He didn't say I had to be an idiot about it.

So.

I walk up the driveway. Before I can even ring the bell, though, the door opens and there's Leah, her head tilted, looking at me like a dog that isn't sure if you've got a treat or not.

"Hi, Kevin." Since she's clueless, she's happy to see me.

I can't speak. My lips won't move.

"Kevin?"

There's a million things to say, but I can't think of a single one right now. I pull the picture out of my pocket.

I hand it over to her. Her eyes go wide and she says nothing at all. She *certainly* doesn't throw herself into my arms and cover my ugly mug with a mass of kisses. Which is fine and is exactly what I expected, so . . .

I worried about what to say at this moment, but you know what? There's nothing *to* say. So I just walk back down the driveway to my car.

Leah comes running behind me, much to my surprise.

"Kevin, wait!"

I turn to take my medicine, but she's just holding out the picture to me. "Here. I want you to have it."

Say *what*? I've been stressing over this thing for days and now she's just gonna give it back to me?

"Why?"

"Why what?"

"Why do you want me to have it?"

She shrugs. "I don't know. Because you want it, I guess."

"Leah, I . . ." I struggle with the words. "I *stole* it."

"Yeah, I know. But . . . I don't know. I guess it's not a big deal. I was wondering where it went. I figured it blew off the mirror and got lost somewhere. Look," she says, "if you'd asked me for it, I would have been fine with it. It's OK for you to have it. Just don't, y'know, put it up on the 'net or anything."

Like I would. I reach out to take the picture, because suddenly I *do* want it. I don't have my tapes anymore and I have no shot with Leah, but at least I can have the picture, right? And guilt-free this time because she's offering it to me . . .

And how pathetic is that? We haven't said the obvious yet. We haven't said that I'm clearly, sadly in love with her and that she's not in love with me.

There, I said it: in love. Sounds really stupid, too.

"Hey," she says suddenly. "I like your bumper stickers."

I've covered up the mayor's stickers with the two I special-ordered: One is red, white, and blue and says, SUPPORT FREE SPEECH. The other is yellow and says, THINK FOR YOURSELF.

"Thanks." I mumble it. I wonder what her boyfriend would think of them and I have to bite my tongue to keep from saying it.

She drops her hand to her side. "Kevin, is something wrong?"

Yeah, everything's pretty much wrong. But I'm not going to tell *her* that.

"Are you angry at me?" She says it with such concern and such worry that there are two things that bubble up inside me. One is *How could I ever be angry at you?* but the other one is—

"Why are you dating him?" And oh *shit* I said it out loud! What the hell?

She blinks. "I don't get it."

"You keep telling me you're on my side on this whole free speech thing, but then you go off with John and—"

"The two don't have anything to do with each other."

"How can you say that? He's like a . . . a . . . Neanderthal." Oh, smooth, Kross—impress the girl you're crushing on by insulting her boyfriend.

"God, Kevin! I'm not *marrying* him. It's just high school."

"Yeah, well . . . I'm not gonna stop. The free speech stuff, I mean. Crazy J sort of made people forget, but I'm not going to let them *keep* forgetting. I'm going to make more noise."

"That's fine. I think it's great. I really do."

"But you won't stand up to John. You won't tell him he's full of it."

"I respect you. I'm *dating* John. I *like* him. We have fun together. I'm not looking for a political ally."

Well, what do I say to *that*?

"I didn't know how you felt," she goes on. "You never told me, and now you come here and get all pissed at me because I never acted on something I didn't know about? Is that it? Did you think I would somehow magically know how you felt about me?"

The worst part? Yeah. Yeah, I did. God, that's pathetic.

"Did you think you could just come here and tell me how . . . Hell, you never even told me anything—you just came here with the picture."

OK, now *that's* the worst part.

"I'm sorry," I whisper.

"What do you *want*, Kevin?"

"To be friends?" I blurt out before I'm even aware I'm going to say it.

She laughs. "Of *course* we're friends. You saved my life. And I think you should go on talking about what you believe in because it means a lot to you. And I believe it, too, but I guess I don't care as much as you do. I wish I did, but I don't. And that really, really makes me honored that you still want to be my friend." She smiles at me, smiles like the picture, and it's a smile *for* me and *to* me and that's just amazing.

"Now take your damn picture." She holds it up again.

I reach out for it. And I can't help myself—I'm smiling at her, matching her grin with my own, smiling even though I hate my smile, my lips peeled back, and I don't care what I look like in this moment and she doesn't care; we're just two friends.

I take the picture from her.

And something occurs to me.

"Hey, Leah?"

"What?"

"Who did you vote for?"

She freezes up. "I don't . . . What do you mean?"

"After the debate. Who did you vote for?"

"What does that matter?"

"It was a secret ballot. No one would know who you voted for. So tell me."

But she doesn't need to. I know. Because if it was me, she would have told me right away. She voted for Riordon. Not even because she believes him, but just . . . because. Because *whatever*. Because it doesn't matter to her.

And it does matter to me. A lot.

It's like a switch is flipped inside my head and my stomach. And all that obsession just . . . goes away.

Fam was right.

I'm suddenly *seeing* Leah for the first time. As a person. Not an ideal. Not some unobtainable *thing*. And you know what? Leah's not perfect. She's not a goddess. I mean, duh, right? But she's just sort of . . . OK.

She's even—God, I can't believe it!—sort of shallow.

Why would I want *that* for a girlfriend or an obsession or whatever?

It all hits me in that moment. I used to think—like, two minutes ago!—I was in love with Leah, but obsession isn't love. I know the truth now. I was just using her. Using some *idea* of her as a distraction from Mom and Jesse.

Yeah, I know her favorite color and where she lives and what she does for Christmas, but I didn't *know* her. Until now.

So, this picture . . . I don't need it or want it anymore.

"You know what, Leah? It's OK. You keep it."

I hand it back to her.

"But . . . But . . ." She looks down at it. "Just because of the debate. Is that all? Just because . . ."

And I smile.

I smile my real, honest smile.

"Don't worry about it. It's not a big deal. Thanks for everything," I say. "Really. I had a good time at your party. I'm sorry again about the picture. That was stupid. Bye."

And then I get into my car, and I don't look back.

Tell the truth, it's the most heroic thing I've ever done.

Safety Valve

EPILOGUE

"CALL ME FROM EACH LAYOVER," Dad says, handing me the pre-paid cell phone. "And call your mother, too."

"I know, Dad."

It's the third day of summer vacation and we're standing near the security gate at the airport. My flight leaves in an hour, but the security line is short, so I'm not worried about rushing.

"It's only got a few hours on it," he goes on, "so don't waste them calling your friends or anything."

"Jeez, Dad, I know."

So, yeah, I'm getting on a plane. Heading to California to see what I can find there, if I can find *me* there, or maybe just another version of me, a better version. Because we can always be better, right?

All I know is this: There's a piece of me missing. It's been missing since Mom and Jesse went out there, and I tried to fill the hole with Leah and that didn't work out so well. So now I'm opening up my own safety valve, like the pioneers did way back when. Going west. Because maybe that part of me that's missing is in California.

Anyway, like Dad said, it's one thing to run away. From Leah. From the Council. From the endless debates. There's nothing *wrong* with running away. The trick is running *back*.

"You better get in line," Dad says. He's right—the line's gotten a little bit longer while we were saying goodbye.

I give him a hug. He pats me on the back. Before I go, though, I fish around in my pocket and hand Dad the key to Brookdale.

"What am I supposed to do with this?" he asks, surprised.

"Just hold on to it for me. And Dad? Whatever you do, *don't* send it to me in California."

He closes his fist on the key and shakes his head slowly. "Why not?"

"Because this way, I have to come back for it."

AUTHOR'S NOTE

EVERY DAY, SOLDIERS, MARINES, AIRMEN, AND SAILORS return from overseas with injuries that take time to heal. In some cases, it takes a lifetime.

If you'd like to support them, consider donating to the Yellow Ribbon Fund. The Yellow Ribbon Fund assists the families and friends of servicemen and servicewomen so that they can visit the wounded as they recuperate at Walter Reed Army Medical Center and Bethesda Naval Hospital.

In addition, the fund also offers mentoring and internship programs to returning servicemen and servicewomen so that they can begin to reintegrate with the civilian world.

Many of those who return from combat overseas are amputees or have sustained otherwise life-altering injuries. Having their friends and families with them while recuperating is the best medicine in the world. The Yellow Ribbon Fund helps make that possible.

Visit the fund at www.yellowribbonfund.org. Even if you feel like you can't do much on your own, you can always consider organizing a fundraiser at your school, church, or community center.

And don't forget—in just about every community in the country, there are many, many residents now serving overseas. Ask around; you'll find it's easy to get names from those who live around you. Then go to your local post office and ask about sending a care package—it will be well appreciated by those serving in the field.

ACKNOWLEDGMENTS

It is both safe and accurate to say that this book would not exist (at least not in any form worth reading) without the persistence and assistance of my agent, Kathy Anderson, and my editor, Margaret Raymo. Ladies, without you this book would have been half as long . . . and nowhere near half as good. Thank you.

Thank you, too, to Lois Szymanski, who told me the story that inspired the book.

The Award for Redundancy Award goes to Robin Brande and Molly Krichten, both of whom read multiple drafts and never complained. (At least, not to me.)

Special thanks to Zac Tine and Eric Lyga for reading that first, awful draft.

Extra-special thanks to Liz Dubelman because I've never thanked her in print and she deserves it.

Last but not least, I want to thank Kenneth C. Wright Sr. His stories of his days as a Marine in Vietnam and his quiet dignity in reliving them made me understand what *real* support entails, not just the easy and superficial kind. Thanks for doing a thankless job.

DON'T MISS THE LATEST FROM BARRY LYGA:

GOTH GIRL
RISING

AVAILABLE FROM HOUGHTON MIFFLIN

ONE

My MOTHER AND I BOTH spent a lot of time in hospitals. Unlike her, I survived.

Before she went and died, my mom told me to stop bitching about my cramps all the time. "It's nothing that every other woman on the planet hasn't gone through," she said.

And besides, she went on, your period is a good thing. It's a sign that you're alive and healthy.

Easy for her to say—cancer was eating her lungs from the inside out, so what's the big deal about some cramps, right?

Still, I knew that what I was experiencing wasn't right or normal. It wasn't what other girls were feeling every month. (I know—I asked around.)

Weird thing, though: After she died, my cramps sort of got better. It's not like they went away; they just stopped being so intense and so consuming. I started to think that, OK, maybe *this* is what other girls felt. Like I had been abnormal before, but now I was somehow becoming normal, that now the world was working properly and everything was good and normal and usual.

Everything except my mom's *face* . . .

My mom's face before they closed the casket looked like a Barbie doll's.

A Barbie doll someone had left in the sandbox too long.

All plasticky and too shiny, but somehow gray at the same time.

And then one day after the funeral—it was a pretty nice day, too—I took a box cutter from my dad's workshop and slashed across my wrist. It hurt, but not that much. Not bad at all.

So I slashed the other one, too.

And that's how I ended up in the emergency room and then in front of a judge and then locked up in a mental hospital.

That was my first time in the hospital. And I got out and I covered up my scars and I went on with my life and I tried to figure out what it was all about, and I'm *still* trying to figure it out.

But it just gets more and more complicated all the time. Every day. The world doesn't slow down long enough for you to figure out anything; it keeps adding things in. Things like geeky guys and comic books and comic book conventions and effed-up teachers and . . .

And another stay in the hospital.

TWO

GOD I'M *DYING* FOR A CIGARETTE. I turned sixteen while I was away but this stupid state says you have to be eighteen to smoke, so they wouldn't let me smoke in the hospital.

When I got home this afternoon, the first thing I did was look for my cigs. But Roger had tossed them already. Now that *he's* quit, he's an effing cigarette *Taliban*, even though it's, like, years too late for that.

"Mom's already dead!" I yelled at him. "Who the hell do you think you're saving?"

And he just gave me his Sad, Tired look. It's one of the three he's got, the other two being Pissed Off and Blissed Out on ESPN.

"You, Kyra." Like it's some big revelation. "Someone has to protect you from yourself. From all the crap out in the world."

"Don't do me any favors," I told him.

He took a deep breath. "It's your first day back home. Can't you behave just a little bit?"

I went to my room. Home all of five minutes and I was already isolated in my room. Living with Roger isn't much different from being in the hospital. He's in charge, just like the doctors and nurses are in charge in the hospital. I have no say. I have no rights.

To make things worse, I'm going back to school in the morning. I don't want to go back to school.

See, I haven't been to school in a while. Six months, which includes all of summer break, when everyone else in the universe was off having fun. Except for me. I got put away. Now I'm supposed to go back to school like nothing happened.

School seems like something that happens to other people.

Last spring, I met this guy. And I guess I fell in love with him a little bit, which was a stupid thing for me to do because it never works out and it's pointless. So I kicked him in the balls and walked away from him and even flipped him off over the Internet.

And then my dad started in on me because, see, before all of this, this kid—this *Fanboy*—had a bullet. And I guess I sort of stole it from him and he figured out I had it and he called my effing *dad* and then all hell broke loose at home because my dad was all freaked out, like I was going to try to kill myself again. And he spent all this time tearing apart the house, looking for this goddamn bullet, which he couldn't find because I'd already given it back to Fanboy . . . right at the same time I kicked him in the balls, actually.

And I kept my mouth shut, too. No matter how much my dad screamed and yelled and ranted and raved, I wouldn't tell him anything about the bullet. Not about where I got it. Not about where it went. Not about the kid who called him at work to tell him about it.

So Roger—my dad, officially—gave up. He sent me to the hospital again.

And now I'm back home. Because as bad as it was, I'm tougher than my mom.

THE LAST TIME I SAW HER

the room the room the room is rosevomit because

THREE

THINGS ARE A LITTLE BIT BETTER at home, of course—I have my *own* room, without a crazy roommate who got knocked up at fifteen and used to let her boyfriend beat her up. So I've got that going for me.

And I have my computer.

It's been *months* since I've been able to do anything on a computer. They had computers in the hospital, but we were monitored and we only got, like, fifteen minutes at a time, so I didn't bother.

I fire up the computer and log on to my chat program and there's Simone, like she's waiting for me. Simone's my best friend—I know all of her shit and she knows all of my shit.

So it goes like this:

simsimsimoaning: *welcom back!!!!!*
Promethea387: *Thanks. Already feel like I'm in jail or something.*
Roger is being a PITA.
simsimsimoaning: *u need 2 get oiut*